Ace Books by P.N. Elrod

The Vampire Files

BLOODLIST
LIFEBLOOD
BLOODCIRCLE
ART IN THE BLOOD
FIRE IN THE BLOOD
BLOOD ON THE WATER

RED DEATH
DEATH AND THE MAIDEN

DEATH AND THE MAIDEN

P.N. ELROD

ACE BOOKS, NEW YORK

This book is an Ace original edition,
and has never been previously published.

DEATH AND THE MAIDEN

An Ace Book / published by arrangement with
the author

PRINTING HISTORY
Ace edition / July 1994

ISBN: 0-441-00071-1

ACE®
Ace Books are published by The Berkley Publishing Group,
200 Madison Avenue, New York, NY 10016.
ACE and the "A" design are trademarks
belonging to Charter Communications, Inc.

PRINTED IN THE UNITED STATES OF AMERICA

10 9 8 7 6 5 4 3 2 1

For Mark,
here's to tracks five and six.
Woof!

Thanks also to
Gloria Shami
for the reality check,
my good friends in
"The Teeth-in-the-Neck Gang,"

And a special thanks to
Roxanne Longstreet
for showing me that the
impossible can *be done*
and *that tip about the creative*
necessity of ice cream.

As this story was written to give entertainment, not instruction, I have made no attempt to re-create the language spoken over two hundred years ago. There have been so many shifts in usage, meaning, and nuance that I expect a typical conversation of the time would be largely unintelligible to a present-day reader. Having had to "shift" myself as well to avoid becoming too anachronistic in a swiftly changing world, modern usage, words, and terms have doubtless found their way into this story. Annoying, perhaps, to the historian, but my goal is to clarify, not confound, things for the twentieth-century reader.

Though some fragments of the following narrative have been elsewhere recorded, Mr. Fleming, an otherwise worthy raconteur, misquoted me on several points, which have now been corrected. I hereby state that the following events are entirely true. Only certain names and locations have been changed to protect the guilty and their hapless—and usually innocent—relations and descendants.

—JONATHAN BARRETT

CHAPTER

—1—

Long Island, September 1776
"But this is miraculous," said Dr. Beldon, lifting my elbow closer to his large, somewhat bulging eyes. Next he ran his fingers over the point where the bone break had been. "It's not possible. There's not a single sign that you were ever injured."

Which was of great relief to me. For a time I'd feared I would never recover the full use of my right arm. Beldon had chanced to call on me this evening just after I'd awakened and had been surprised to see that the sling I'd worn for nearly a week was gone.

"And there is no more discomfort when you move it?"

"None," I said. Days earlier, Beldon had expressed to me the need to rebreak the bone so as to properly set it again, but I'd been putting it off. Now I was very glad of that procrastination.

His fingers dug a bit more deeply into the muscle. "Make a fist," he ordered. "Open. Close. Now stretch your arm straight. Twist your hand at the wrist." Eyes shut, he concentrated on the movement. "Amazing. Quite amazing," he muttered.

"Yes, well, God has been most generous to me of late," I said with true sincerity.

Eyes open, now his brows went up. "But, Mr. Barrett . . ."

"You said yourself that it was a miracle," I reminded him. Our eyes locked. "But I don't think you need take any notice

1

of it. Should anyone be curious, you may certainly inform them that my arm has healed as you expected."

He didn't even blink. "Yes. I shall certainly do that." The only clue that anything was amiss was his slight flatness of tone and a brief slackening of expression.

"Nothing unusual about it at all," I emphasized.

"No . . . nothing un . . ."

I broke off my influence upon him and asked, "Are you finished, Doctor?"

Blink. "Yes, quite finished, Mr. Barrett, and may I express my delight that you are feeling better?"

We exchanged further pleasantries, then Beldon finally took his leave. My valet, Jericho, had silently watched everything from one corner of my room, his dark face sober and aloof yet somehow still managing to convey mild disapproval.

"It's only to spare us all unnecessary bother," I reminded him, shaking my shirtsleeve down.

"Of course, sir." He stepped forward to fasten the cuff.

"Very well, then. It's to spare *me* unnecessary bother."

"Is the truth so evil?" he asked, helping me put on my waistcoat.

"No, but it is unbelievable. And frightening. I've been frightened enough for myself; I've no wish to inflict that fear upon others."

"Yet it still exists."

"But I'm not afraid anymore. Bewildered, perhaps, but—"

"I was speaking of other members of the household."

"What other members? Who?"

He made a vague gesture rather akin to a shrug. "In the slave quarters. There are whisperings that a devil has jumped into you."

"Oh, really? For what purpose?"

"That has not yet been decided."

"Who is it that thinks so?"

His lips closed, and he busied himself at brushing lint from my shoulders.

"I hope you have discouraged such idle gossip," I said, adjusting my neckcloth. It had become rather tight in the last few moments.

"I have. There will be no problems from it. I only mentioned this because you were seen."

"Doing what?"

"Something . . . extraordinary. The person I spoke to said he saw you . . . flying."

"Oh."

"Of course, no one really believed him, but his story was disturbing to the more gullible."

"You hardly surprise me." One or two of our slaves, not as well educated as Jericho, would certainly be prey to all sorts of midnight imaginings, especially if they'd been listening to fanciful tales before bedtime.

"Can you fly, Mr. Jonathan?" Jericho's face was utterly expressionless.

I gulped, my belly suddenly churning. "What of it, if I could?"

There was a considerable pause before he replied. "Then I would suggest that you be more discreet about it."

My belly stopped churning and went stone still. "You . . . you've seen me?"

"Yes."

Oh, dear.

He stopped brushing at lint and turned his attention to the shelves in my already orderly wardrobe.

"You seem to have taken it rather calmly."

"I assure you, I was most troubled when I saw you floating over the treetops yesterday evening . . ."

"But . . . ?"

"But you looked very happy," he admitted. "I concluded that anything capable of giving you such wholesome joy must not be a bad thing. Besides, my *bomba* has told me tales of his childhood that talk of men turning themselves into animals. If a man can learn the magic to become an animal, then why can a man not learn the magic to fly?"

"This is not magic, Jericho."

"Are you so sure? Then what is it that turns a tiny seed into a tree? Is that not a kind of magic?"

"Now you're speaking of science or philosophy."

He shook his head. "I speak only of what's been said. If I choose to ascribe all that has happened to you to magic, then it *is* magic."

"Or superstition."

"That comes in only when one is afraid or ignorant. I am neither, but I have adopted an explanation that is tolerable to me."

"Maybe I should adopt it for myself, as well. Nothing else I've considered has come close to explaining things so handily. Especially things like this." I touched my miraculously healed arm.

"And this?" he asked, his hand hovering over a small mirror that lay facedown on one of the shelves.

"Yes, that, too. You can get rid of it, y'know." Since my change, I'd found that particular vanity item to be singularly useless, not to mention unsettling. I'd more or less known what to expect, but it had still given me a sharp turn to look into a mirror and not see a damned thing. I'd briefly and irrationally worried that that was what I'd become: "a damned thing." Father and I had discussed it thoroughly, for I was very upset at the time, but we'd been unable to explain the phenomenon. Perhaps Jericho was right and it was magic.

"As you wish," he said, tucking the offending glass into a pocket. "Does Mr. Barrett know about the flying? Or Miss Elizabeth?"

"Not yet. I'll tell them all about it later. The news won't grow stale for waiting. And I promise to take your advice and be more discreet."

"I'm relieved to hear that."

After a moment, I added, somewhat shyly, "It's . . . not really flying, y'know."

He waited for me to go on.

"I sort of float upon the air like a leaf. But I can move against the wind or with it as I choose."

He thought that over for a long time. "And what is it like?"

A grin and a soft laugh bubbled right out of me. "It's absolutely wonderful!"

And so it was. Last night I'd done the impossible and broken away from the grasp of the earth to soar in the sky freer than any bird. It was surely the most remarkable portion of the legacy I'd come into since my . . . death.

Or rather, my *change*.

The details of that particular story—of my death and escape from the grave—have been recounted elsewhere. Let it suffice for now that upon my return, I soon discovered I'd acquired the same characteristics that governed the waking life of a certain Miss Nora Jones, a lady with whom I had shared a very intimate liaison.

Like her, I was now able to influence the very minds and thoughts of anyone around me, thus allowing me to resume my former life with my family almost as though nothing had ever happened. I had learned the secret of how to heal swiftly and completely. And I was able to fly . . . so to speak. Though I'd never actually witnessed Nora indulging in such a display, I had no doubt that she was capable of doing it, since my own condition now so completely mirrored her own.

Mirrors. Yes, well, you've heard about them already.

Like her, I was also unable to bear sunlight, which might be considered a heavy burden, but for the fact that my eyes were so improved. The night had become my day; the stars and moon my welcome companions in the sky. When the sun was up, I slept—or tried to; I was having some difficulties there, but more on that later.

My strength was that of a young Hercules, and my other senses enjoyed similar improvements. Each evening I discovered a new delight to the ear, a fresh appreciation of touch, and, though I was not required to breathe regularly unless I chose to speak, I could pick out and identify a scent almost as well as one of our own hunting hounds. Taste had also undergone considerable alteration, though I never exercised it upon what might be considered a normal meal.

For, like Nora, I had come to subsist solely upon *blood* for my sustenance.

But again, more on that later.

"What are you writing, little brother?" asked Elizabeth, peering across the library as she walked in. Her nightly practice at her spinet had ended, but I'd been so absorbed in my work that I hadn't noticed when the music stopped.

"A letter to Cousin Oliver," I replied.

The early part of the evening had passed pleasantly enough amid familial congratulations on my recovery. Diverting attention from myself, I had given all the credit to Dr. Beldon, much to his great enjoyment. Father and Elizabeth, who, along with Jericho, knew the full truth about my changed nature, required a more detailed account from me, which I'd promised, but had yet to provide. By subtle gesture and with a well-placed word or two, I gave them to understand that my healing was connected to my change, and thus not a topic for general discussion. We'd quietly arranged to talk later. As I had no interest in Mother's card game and was too restless to read, I'd taken sanctuary in the library to deal with some necessary correspondence.

"But you just sent one only . . ." Her voice trailed off.

"I know, but much has occurred since my last missive."

She thought about that awhile, then came over to stand next to Father's desk, where I happened to be working. "I have something for you," she said, pulling a flat packet from her skirt pocket.

I instantly recognized it. "My journal!"

She gave it over. "I kept it from your things when Mother was having your room cleaned out. I was afraid she'd either throw it away or read it herself, and I didn't think you'd have liked either of those choices."

"You're right, I wouldn't. Thank you."

"I didn't read it," she added.

This surprised me, not because Elizabeth was a prying sort of person, but because at the time she'd thought me dead. "Why not?"

"I couldn't bring myself to. These are your words and your thoughts, I just couldn't bear the idea of reading them so soon after . . . anyway, I wanted only to keep them safe. From her. I don't know what I hated most, her utter coldness over you or the way she ransacked your room like a bloody vulture."

Mother again. "It's all over now."

She put her hand on mine. "Yes, thank God."

"It would have been all right if you had read it. There's nothing in here that I wouldn't have minded sharing with you and Father."

She smiled at that. "But you're back and there's no need, is there?"

"May there never be another," I solemnly intoned, putting my hand over my heart.

That brought out another smile, which was most pleasing. Her good humor and mine restored, I picked up my pen and regarded the sheet of paper before me, wondering what to put down next.

"Mind if I keep you company?" From one of the desk drawers she pulled out a penknife and some goose quills.

"I should welcome it," I said absently.

Apparently Elizabeth was prepared to wait for Father to join us before calling for my promised explanation. Taking a chair next to the desk and close to my candle, she began carving a point on one of the quills. "Are you going to tell Oliver about what's happened to you?"

A brief laugh escaped me. "Hardly, or he'd think that the Fonteyn half of my blood had finally boiled my brain. Did I ever mention to you that tour we took of Bedlam?"

"In noxious detail." She steadily sliced away on a quill, pausing only to narrowly inspect the results of her work.

"I've no wish for Oliver to regard me as a potential inmate, so be assured that the details of my recent experience will find no place here."

"Then what—"

"Nora."

Her name temporarily halted Elizabeth's inquiries, and I took the opportunity to dip my pen into the inkpot. After reading again my few lines assuring Oliver of my continued good health and a wish for the same for him, I had to pause yet again and think how to proceed. Before leaving England for home some months ago, I'd asked him to keep an eye on Nora for me and in such a way as to leave no doubt that my relationship with her had quite ended. My lightness of attitude quite puzzled my poor cousin, considering his awareness that Nora and I had been passionate lovers for nearly three years.

But, of course, Nora had caused me to forget all that.

I wasn't sure if I should curse her or bless her for what she'd done to me. Some nights I did both. This was one of those nights, and they happened more and more frequently as my memories of her returned. Though she had committed a great wrong against me, I yet loved her and missed her terribly.

"Ow!"

Elizabeth had had a mishap with the razor-sharp penknife and nicked a finger. She ruefully held it close to the candle to inspect the damage, started to put her finger to her mouth, then stopped, her eyes suddenly shifting up to meet mine.

"Be more careful," I said, trying not to stare at the drop of blood welling from the tiny cut.

She lowered her hand slightly. "Does this trouble you?"

"Why should it?"

"Because you've an odd look on your face. Are you hungry?"

"No, I am not hungry." Not yet. Later, after everyone was asleep and the world was quiet, I'd slip out and . . .

"Then what?"

"I can smell it," I whispered, not without a feeling of awe.

She brought her finger close to her nose and sniffed, then shrugged at her failure to sense it. "A little speck like this?"

"Yes. It hangs in the air like perfume."

"That must be interesting for you," she observed. The bleeding had stopped, so she wiped away the blood on her handkerchief. Picking up the quill, she gingerly resumed her delicate work with the knife.

Disturbing, more like, I thought, unable to ignore the scent and the reactions it aroused within me. I raised one hand to cover my mouth and ran my tongue over my teeth. There, the two points on my upper jaw . . . a slight swelling, not painful . . . quite the opposite, in fact.

"Jonathan?"

"It's nothing," I said, a bit too quickly, letting my hand drop away.

But she seemed to know what I was hiding. "Sweet God, Jonathan, you've nothing to be ashamed of."

"I'm not," I said. "Really."

"Then why the glower?"

I made a fist and bumped it lightly against the desk, then opened it flat. "I'm not sure I . . . that I'm . . . comfortable with this part of what's happened to me."

"You do what you do because you have to."

"Yes, but I've . . . I worry about what people might think should they find out."

"But no one else knows but me, Father, and Jericho. We don't speak of it, and you're not likely to blurt it out in company."

"As if it's something shameful."

"Something private," she corrected. "Like your journal."

Unable to endure her steady, sensible gaze, I shoved my pen into a cup of lead shot and stood up to pace.

She continued to watch me. "Come now and listen to yourself. Worrying about what others may think is the sort of thing that bedevils Mother. There's no need for you to pay any mind to that same voice, or you could end up like her."

All too true. I *had* been haunted by a miserable chorus of dark voices muttering of nothing but doubt and doom. "It's just that most of the time everything is as it was for me before my . . . return. And yet"—I gestured vaguely—"everything is so different. *I'm* different."

She did not—thank God—gainsay me. The changes within that had literally brought me back from the grave were profound, and their full influence upon how I now lived were only just being realized. I slept, if one could call it that, the whole day through, unable to stir for as long as the sun was up. Since the household held to an exactly opposite habit, my enjoyment of its society was unhappily limited. The rest of the time I was alone. Very much alone.

And as for Elizabeth's little accident . . . well, it was yet another reminder of an appetite that the world would doubtless look upon as disgusting or at the very least react to with alarm and fear.

I paused by the bookcase and stared at the titles within without reading them. "Remember the night I . . . came back?"

She nodded. It was not likely that either of us would forget.

"After we'd captured the rebels, two of Nash's Hessians escorted me to Mrs. Montagu's. I thought I'd gotten rid of them, but they came back and saw me in her barn with her horses . . . feeding myself."

"Then what?"

"They ran like rabbits. They were terrified. One of them called me a name, '*blutsauger.*'"

She stumbled over my no doubt questionable pronunciation. "Bluet-saw—"

I repeated the word for her. "It means 'bloodsucker.' Hardly flattering."

"Certainly not in the context that it was given."

"Not in any context."

"What of it? You're a 'bloodsucker,' I'm an eater of animal flesh."

"That's not the same."

"It would be if dining on a good hot joint was thought to be repugnant by most people. It's not like you to be feeling sorry for yourself, little brother. I hope you can get over it."

I idly poked at a crescent of dust gathered in a tight corner of the bookcase woodwork. One of the maids had been careless over her cleaning chores. Woe to her if Mother noticed. "Perhaps the Fonteyn blood is doing its work upon me after all, and I shall become mad."

"I think not, since you've been diluting it so regularly with that of our livestock."

My openmouthed stare was returned with a flash of her bright eyes as she cocked her head to one side. It was meant to convince me that I was taking myself far too seriously. "I do believe you have a fool for a brother," I said wearily.

"Better a fool than a corpse," she responded bluntly. "You're not going mad, you're just getting used to things. I still am, myself."

"And what do you do about it?"

"Ask God to sort it out for me, say 'amen,' and go to sleep." The point of one quill cut to perfection, she put it aside and picked up another. The feathering had not yet been trimmed away and she made a fine mess on her wide skirts as she worked to correct the oversight.

"Would that I could sleep," I muttered.

"More dreams?"

"Nothing but, and no waking to escape them is allowed."

"Dr. Beldon couldn't help?"

"He let me try some of his laudanum."

"And it didn't work?"

"Not really. He made up a draught and told me to take it when I was ready to retire, but I knew I'd never be able to keep it down. So I went out to the stables and drew off blood from one of the horses to mix it in and was able to drink that. It put me into quite a stupor, but the dreams were still there and more disturbing than usual. Never again." I dropped into Father's big chair by the dormant fireplace. "Damnation, but the only rest I've gotten since my return was when I was forced to shelter in the old barn."

"Perhaps you could go back and try it again."

"Why should my sleeping there be any different than here in my own bed?"

"I don't know. If you went back you might find an answer."

"It's hardly safe."

Her brows drew together as she glanced up from her fine carving. "No one goes out there anymore."

"The Hessians might. You know they wanted to take Rapelji's house away from him for their own lodging? He's lucky they changed their minds and took over the church instead."

"Not so lucky for the church."

"Better to have them there than at Rapelji's or even in our own house. I've been down to The Oak to learn the news, and they're a pretty rough and savage lot. And they enjoy it."

"I've heard the stories, Jonathan," she said dryly. Because of the recent occupation, Elizabeth had hardly been able to stir a foot outside the door for fear of being insulted by the very army sent to protect us. "Anyway, you've wandered off the subject of the barn. Why don't you try spending the day there? Jericho can run out and check on you if you're that worried."

I grimaced. "It's so open and unprotected, without doors or shutters. I only used it because I had no other choice."

"But you were able to find rest then, with no dreaming."

That was inarguable. I was about to raise more objections anyway, just to keep up the flow of talk, when Father came in, shutting the library doors behind him. He was a tall man with a spare figure and a still-handsome face, but lately more lines had begun to clutter his normally amiable expression. Imprinted there by the upheavals in our own lives and by the larger conflicts outside our home, they seemed to lift when he looked upon us, his children.

"Is the card game finished?" Elizabeth asked.

"No, they're still at it," he replied, meaning Mother, Dr. Beldon, and Mrs. Hardinbrook, who was Beldon's widowed sister. "They've changed to something that needs but three players to work well, so I made my escape."

"Why do you play if you don't enjoy it?"

"It soothes your mother's soul." He strode toward the cabinet that held a small supply of wine and spirits, then changed his mind with a sigh. "No. I'll be damned before I let that woman drive me to drink."

"That woman" referred to Mrs. Hardinbrook, not Mother.

"What did she do tonight?" I asked.

Father rolled his eyes, looking glum. "She opened her mouth, and that's more than enough. How she does clack on. I don't know as I've ever seen her pause for breath. At least when we're at cards she shuts up for the play."

"And when Mother is talking," Elizabeth put in.

Father grunted agreement to that, then turned all his attention upon me. "All right, laddie, what's the rest of your tale? Just how did your arm heal so quickly?"

Elizabeth left off her carving of pens and put her hands in her lap.

I gulped. It's one thing to promise an explanation, but quite another to actually deliver it, particularly when one doesn't know where to start.

"Well, it's connected with how I . . . escaped my grave." My last words came out in a rush, as I wanted to get past them as quickly as possible. I did not like to think about that time; it always made me feel ill. They could see how difficult it was for me to talk, and waited me out. Suddenly restless again, I launched out of Father's chair and stalked up and down the room.

"I . . . floated out," I finally said.

They exchanged looks. Father's brows went up. Somehow, this had been so much easier to talk about with Jericho, but then he'd already known something of the subject.

"That's how I got out without disturbing the earth. I can make my body . . ."

They leaned forward, silently encouraging me to continue.

". . . make it . . ."

"What?" demanded Elizabeth.

And the words just would not come. Their combined gaze left me entirely flummoxed over what to say next. I was being foolish again, worried they wouldn't believe me, or worse, that they'd be afraid of me. But they'd accepted so much already and now seemed willing to accept more, so such worries were certainly all in my own head.

"Jonathan," Father prompted, his expression kindly.

I nodded. "Yes. I'm trying. What it is . . . is that I have the ability to make myself insubstantial, allowing me to pass through solid objects. To float."

"Float?" he echoed.

"Yes, sir."

Neither said anything for a time, but they did exchange looks once more. They did not, thank God, laugh.

"Well," he finally said. "What has that to do with your arm healing?"

It was my turn to stare. The floating and the restoration were so linked in my mind that it had been natural for me to conclude that others would also see the connection.

"Uhh . . . that is . . . when I ceased to float around, I was all better."

Another lengthy silence.

"I know I'm not doing this very well—"

"No, not at all," agreed Elizabeth.

"It's like that business with mirrors. I've no explanation for it, it just *is*."

"Perhaps," said Father, "if you gave us a demonstration?"

I'd foreseen the need for one from the start. That knowledge did not make it any easier, though. I nodded, went to the windows and closed the shutters to prevent anyone from spying, then turned to face Father and Elizabeth. Holding my hands up before me that I might observe my progress, I willed myself to slip slowly into . . . whatever it was. The room seemed to fill with fog as I grew more and more transparent.

Elizabeth rose straight up from her chair to gape. Father staggered back, bumped against his desk, then suddenly sat down. On the floor.

Immediately becoming solid again, I started forward, but abruptly froze in place, held back by doubt, by their wide-eyed stares.

"Good God," Father whispered.

"I'm sorry," I said.

He gave himself a shake and inhaled deeply. Stood up. Stared some more. "Sorry for what, laddie?"

Then I seemed to see myself through his eyes. They were the only mirrors left to me. They showed an uncertain young man who might as well apologize for the color of his hair as for this new . . . ability. "Excellent question, sir."

He glanced at Elizabeth, who had gone very white, and touched her arm in a reassuring gesture. "You just surprised us, that's all. Nothing to apologize for." He put his hand out to me. I hesitantly came closer and took it. His grip was warm, encouraging. "You're solid enough, now."

Elizabeth took my other hand, but said nothing.

"Perhaps you could do that again," he suggested.

And so I did. Eyes shut so that I did not have to watch them fading into the fog, I repeated my action.

"He's so *cold*," said Elizabeth, her voice distant though I stood right next to her.

Then I let go of all ties to solidity. The pull of the earth, the feel of my clothes, the familiar constraints of my own body ceased to be. I held myself in place by thought alone.

"My God, he's vanished!" Father whispered.

But I'm right here, I protested, but of course, I had no mouth with which to speak. Opening my eyes now was something that could be exercised only in my mind, for in this state I was unable to see anything. Enough. I instantly resumed form again.

They yet held my hands and continued to do so. Father's grip increased somewhat, Elizabeth appeared too shocked yet to react.

"I vanished?" I asked. "Is it true? Father?"

He exhaled, turning it into a sort of laugh. "Clean away."

Oddly enough, after all the practicing I'd done, observing myself as I became more and more transparent until the gray fog engulfed everything, it had never occurred to me that I could become entirely invisible during the process.

"You're all right?" Elizabeth asked shakily.

"Yes."

"It doesn't hurt or anything?"

"Not at all."

"What does it feel like?"

"Sort of . . . like holding your breath, but not having to let it out for more air."

She thought that one over a bit. Father asked me to do it once more. I obliged, this time willing myself to travel some distance across the room before reappearing.

"Well-a-day," he said, borrowing one of my own expressions. "You said you floated, though?"

As the worst of the surprise was past, I was more willing to oblige their curiosity. This time I did not let the fog swallow me completely and held myself in a near-transparent state. Weightless, I drifted upward until I was right against the ceiling. I felt its restraining barrier, but knew I could seep through it to the floor above, if I wished. I did seriously consider it, but decided not to; tonight's performance was quite sufficient.

Growing gradually more solid, I sank to the floor.

They had a hundred questions for me, which I tried to answer, though some were unanswerable.

"I really don't know how it works," I said after nearly an hour of talk and a number of demonstrations that left me fatigued from the effort. "I don't know how it healed me. God knows, I wish I did."

"If it pleases God to keep the secret to Himself, then so be it," said Father. "You're whole again and that's what matters. We shall have to content ourselves with that and give thanks for it, for it seems a mighty gift."

"If not an alarming one," Elizabeth added.

"I'm very sorry for that."

Father laughed a little. "Don't see how it could possibly have been avoided, laddie. Have you any others we should know about?"

I shrugged. "I can't really say. That's why I was writing to Oliver tonight. I wanted him to pass a letter on to Nora for me. I've asked her a number of questions about what's happened to me, but it's going to be months before I hear from her . . . if she even answers."

"Why do you think she won't?"

"Because she made me forget so much."

"But from what you've told us of her, she strikes me as being a woman of honor."

"And overly secretive. She could have told me what to expect—" I broke off and firmly smothered that tiresome lament. "I'm sorry. When it comes to Nora, I sometimes just don't know what to think. She's gifted me with a very fine double-edged sword, but failed to give instruction on how to safely wield it. If I'm not careful, I could injure myself or others."

"You're doing the best you can, laddie, no one can expect more than that. Anyway, there's no reason to think she won't answer. You might want to send more than one letter by different ships, though. Times are so unsettled that a single missive might not get through."

"Yes, I'd thought of that."

"Good. Get all your writing done tonight and I'll see that it's sent out for you tomorrow."

"Thank you, sir."

The words had hardly left my lips when the library doors were thrust open with a great deal of force. Mother stood on the threshold, glaring at the three of us turn on turn.

"What's going on here, Samuel?" she demanded.

"Nothing, as you see," he said, spreading his hands. "We were just talking."

"Talking? I'm sure you were." Despite the heavy powder coating her face, we could see that she was very flushed. "About what, may I ask?"

"Nothing important."

"Yet you still have to shut the doors?"

"We had no wish to disturb your card game."

"And the shutters?"

"There was a draft."

"You've an answer for everything except what's been asked, don't you?"

To that, Father made no reply. I wondered where Beldon had gotten to, as it looked to be one of those nights where his medical talents might be required.

"Jonathan Fonteyn."

I *hated* the contemptuous tone she always used when addressing me. "Yes, madam?" I whispered back.

"What were you talking about?"

"Nothing, really. I'm writing some letters, and Father promised to post them for me."

"And what are you doing here, Elizabeth? I'm sure that such conversation can't possibly be of any interest to you."

"I was just cutting some pens."

"No doubt, I can see the mess you've made all over the place. You can leave off with that. It's late and past time that you went upstairs."

Elizabeth pursed her lips and said nothing.

"Well, girl?"

"I shall be along shortly, Mother, as soon as I've cleaned up."

"You'll do as you're told and be along now."

"She's no longer a child, Marie," said Father.

"So you've noticed," Mother snarled back. "So you've *both* noticed! You think I'm blind to it? You think I don't see the three of you, the whispers, the looks you pass each other? It's disgusting."

"Marie, that's quite enough. You've made a mistake—"

"Yes, I'm always making mistakes. I'm always the one who's wrong, the one who imagines things. You'd like that, wouldn't you?"

Father said nothing. His face had become a hard, expressionless mask, as had my own, as had Elizabeth's. When Mother was in this kind of mood, no appeal to reason would work on her.

"The devoted father and his two *loving* children," she sneered. "God should strike the lot of you dead where you stand."

"Oh, Marie," sang out Mrs. Hardinbrook, coming up behind Mother. Her voice and manner were light and innocent of the situation she was walking into.

Mother's face underwent an immediate change. The Medusa abruptly transformed back to being a middle-aged matron, smooth of countenance and unblemished by vile thoughts.

"Yes, Deborah, what is it?" she cooed.

"We still have another hand to play out. I hope you will come back and finish it? Please say you will."

"Of course, of course. Do lead the way, my dear."

Mother shot us one last venomous glance before turning to follow Mrs. Hardinbrook. She pointedly left the doors open.

Father let out a pent-up breath and sat heavily in his chair. He didn't look well. "God," he said, putting his head in his hands. He rarely ever succumbed to the strain. Seeing him like this was enough to tear my heart in two. I went to him and knelt next to him, feeling dreadfully helpless and angry all at once.

Elizabeth crossed to the cabinet, poured out a portion of brandy into a cup, and took it to him. This time he had no objection to drink. When he'd finished, she poured one for herself and took it straight down as though it were water. I could have used one for myself, but knew better than to try.

"That Hardinbrook woman may be a clacking toad-eater, but she's a damned useful clacking toad-eater," Father finally said.

"I'll not say anything against her," I added.

Elizabeth looked past us to the open door, as if fearful that Mother might return. "What are we to do?" she asked Father.

"We needn't do anything. The fit will pass and she'll be all right. She won't remember any of this tomorrow."

She put down her cup and stood before him. "She's getting worse, Father. The things she said about me and Jonathan are bad enough, but to include you in with her filthy accusations is beyond endurance."

"What would you have me do?" he asked, all subdued.

She dropped her eyes.

"I could possibly send her away somewhere, but what good would come of it? She's all right here most of the time, and Beldon and his sister usually keep her in hand. I'm sorry for what she's doing to you two—"

"And to yourself, Father," I said.

He shrugged, as though his own pain was of no consequence. "I am sorry for that and if I could stop it, I would."

"Why can't you send her away?" Elizabeth murmured, again not looking at him.

"Because I made a promise when I married her. I promised to take care of her. Always."

"But she's getting more impossible every day. She's getting worse."

"And would become much worse if sent away. It's the same as if she were ill in bed with a fever. The fever she suffers from is in her mind rather than her body, but the principle is the same. She needs care, and it is my responsibility to see that she has it. For the sake of the promise I made those years ago and for the memory of the love we once had, it is my chosen duty. I will not dishonor myself by ignoring that duty just because it has become unpleasant."

"And what are we to do, then?"

"I have no answer for you, daughter. I'd rather hoped you'd give me one."

Elizabeth raised her head. She was blushing right to the roots of her hair. "I think I understand you, sir."

He lightly touched her hand. "I thought that you would. What about you, laddie?"

"We all have our duty, sir. I will not shirk mine."

"Good."

"But . . ."

"Yes?"

"If now and then, when we get filled up with it, would you mind very much if we complained a bit?"

He laughed. Some of the deeper lines lifted slightly. "Not at all. That is, if you don't mind my joining you."

It was late, and the house was very silent. I'd opened the shutters again to enjoy the air. It was damp and heavy with the sea smell, but clean. A draft stirred up the slivers of quill and feathers from Elizabeth's abandoned work. I put the finished pens in the cup of shot and used the edge of one packet of finished letters to sweep the leavings off the desk and into one hand. Some of the stuff dropped onto the floor, but the rest I threw out a window. My letters, sealed and addressed, I placed under the shot cup where Father might easily find them. There was a good four months' wait ahead of me—more likely six with winter coming on and slowing the passage of shipping—

before I could even begin to look for a reply from either Nora or Oliver.

I had a hope, and no more than a hope, that once Nora knew of my situation she would answer by coming herself. Though to think that she'd cross all the way from England during the worst months of weather was rather a lot to expect of her. Not only was the risk of a winter crossing very bad, but there was also her special condition to consider. Confined to whatever sanctuary she could manage during the day was limiting enough, but the question of how she could feed herself during the voyage was not one I could readily answer, nor did I care to think on it much.

Mine was a fool's dream, though. She would not come; it was an impossible expectation. A letter. I would gladly settle for a letter.

But six months . . . damnation, that was an *eternity*.

My candle had burned low. With everyone asleep and the need to pretend its necessity removed, I blew it out. The gentle silver light of the night sky advanced into the room. It seemed to carry a world of scents to me: earth and plant, wood smoke and stable, sea and shoreline.

Time to sup.

CHAPTER
—2—

Up in my room, I quietly changed into clothes more suitable for an outdoor excursion: dark coat, waistcoat, and breeches, my plainest shirt, simplest neckcloth, and the older of my two pairs of riding boots. Not that I was planning to give Rolly any exercise—I'd save that pleasure for tomorrow night—but boots were more practical for roaming the countryside than shoes.

Not that I planned to do much walking, either.

Leaving my other clothes on the bed for Jericho to see to in the morning, I also left him a note explaining my absence. He could talk to Elizabeth if he wanted more details.

I opened the window, intent on using it for my egress from the house, then had second thoughts, remembering my promise to Jericho to be more discreet. No one was in sight down in the yard, but that meant nothing. Though the prospect seemed unlikely, anyone wishing to spy on me could hide himself easily enough, even from my improved vision. I might be able to see as well in the dark as others could during the day, but I had yet to learn how to see through things. There were any number of trees, bushes, and buildings offering protection for a determined observer of demon-possessed mortals.

Good lord, but I hoped Jericho had successfully repressed *that* gossip. Not wishing to add to it, I stood well back from the window before relinquishing my hold on the physical and floating out. Briefly, I sensed the frame loom around me, then felt the tug of the wind drawing me forth into the open sky.

If not for my earlier practice before Father and Elizabeth, I might have found this experience of traveling blind to be extremely confusing. Indeed, to suddenly be without a body in the conventional definition, one might expect to maintain a certain level of confusion for some goodly length of time before finally mastering such an unusual sensation. I'd adapted remarkably quickly to it, though, and suspected that my casual assumption of this ability to be linked to the more obvious inner changes. While a caterpillar has no understanding of flight, after its metamorphosis into a butterfly it has no difficulty taking to the air. A similar gift of understanding must have somehow slipped into my being during my own metamorphosis in the grave.

Drifting high and far from the house, I very, very gradually assumed enough solidity to allow me to see exactly where I'd gone. As this action lent weight to my form, I lost some height, but not much. I held in place, arms spread wide like wings, and looked in wonder at the gray land below. It reminded me of the time Oliver and I had climbed to the roof of one of the buildings in Cambridge to take in the view. To ourselves, we seemed as aloof as gods from the small people and animals that crept about on the miserable ground beneath us, but in the end could not escape the fact that our means of rising above them, our lonely tower, tied us just as firmly to earth. Now I had no ties at all, except for those of memory, which could easily be set aside. For now, I was a bird or a cloud, with no concern for anything but to enjoy this strange freedom for its own sake.

I soared above the tallest trees, or dipped down to rush between their boughs like a hunting hawk, then down still more to coast just above the fields and pastures. Any wall or fence that presented itself I merely skipped over, smoother and faster than any jump I'd made while on Rolly's back.

Ah, but most pleasures have their price, and as with any exercise, I found myself growing weary for want of refreshment. A week ago, I might have satisfied my need with wine and a meat pie, but a week ago I was not able to fly. As my means of travel had changed, so had the demands and tastes of my appetite.

So far, the army had not completely stripped us of our stock. Some of our horses were pastured close to the house, and those were the ones I usually fed upon. We also had cattle, but I preferred horses, as they were groomed regularly and thus much cleaner.

I took on more substance to see better and found I'd traveled well to the south and had to circle back again. Just within sight of the house, I swooped low and solidified, my feet touching lightly down on the cropped grass of a small field. The horses dozing at the other end paid me no notice, but their ears flicked in my direction as I walked toward them. The interest became more marked when I reached into a pocket and pulled forth a small apple. Holding it high so they could see it, all I had to do was wait.

Eventually, Desdemona, who had a greedy temperament, decided that she deserved the bribe more than the others and ambled over to take it. While she crunched away on the apple, I got hold of her halter and soothed and stroked her until she went very still.

The smooth warmth of her silken coat proclaimed that she was well-cared for and in fine health. What little blood I needed to maintain my own strength she could easily spare with no ill effect. I knelt and felt out one of the surface veins in her near foreleg, brushing at it with eager fingers. My belly was twisting in a most pleasurable way, anticipating what was to come. My mouth and tongue were dry, but that would soon be amended.

The corner teeth in my upper jaw had grown longer than any of the others and tilted slightly outward. An odd sensation, that, but I quite liked it. I liked it even better when I bent over the vein and used them to gently and quickly cut through the intervening flesh.

God, but that rush of red heat was wonderful. It rolled right through me, sating, satisfying, comforting, sweeping away all the dark doubts I'd harbored. This was food in its purest form, as basic as a mother's milk. How like a suckling infant I felt, too, drinking in incredible, reviving nourishment such as I'd never known before. Consciously known, that is. Our memories of babyhood, of nursing, of that last physical link we have to our mothers is inevitably severed as we grow older, but the craving and need for fulfillment is ever with us. Others might strive their whole lives to recover that sweet estate in one form or another, but my own endeavors had apparently ended, if this serene gratification was anything to judge by.

The wounds I'd made were small, and the blood flow gradually ceased. I lapped up the last of it and drew away, giving Desdemona a reassuring pat and a second apple from another pocket. As though nothing at all had happened or was amiss, her velvet lips plucked up the fruit and she quickly disposed of it as I let myself grow lighter and drifted out of the pasture.

I went solid again on the other side of the fence, leaning on it and breathing in the early morning air. Dawn was not very far off, but I had more than enough time to get to the old barn before the rising sun became a problem.

I left the fence and struck out over the fields. Not that the novelty of flying had worn off, but I was finding the steady march enjoyable for its own sake. It also allowed me to exercise my improved senses, as they were always so muffled when I ceased to be corporeal. Eyes and ears open, I drank in sights and sounds as eagerly as I'd drunk in Desdemona's blood, for I craved nourishment for my mind as much as for my body.

Damp grass and leaves underfoot, night birds making their final calls to one another and day birds sleepily rousing themselves, the wind cool on my face, it was as though I were noticing it all afresh, like a newborn child. But unlike that imaginary babe, I could identify and appreciate it all. Science, philosophy or magic, whatever force had brought me back from the grave had taught me to value the beauties of the world anew. Things that I'd once dismissed as commonplace now caught my notice; the graceful shape of a branch or the soft pattern of moss on a rock. I wanted to see and touch everything, to know and understand all. I'd been given a second chance to do so; I would not waste it.

Though it was unlikely I'd run into an inconvenient sentry here on my own land, I took care not to make too much noise. I'd be able to deal with any trouble easily enough, but there was no point attracting it in the first place.

The worries I'd confided earlier to Elizabeth came back to me now, for they were not without foundation. The Hessian troops so recently thrust upon us by the rebellion were yet here and seeking shelter in every possible hovel. Some were lodged in private homes or had taken over the churches and inns and, along with the English soldiers, were stripping the Island of all stock and produce. We'd mostly been spared thus far, but were expecting the worst. Unless General Howe finally decided to take his men and pursue Washington's rabble across the water to Manhattan Island, there wouldn't be much left for the coming winter.

Of the battle that had taken place last month between those two commanders we'd heard many conflicting tales and hardly knew which to believe. The one common thread woven into them all had to do with the horrific brutality of the Hessians. Their own officers had been shocked by their vicious behavior. Stories came to us of surrendering rebels receiving no quarter, even sorely wounded men were heartlessly run through by bayonets, or shot, or clubbed to death by musket stocks.

My own contact with them had not been so violent. Indeed, I was treated with a degree of respect by some of the ones staying in Glenbriar for my assistance in capturing two rebels not long past. The fact that I'd later been instrumental in helping the rebels get away had happily escaped notice, so far. But this advantage was small and limited only to those who knew me. It was a wise man who stayed out of their way altogether.

The barn stood out from the shelter of some trees, though ivy had taken it over and blurred its lines. There had been a stormy night since I'd last been here, and my footprints in the dirt inside the doorway were gone, though the ones deeper within remained. I followed these in to a far corner where a shoulder-high partition had been built out from the wall to make a dim stable. The floor here also retained the marks of my previous occupancy. I now added to them, pacing slowly up and down, up and down, waiting for the sun to arrive.

If I hurried, I still had time to hurtle through the sky and make it back to my own room before it was too late. The safety of the house was certainly more attractive to me than spending the day sprawled in this filthy barn, but the comfort I should have drawn from my bed had eluded me since my return. Instead of rest and sleep, I endured endless hours of bad dreams and foul dreads which served only to remind me of things I'd rather forget. These bouts of darkness left me weary to the bone upon awakening; sometimes it was hours before I could fully shake it from my mind.

And with each passing day and emerging night, I was growing more and more *tired*. Though I could often dismiss it awhile—especially after feeding—I was never truly without it. In odd moments here and there, the weariness dragged at me, as though the earth were trying to draw me back into itself once more, to return me to the grave.

Nora, if I could trust my memory, had not suffered from such continual exhaustion. Occasionally she'd fall prey to a fit of melancholia, but it never lasted long, particularly when we were together. But these instances were hardly different than what I'd seen in others and in myself at the time, brief and transient. My present state was nearly constant.

Dear God, but I needed *rest*.

The events of the evening seemed to crowd one atop the other like bees in a hive. Buzzing and darting and often imparting a sting or two, I knew I was destined to have a raw time of it for the day. Before my change, such a state of mind had always deprived me of sleep; it would be no different now.

I sat in the darkest corner of the stall and grimly waited for the sun to roll above the horizon.

Soon. Just another moment or two. My limbs were already growing sluggish. No sense in letting myself freeze for the day in what would soon become an uncomfortable posture, I lay flat, eyes shut, waiting . . .

. . . waiting.

I sat up, certain that I'd heard something, then stopped, cold as a stone.

Utter confusion seized me. I could not move or think for some moments, not because of the approaching sunrise, but out of pure shock and disorientation.

I was no longer in the barn.

That bit of realization was the only fact to impress itself upon my mind. Like an unwelcome lodger, it remained there, crowding out all other thoughts. I wasted much time trying to understand what had happened to me. In one instant I'd been stretched out for the day on the hard floor, and the next I was suddenly on the grass under an open sky.

Someone must have moved me, I thought. Then I abruptly knew that I had slept the day through. It was happily anticipated sunset, not a dreaded sunrise to which I'd awakened.

After so many days without it, I'd finally achieved it. *Rest*. No bad dreams, no dreams at all, only sweet oblivion.

Thank God.

But how had I come to be outside the barn? Perhaps Jericho had come by to check on me and had taken it into his head to shift my location, though why he would do such a thing was beyond imagining. Where—?

Brain working again now that the surprise had passed, I stood and brushed myself off and looked around. I had heard something, and the noise was still with me. Human noise, human speech.

German speech, fast and for the most part unintelligible to me.

Hessians. Damnation. The Hessians had arrived.

Now it seemed obvious that they had been the ones who had moved me from the barn, and, irksome as it might be, I'd have to have words with them, or at least with their commander. Hopefully, he would know more of English than I did of German, and I could righteously demand an answer to why they were trespassing on my land.

Suffused with anger at their intrusion, I glared around and immediately spotted a sentry. I'd been taken to one side of the yard next to the barn, the outer wall of that structure being on my right. The man stood poised at the far corner, peering around it to what I concluded was some activity that did not directly affect him, but held his extreme interest. I stalked up and dropped a heavy hand on his shoulder.

"Entschuldigen Sie. Your commander, where is he?"

Alas, I discovered that what my tutor, Rapelji, had taught me was true: for every action, there is an equal and opposite reaction. My brusk though friendly greeting was violently met. The man whipped around, stared at me all wild-eyed, then let forth with as bloodcurdling a shriek as had ever been my misfortune to hear. Before I could do or say aught else, he backed away, his mouth hanging open. Though he'd lost breath for further screams, he was yet capable of an awful gasping and gagging. I thought he was having some sort of fit and stepped toward him, reaching out.

"Nein! Nein!" came his hoarse reaction as he backed off even farther.

He seemed to be perceiving me as some sort of threat. Before I could make any attempt to reassure him otherwise, he rushed around the corner of the barn, yelling incoherently.

Damnation again. I went after him, rounding the corner—and got my second shock of the evening as I was met by a phalanx of nervous-looking Hessians with their muskets all leveled and pointing at me. Instantly, I threw my hands high.

"*Freund!*" I squeaked. "*Ich bin ein Freund! Freund!*" The words for "Don't shoot" were unfortunately not a part of my limited German vocabulary.

My babbling gave them pause, though, for those first few critical seconds and they did *not* turn me into a sieve with their musket balls.

While they hesitated, I added, "*Where is your commander?*"

That struck a nerve. They were apparently disciplined enough to cleave to the military virtue of passing any difficult decision over to a higher authority. Some of them wavered, relaxing their tight hold on their weapons and looking to their left for guidance. Not turning my head from them, I let my eyes travel in that direction. There were several lighted lanterns about, making no difference to my vision, but helpful to their own. Standing in one such puddle of light in the doorway of the barn was a stocky man in an officer's florid uniform. I was not familiar with the trappings of Germanic rank—he could have been a lieutenant or a general for all I knew—but hopefully he would take charge now and persuade his men to calmness.

"*Good evening, sir,*" I said, trying to steady my voice.

He looked me up and down as though I were some sort of lunatic on display in a town marketplace and made no reply.

"*My name is Barrett. I live here.*"

His brows lowered and his full lips pushed out into a truly terrifying pout.

"*This is my land,*" I clarified.

The soldier that I'd first encountered hesitantly stepped forward and saluted. The smartness of the gesture was somewhat diluted by his twisting around to keep me in sight. The officer fixed his eyes on him and gave a brief, guttural acknowledgment, apparently permission to speak. There followed a quick burst of wordage, accompanied by gestures, as the fellow accounted for himself. He pointed at me quite a lot, and at the interior of the barn.

Oh, dear. Like the sunrise I'd missed, the reason for all the uproar suddenly dawned in my brain. Oh, dear, oh, dear, and damnation again and again and . . .

"*You!*" The officer was addressing me. "*Come here.*"

Experimentally, I lowered my arms. His men did not fire. I walked over slowly, trusting that they feared him more than me. When close enough, I made a formal bow and reintroduced myself, this time with more dignity and less haste, and inquired after his own identity.

"Muller," he said, adding in something about his rank that was too quickly spoken for me to catch. He gave a curt sketch of a bow, then jerked ramrod straight, the better to look down his nose at me.

I asked him, as politely as I could, why he was here.

He countered with the same question.

I repeated that this was my land, that I lived here.

"*You live in a—*"

"*Pardon?*" I did not know the last word.

He pointed meaningfully at the barn.

I looked insulted and told him that my house was elsewhere on the property.

"*Why were you in the barn?*" he demanded.

My explanation that I'd had a long day of walking and had stopped for a rest did not sit well with him.

"*He was dead,*" put in my former guard, somewhat fearfully.

"*Asleep,*" I corrected firmly, keeping a bland face.

"*Dead,*" the man argued back.

I rolled my eyes and shrugged, trying to give the impression that the man had lost his senses. Few of the other men were willing to give up what must have been a vivid first impression of me, either. Several nodded agreement with the guard and made surreptitious gestures with one hand that supposedly protected them against the evil eye. These may have been the very ones who had first entered the barn and found my seemingly lifeless corpse, probably not the first they'd encountered in their military ventures, but very certainly the first that had ever revived.

"*Why are you here, sir?*" I asked the officer.

But he was not to be distracted into going on the defensive and demanded a further accounting to justify my own presence.

"*My German is poor, sir. Do you speak the English?*"

"*Nein,*" he said flatly, as though I'd insulted him.

"*The French?*"

"*Nein.*" This time it was a sneer.

Sighing, I decided to forgo asking after his skill at Italian or Latin, then an idea flashed up. "*Do you know Lieutenant Nash of the British? He is my friend.*" Well, that was stretching things a bit, but perhaps a familiar name might improve this fellow's disposition.

"*Nein. What are you doing here?*"

I repeated myself.

"*He was dead,*" insisted the guard.

The other men nodded.

The officer glared at him.

"*It's true! We found his—*"

Again, I had no understanding of this last word, but could guess that it meant "corpse" or "body." His gestures were eloquent as the man babbled on, anxious to prove his case that I was, indeed, deceased. His allies offered agreement whenever he paused for breath, then Muller had enough and cut him off with a sharp order. He was very good at glaring, and liberally demonstrated this talent to us all. The men came to attention for him, but it was uneasily held by the guard's allies. When things were quiet again, Muller growled at the guard, who saluted and went into the darkness of the barn.

When he emerged a moment later, he had another man with him, a civilian. The poor fellow's hands were bound and there was a rough sack over his head, but I instantly recognized him.

"Jericho! What in God's name have they done to you?"

Heedless now of their threat, I rushed over to him and tore away the sack. Jericho's face was covered with an uncharacteristic sheen of sweat, and he was very white around the pupils. His lip was split, and a bad bruise was swelling one eye shut. His clothes were covered with dust and torn, and his movements were slow, silent and plaintive indication of his ill treatment.

I rounded on Muller, so white-hot with outrage that I was unable to speak. Apparently my expression was eloquent enough, for this stone of a man actually flinched before recovering himself.

"Who did this?" I snarled, forgetting myself and using English, but Muller seemed to understand my meaning.

"Keiller," he said to the guard.

Keiller responded with another rapid explanation. I didn't bother to try following it, having no interest in excuses. Instead, I found my penknife and cut away Jericho's bonds.

"Are you badly hurt?"

"I shall be able to walk home," he said. "And if not that, then I shall certainly crawl."

"What happened?"

He rubbed his wrists. His hands were shaking. He was shaking all over.

"You came out to check on me, is that it?" I prompted.

He nodded. "It was getting on to dark. I was waiting for you to wake up when they came. They . . ." He gulped, clearing his throat. "Upon finding a Negro man with a dead white man, they concluded that I had killed you."

"Oh, my God."

"They were . . . their reaction was not gentlemanly. I . . . they were—" He was swaying on his feet.

"Sit down, man," I said taking his arm.

"*No.* Not before them, I won't." He straightened with a glare every bit as formidable as Muller's. "They were going to hang me, Mr. Jonathan. Kept waving a noose under my nose and laughing. Perhaps it might not have happened, but I am most pleased that you woke up when you did."

I stared at him, a great knot in my throat, once more at a loss for words. The situation was all but beyond speech, yet somehow I found it and turned it upon Muller.

"You barbaric son of a whore—" I began. Muller may not have understood my words, but he could make sense of my tone well enough.

"Mr. Jonathan, now is not the time to antagonize the man," Jericho cautioned.

"He and his lot should be flogged for what they've done to you."

"Agreed, sir, but presently they have the numerical advantage."

I had more, much more, invective in me, but Jericho's reasoning had penetrated the anger fogging my thoughts. When I was once more my own master, I saw that the best course of action was for us both to get away as quickly as possible. Muller would doubtless object, but that was something that could be easily overcome.

"*Herr Muller, we are going home now.*" I stated this as inarguably as possible, looking directly into his eyes. "*You will excuse us.*" It was very polite, despite my hot feelings, but polite German was all I had. Fortunately, it served. I did not know Muller well enough to be able to read any subtle changes in his otherwise fierce expression, but my influence must have worked. He made no objection when I put a supportive arm around Jericho and led him away. His men, taking this as assent, parted before us. Some were very anxious to keep a goodly distance.

"By God, this is enough to turn me into a rebel myself," I growled as we left them behind.

"I would not recommend it, sir."

"Damnation to the bastards. Why not?"

"Because if this is how our friends treat us, how much worse might we receive from our enemies?"

"I'm so sorry, Jericho. This is my fault."

"Hardly, Mr. Jonathan." He paused in his walk, gasping a bit. "May I ask to simply lean on your arm, sir? I fear your well-intentioned assistance is somewhat painful to my ribs."

I let go of him and offered to run ahead and fetch the carriage and Dr. Beldon, but Jericho insisted that we could be home by the time I'd returned with help, and so it proved. With him holding onto me for balance, we hobbled up one of the graveled paths to the house. When we were close enough, my shouts brought forth one of the stable lads and all of the dogs. The noise attracted more people, more help, and finally Dr. Beldon arrived to assume his duties as a physician. I was very glad to turn the responsibilities of caretaking over to him.

"Jonathan?" My father came striding over even as Beldon supervised Jericho's removal into the house for treatment. "What in God's name is going on?"

After several unavoidable repetitions as more of the household came by to listen, I concluded my story to Father in the library. He understood from Elizabeth the purpose of my visit to the barn, and neither of them offered any objection to my slightly expurgated version of the facts. The important issue for us was that there were unwelcome Hessian soldiers squatting on our land.

"Beasts," said Elizabeth, in reference to Jericho's beating.

"You shouldn't have been out there to start with," said Mother, sniffing. "Perhaps next time you'll stay home."

Since her comment had added nothing of merit to the conversation, I readily ignored it, as did everyone else. Perhaps we'd gotten used to them after all this time, making the task easier.

"Samuel, tomorrow you will immediately go and seek recourse about having them removed from the property," she said. "This is intolerable. Next thing you know they'll be begging for food at our very door."

"It's more likely that they shall simply take it where it stands in the fields," he said.

"Then you will find a way to prevent that. They're here to fight the rebels, not steal from the King's loyal subjects. If they want food, they can take it from the seditionists but not from us."

"I'll do what I can, Marie."

"See to it." She jerked her chin up in a most insufferable manner, but my father suffered it. Argument with his wife was both aggravating and futile, so once more he refrained from doing so. She turned a cold eye on me. "And this time you will help him, Jonathan Fonteyn. You've no illness or injury to excuse you from an honest day's work anymore. This constant shirking is to end. I didn't spend all that money on your education for you to lie about the place doing nothing. What would people think?"

I considered that other people would hardly find my apparent inactivity to be in the least interesting, but kept that opinion to myself. "I'll do what I can, madam," I said, assuming Father's acquiescence. It seemed the wisest course.

Her expression was such as to indicate she found my response to be irritating, but not so much so as to upbraid me for it.

Dr. Beldon came in just then. "Your man is going to be all right, Mr. Barrett," he told me. "There's some extensive bruising and a couple of cracked ribs. He is in some discomfort and will be for some time, but he should eventually make a full recovery."

"Thank heaven for that. And thank you for your kind help, Doctor."

"To be sure, I am only too happy to—"

"That's another mistake that should be corrected," Mother interrupted.

Beldon cut himself short. He'd had much practice at it in her company.

The corners of her mouth turned down more deeply than usual as she looked at me. "If you'd sold that creature off and hired a proper English servant as I'd told you to do years ago, none of this would have happened."

I took in a sharp breath and glanced at Father. He shook his head ever so slightly. That particular conflict had long been put to rest; Mother was talking only to hear the sound of her own voice. She was overly fond of it, I judged.

"Well," said Father, standing up. "There's naught to be done about any of this tonight, so let's try to forget about it for a few hours. Marie, would you like to partner me at cards against the doctor and Mrs. Hardinbrook?"

Good God, but he *was* anxious to distract her to make such a proposal.

"Not yet, Samuel. I've some news of my own to impart."

He tried to put on a friendly, interested face, and almost succeeded. Mother's idea of news often turned out to be disappointingly trivial.

"I received a letter today from one of my cousins in Philadelphia. She says that conditions there are perfectly horrifying. The streets are awash with traitors, and their treatment of loyal subjects is a disgrace. She has wisely accepted my invitation to stay here until things are put right again."

"Really?" said Father, sounding a touch faint. "Which cousin might that be?"

"Cousin Anne Fonteyn, of course," she said impatiently, as though Father should have somehow divined her thoughts and known.

"Cousin Anne?"

"Yes, Father's youngest brother's daughter. You *know* her."

"Yes, I seem to recall . . ."

"Oh, for heaven's sake, Samuel, if you don't remember her, then say so, I can't abide it when you dither like that."

Father's expression grew harder, but he did not give in to his emotions.

Elizabeth's eyes met mine, silently communicating her anger and sympathy for his plight. I could almost hear her previous night's refrain: *she's getting worse.* To some extent I could agree with her, but could not help thinking that Mother was not worsening, only growing less inhibited in expressing her casual cruelties. It was when those expressions were questioned that she became worse.

"They'll be here any time, now, I'm sure."

"They?" asked Father.

"She said she was not traveling alone, as it's much too dangerous. I expect she'll have some servants with her. The other cousins are choosing to remain in the city."

Thanks be to God for his mercy, I thought.

"I don't want her to think that we're a tribe of uncivilized savages. All will have to be in readiness for her arrival, including getting rid of those soldiers." She made them sound no more threatening than an inconveniently placed wasp nest to be smoked out by one of the groundsmen. "I won't have them running about as though they owned the place. What would people think?"

"For a woman with such keen concern over the opinions of others, one would assume she'd have an equal regard for those of her own family," I later confided to Elizabeth when everyone had gone.

"Oh, bother it, Jonathan. The woman has no regard for anyone but herself." Elizabeth had taken her favorite chair near the settee. She'd found a piece of string somewhere and endlessly curled and uncurled it around her fingers.

"The woman?"

Elizabeth paused to wearily rub the back of her neck. "I'll call her 'Mother' to her face, but don't expect me to maintain any pretense of affection in private. She's no mother to me beyond the fact that I lived in her womb for some months before finally escaping."

"Good God!"

"No need to be so shocked, little brother, for have you not had the same thoughts yourself? I see that you have."

"Perhaps not so crudely put—"

"I know and I'm sorry, but that woman angers me so. Were a stranger on the lane to treat me as she does, I'd have nothing more to do with her, yet we have to put up with it day after day after day, and it's far more dreadful for poor Father." She twined the string around one finger tightly, turning the unadorned remainder of her flesh quite red from the constriction.

"At least he's able to find some solace with Mrs. Montagu. I think that's why he proposed an early card game."

"Yes, get the evening's torture out of the way so he's free to leave. I'm glad he has Mrs. Montagu; she must be of considerable comfort to him. I wish she could be our mother instead. In a way she was for all those years that that woman lived away from us. But she's Father's solace, not ours. I wish

I could find some for myself." She unwrapped her finger and studied the ridges the string had impressed into her flesh.

"What do you mean? Take a lover?" I all but whispered the last word.

"Take a . . ." Her mouth sagged. "Oh heavens, Jonathan, of course not. What are you thinking?"

My face went hot. "That's the problem, I wasn't. Please forgive me."

She thought about it awhile. "No need, I can see where you came up with that, and were I that sort of woman, I might consider it, but since I'm not, I shan't."

"But Mrs. Montagu is a perfectly respectable lady," I protested.

"Of independent means and with her own house, things which are denied me. What were you thinking this time?"

"If I answered that, I should be repeating myself," I said glumly.

She laughed again, as I'd hoped she would, but sobered after a bit. "It's just not fair. Men can follow all sorts of interesting pursuits, but women must be satisfied with babies and running the house and doing what other people tell them."

"Were you a man, what would you do?"

"Want to turn back into a woman, but as a woman, I might like to go to Cambridge as you did. I could study law or medicine, but perhaps not the clergy, as the work is much too hard: sermons every week, tea parties, and having to be nice to everyone, including people like *her*."

Mother. "What makes you think law or medicine is any less toilsome?"

"It's not, I'm sure, but I've a better head for it. I see how Father enjoys what he does; he plows through his law books like a farmer in a field and he's brilliant at it. I've also watched Dr. Beldon. He may play the toady for a place at table here, but he's a very good physician. I wonder why he doesn't set up his own household; he could easily support himself."

"It's too much to do. If he's busy running his own house, he might not have time for his practice."

"Then he should marry. There must be some woman out there who enjoys housework."

"I hardly think that wedlock is anything he'd want to try." I leaned back on the settee and put my feet up on the arm of Elizabeth's chair. "For a man of his nature, he's better off simply hiring a housekeeper."

"Has he been any problem to you lately?"

"Not at all. He's a gentleman."

"And extremely fond of you."

"I'm aware of that, dear sister. However, it is not within me to return his regard in a like manner. He understands that."

"It's all rather sad, isn't it?"

"I suppose it is."

"Your boots want a polish," she said after a moment's idle study, having apparently forgotten her length of string along with Dr. Beldon.

"Another time." Head cradled back in my clasped hands, I shut my eyes and sighed with vast contentment. "It worked, y'know."

"What worked?"

"Your idea about my sleeping in the barn."

"Really? With all the excitement about the Hessians, I forgot to ask. No bad dreams?"

"Not a one. I had no sense at all of the passage of the day— that's what left me so confused, else I might have handled things differently when I woke up."

"That's wonderful, but what will you do tonight? You can't go back to the barn."

"No, I can't, but the experiment was a success, and from that point perhaps I may determine why it was successful. What quality is there about the barn that allowed me to find true rest?"

"Darkness?" she suggested.

"I have that up in my room."

"Fresh air? I know there's none once Jericho closes the shutters and windows and puts up the blankets."

"That's something to consider. I could try sleeping in the basement today, plenty of air there every time the door opens. On the other hand, I do not breathe regularly, so why should I require fresh air, particularly when I am in a state that so perfectly imitates death?"

She tapped one of my ankles. I opened my eyes. Her own were sparkling with intense thought. "Consider this: where would you be had you not come back to us?"

"Out in the barn?"

"No! I mean where would you be if you hadn't come back? If you were still—"

Ugh. I hated to think about that.

She answered for me. "You'd be in your grave. In the *ground*."

"My body only, I should hope and pray that my soul might be more happily lodged in heaven."

"Exactly. But both your body and soul have returned to the earth. Might we consider that between your death and return that some sort of compromise is required?"

"What are you leading to?"

"Well, just look at it. The only time you obtained any rest has been in the barn, on the *bare earth* of the barn."

"Surely you're not asking me to return to my grave?" I found this idea to be not just repugnant, but enough to make my bones go all watery.

"Certainly not!"

"Then—oh, yes, I think I perceive it now. You're recommending that I simply sleep on the ground, preferably in some sheltered, sunless area."

"I—"

"But I've already proposed to sleep in the basement."

"With the scullery boy tripping over you and getting a fright like those Hessians? No, I'm thinking that you might take a quantity of earth with you when you go to bed this morning."

"Take the grave with me instead of me going to the grave? Oh, that makes lots of sense."

"It's worth a try. Why don't you like it?"

"Because the idea of pouring a bucketful of earth onto the fresh, clean sheets of my bed and then cheerfully wallowing in it for the day is hardly appealing."

"Jonathan, you ass, put it in a sack or something first."

"Oh. Well, I would have thought of that eventually."

Her mouth curled to one side, indicating that she didn't quite believe me.

"I'll think about it," I promised, which satisfied her, though her mouth remained twisted, albeit for a different reason.

"Move your boots, would you? You stepped in something awful and I'm tired of smelling it."

I shifted my feet from her chair arm and sat up. "So you don't think I should sleep in the basement?"

"Only if you insist. You'd have to have a little 'talk' with Mrs. Nooth, though, perhaps with the whole kitchen staff."

"No, thank you. The last time I did so much 'talking' I got a wretched headache for my trouble." Headache . . . that reminded me of something. "Do you know anything about this cousin who's about to inflict herself upon us?" It occurred to me that out of self-protection I might have to exert a little influence over her when she arrived.

Elizabeth chuckled. "I talked to Mrs. Hardinbrook about her—or rather she approached and talked to me. She hardly ever does that unless she wants to inform me of some glowing virtue about her dear brother that I may have overlooked in the last three years."

"What did she say about the cousin?"

"Only general pleasantries of how *nice* it will be to have fresh company, but might it not be just a *little* bit crowded? She does like to clack on, you know, but it was a touch forced this time. I can only conclude that she's worried her position as the household's chief toad-eater is about to be usurped."

"Yes, and if it does get too crowded, Mother will choose blood kin over her best friend."

"Otherwise, what *would* people think?" Elizabeth did a credible, if supremely unflattering imitation of Mother's favorite worry.

"Perhaps we may be sincere in our welcome of Cousin Anne, then. Unless she turns out to be as bad as Mrs. Hardinbrook . . . or worse."

"That would take a bit of effort. Anne may share our Fonteyn blood, but please God, perhaps she's been spared the Fonteyn temperament."

"Amen to that," I said fervently.

CHAPTER
—3—

"Samuel, have you done anything about those soldiers on our land?" Mother demanded as she'd done every night at dinner for nearly two weeks.

"I have."

"And what of it?"

"The situation is under the most urgent scrutiny."

Not quite a lie, but hardly the truth, which Father had confided to me some time ago. The Hessians currently sheltering in the old barn at the edge of our property would remain there until further notice. Without permission or even a hint of payment, they'd made themselves at home by felling trees and slaughtering some of our cattle that had strayed too close to their sentries. Father's protests to their commanders were politely accepted, and he expected them to be just as politely ignored. It looked to be a long winter ahead for us all.

"I want them out of there as soon as possible. We'll all be murdered in our beds and it shall be your fault."

Thus spoke Mother, and Father had the great good sense not to respond to her statement. Since I was in the next room (trying to read) and alone, I was allowed the luxury of privately making a face and shaking my head.

"Oh, but we are very safe, Marie," said Mrs. Hardinbrook. "I must confess that until Lord Howe landed I had my worries, but now that his brave men are all over the Island—"

"Like ants on a corpse," muttered her brother.

"Really, Theophilous! We *are* eating!"

"My apologies, sister, but in case you haven't noticed, it is those so-called brave men who are causing Mrs. Barrett so much distress."

"Well, of *course* there are bound to be *some* soldiers who may behave in a less than honorable manner, but I'm sure their officers keep them in line."

"I think you'll find the officers are quite as bad. And as for those Hessian troops—" He broke off as though realizing that a detailed description of their atrocities might prove to be more offensive than instructive.

"They *are* foreigners, after all," said Mrs. Hardinbrook. "What do you expect?"

Like Father, Beldon chose not to provide an answer.

Mother was quick to step in where he had fallen back. "To be treated with the respect that is due to any loyal subject of the King."

"Amen to that," enthused Mrs. Hardinbrook. "Perhaps, Theophilous, you have not had the chance to meet some of the nicer officers, and therefore you've gotten a poor impression of our defenders."

"I've met enough to know that being an officer does not mean that the fellow is automatically a gentleman. My God, Deborah, if you'd seen what had happened to that poor Bradford girl this morning—even the beasts in the wild do not violate their young with such—"

"*Dr. Beldon*." My mother's voice came down like a hammer. "I will not tolerate such talk at my table."

An awkward silence followed—a frequent occurrence in this house—then came the sound of a chair scraping over the floor as Beldon stood.

"Forgive me, Mrs. Barrett. I forgot myself and let my instincts as a physician overcome my manners. You are quite right to remind me."

It was humbly spoken and apparently enough to appease Mother. Beldon next excused himself, and I heard the dining room door open and close.

"As I was saying, Samuel . . ." she resumed.

But I stopped listening when Beldon walked into the library, his face flushed and hands twitching. He gave a slight jump when he saw me sprawled in my usual spot on the settee, mumbled something about not wishing to intrude, and turned to leave.

"No, it's all right, I should greatly appreciate some company, Doctor, if you don't mind. Perhaps you would like to have a glass of Madeira to help your digestion?"

I gave him no chance to refuse and was up and pouring the stuff myself, rather than call and wait for a servant to do it.

Nonplussed, for I had never really encouraged his company before, he accepted the drink and took another seat across from me. "You're very kind, Mr. Barrett," he said, cautiously.

I shrugged. "Mother is in one of her more acid tempers tonight."

"You heard?"

"It was impossible not to."

Now he had a turn at shrugging and downed a good portion from his glass.

"What's this about the Bradford girl?"

Beldon was a gossip, albeit a pleasant one, but this particular subject was not one he was willing to explore. "I've no wish to be indelicate, Mr. Barrett."

"Nor have I. My interest is anything but prurient, I assure you. Will the girl be all right?"

He made a face. "In body, if not in soul."

"What happened?"

"I . . ." He labored a bit, then finally sighed. "I was taking the air this morning when I saw one of the village midwives hurrying along the creek road. As I'd not heard any of the ladies on the farms in that direction were in an expectant state, I made bold to question the woman about her business. I got a short answer for my trouble, but she didn't protest when I came with her.

"We got to the Bradford house and found the girl still in a much agitated state, but able to tell her story. As soon as we got her calmed down, we both examined her injuries and made careful note of all she said about her outrage. Before another hour had passed I lodged a complaint with Lieutenant Nash about the incident. He said he'd look into it." Beldon's tone implied that he had little faith in Nash's investigative abilities.

"You've spoken to Father about this, I hope?"

"Yes, and he's also made a protest. I think it may count more with Nash than mine, but whether any of it will count for anything remains to be seen."

"I think that it was most generous of you to do so much and

have no doubt that redress will soon follow."

"One can but hope. It's just the girl and her widowed mother, and they're all alone but for a few house servants and some field slaves. Their land's just enough to support them, but little else. When one has no money, one has no power. I just wish I could do more for them."

"But surely you've—"

"I mean that the girl has had more than her honor taken from her. There's such a thing as innocence as well. She's hardly more than fifteen and will likely carry this wretched burden with her all the rest of her life. It's enough to crack a heart of stone."

"But not, apparently, Lieutenant Nash's?"

"He's a self-important little coward hell-bent on avoiding any problem that falls his way. I suppose he thinks that by not dealing with it, and telling his superiors that all is well, he'll finish out this campaign with a promotion."

"Coward?"

"To anyone in the army above the rank of lieutenant. I've seen his like before."

I did not question him on that point. He'd once served in the army years back during the war with the French, and loathed to speak of it. That he even made a reference to it now indicated to me the depth of his feelings.

"Is there no more to be done? Can we not speak to someone other than Nash?" I asked.

"I suppose so, but there's so much going on that I doubt anyone will listen. Poor Miss Bradford is but another report to those in charge. They've more pressing matters on their mind than to seek redress for some penniless, friendless farm girl. It's also sick-making to think her attacker is yet unpunished. He's probably boasting to others this very minute about what he's done and perhaps plans to repeat his crime."

"Did you get his name?"

He shook his head. "She described him well enough, though. It was definitely an officer, from the look of his uniform. Had a scar shaped like a backwards 'L' on his cheek. Shouldn't be hard to find him, but Nash put me off. Damn the man." He finished his Madeira.

"Another glass?"

"No, thank you. I appreciate your listening to all this. It's very kind of you to be concerned."

"At your service, sir."

He stood. "I think I'll just check on Jericho, then have a walk about the grounds."

I lifted my brows. "No card game with Mother?"

He shot me a guarded look. He was well aware of how things were in this family, with Father, Elizabeth, and myself drawn close to support one another against Mother's ill temperament. As a physician, he was often called upon to treat Mother's more severe attacks, but as a toad-eating dependant, he had to pretend, like his carefully blind sister, that nothing was wrong. It often left him adrift somewhere in the middle of the mess, and I felt sorry for him about it.

He perceived that I was not mocking him with my question. Such abuse came often enough from "dear Deborah," so I found no fault with his brief doubt against me. He shook his head and smiled shyly. "I don't think so. Haven't the stomach for it tonight. Good evening, Mr. Barrett." His step was slow as he left, his shoulders a little slumped. Sometimes sympathy can be as heavy a burden as contempt.

I put my book aside and ground my teeth for several minutes, which accomplished nothing. I'd been doing quite a lot of that lately: nothing.

It had been necessary for me to "talk" with the kitchen staff, after all, so that they would take no notice of me sleeping the day through in a remote corner of the cellar. It was very rough sanctuary compared with my excellent bed upstairs, but safe from fire and discreet. I rested better than a king lying on the tamped-down earth there. No longer prey to the distraction of constant fatigue, I now chafed for something to do.

My very early morning activities of exploring the sky above our lands had not yet palled, but there was a certain hollowness in such a solitary pursuit. To share the experience with a companion would have been a blessing, but that, I found, was an impossibility. My talent for vanishing was confined to myself alone. A few nights ago, Elizabeth had bravely agreed to participate in an experiment to see if she might be able to disappear with me. She'd been less than enthusiastic, but balanced it with cautious curiosity. Putting my arm around her, I gradually ceased to be, but she remained solid as ever and shivering with sudden chill.

"You seem to draw all the warmth out of the air when you do that," she observed upon my disappointed return.

"I wonder why that is? Perhaps I could ask Rapelji about it."

"You could try, but don't let Rachel or Sarah hear you or it will be all over the Island by noon."

"It was but jesting speculation, sister. What Rapelji and his housekeepers don't know won't hurt me. I'll keep my questions to myself."

Alone. I was tired of being alone. I was tired of being in the house. Any rides I took on Rolly were limited to the immediate grounds, as it was dangerous to go any farther after dark. I had no fear for my own security so much as that of my horse. Rolly was too dear to me to lose him to a stray musket ball or to a greedy soldier looking to confiscate some four-legged booty.

Well, if I couldn't distract myself with riding, then at least I could walk, and I had a mind to walk a goodly distance tonight. After a quick stop in my room to ready myself with hat, stick, and some spare coin, I made my escape out the side door. My only encounter was with Archimedes, Jericho's father and valet to mine. A naturally taciturn man, he merely raised an eyebrow at my leaving. I nodded back and told him I was going for a walk, should anyone ask after me. His brow twitched and his lips thinned. By that I understood that Father would shortly know of my nocturnal ramble. It hardly mattered. Father knew I would be safe enough.

It was much too early, and I was too close to the house, to try taking to the air; also, the wind was very gusty and strong with the promise of rain in it. I thought of going back for my cloak, but decided my plain blue wool coat would suffice. I was not at all cold.

Yet another immunity, Nora? I thought, trudging off into the dark that was not dark to me. To my best recollection, she'd never complained of the cold, not even during the worst of England's weather.

I left our long drive and turned onto the Glenbriar road. If I was careful and quiet, I would not need to worry about sentries until quite close to Glenbriar, and even then they were of little concern to me. The ones under Lieutenant Nash's immediate command all knew my face, though God knows what else they knew about me if those two Hessians I'd frightened a while back had been talking.

The walk was more invigorating than fatiguing despite the rough tug of the wind. I was not hungry, not yet, perhaps not even for the night, having learned that nightly feeding was not always necessary for my needs. Every other evening suited for me, that is, if I did not indulge in skyward antics, an exercise which naturally roused a good appetite.

I passed many familiar landmarks, marveling at them anew in the bright silver glow that seeped through the roiling clouds high above. Diffuse and shadowless, but occasionally uneven, it was like watching sea waves dance as the light fluttered over the ground and wove between the trees and hedges. I could have read a book by it, but for the distracting motion. On the other hand, why should I read when such fleeting natural entertainment offered itself? The book would be there when things calmed again.

The buildings gradually increased in number, and I caught the attention of a few dogs as I passed down the lane. Shutters opened or remained shut, depending on the courage of the occupants. I was challenged by two gruff sentries, but they recognized me and let me pass unquestioned. They were not the two who had called me "*blutsauger*."

The Oak was a venerable old inn that had started as a simple tavern back when the first settlers had come to take land from the local Indian tribes. It was said that many a grant and swindle had occurred over the tables there and little had changed since that time. It had grown quickly through the years and boasted several comfortable rooms now. Mr. Farr, the owner, brewed excellent beer and ale and had a good cook, but alas, I was no longer permitted to partake of those particular earthly pleasures again.

As Glenbriar was but a small village, the keeping of early hours had been the rule, but not anymore. The soldiers had turned the inn into a kind of headquarters, and they kept whatever hours their mood demanded. Perhaps Mr. Farr was making a healthy profit; he certainly deserved some compensation for all the inconvenience.

"Good evening, all," I said, crossing the threshold.

The common room held all varieties of soldiers, most of them divided into groups by subtle variations of their uniforms. There were a number of familiar village faces as well, also crowded together. I saw scant evidence of them mingling with one another. Because of the disruptions, outrages, and out-and-out theft by our saviors, there was little love between the civilians and the military.

"Mr. Farr." Smiling, I approached him where he sat smoking at his favorite spot near the fire.

He stood, looking all pale and awkward. Like many others in our community, he'd heard of my death and burial. And by now he'd also heard my sister's story that it had been a visiting cousin of mine of the same name who had died, not me. As with many other folk, he was in sore confusion over what to believe about the incident. He'd seen me more than once since the night of my return, but still suffered from a base and lingering fear of me. Without an overworking of my usual manner, I always tried to put the man at ease whenever possible.

I shook his hand and inquired after his health and got a halting reply about the ache in his bones, an unfortunate reminder for him. The last time I'd been by, my broken arm had been in a sling. His eyes traveled down to that particular limb, and he made a similar inquiry after my well-being.

"Feeling quite the best these days, Mr. Farr. Dr. Beldon is a miracle man. Patched me back together better than before. I'm sure he'd be more than happy to help if you wished to consult him yourself."

"Er—ah—yes, I s'pose I might do that some time, sir. Can I get you anything?"

"Not just now, thank you. I came by to talk with Lieutenant Nash. I hope that I may find him in?"

"He'll be in t'other room there. Quieter." He indicated a door off to one side. I excused myself to Farr, knocked twice to announce myself, and went in.

Nash was nearly finished with his supper. Quite a boneyard of chicken leavings was piled on his plate, and he was in the act of washing down a last crust of pie with his beer when I entered. He hastily swallowed, coughed, and stood up, wiping his mouth with the back of his hand.

"Good God, it's Mr. Barrett!" he exclaimed. His pleased surprise was highly gratifying. I hadn't known what sort of welcome to expect.

We shared a greasy handshake and he invited me to sit with him. I declined his offer of refreshment.

"How have you been, sir? Arm all better, I see?" he asked, settling himself once more.

"All better," I echoed and once again gave the credit to Beldon.

"That is good to hear. It was bothering you quite a lot the last time I saw you. Figured that's how we lost track of you that night."

I'd been "helping" Nash chase down some escaped rebels then, and he was right, my arm had caused me much discomfort at the time. "Yes, I'm sorry about that."

"Where did you get to, anyway?" he asked, his eye still sharp after what must have been a sizable flagon of beer.

Oh, dear. If I had one more mixed blessing to thank Nora for, it was being forced to learn how to lie quickly and well. I hated it, as any lie was a dishonor, but the alternative was even more dishonorable, depending on the circumstances. This time I judged them to be safe enough for me to bluff my way through.

"I'm not really sure, Mr. Nash. I recall trying to chase down those murdering thieves, and then I got all turned around in the dark. Very alarming, that. I've lived all my life here and know every stick and stone and then to get lost . . ." I gave out with a deprecating laugh. "When I got tired of blundering around, I gave my horse her head and she took me straight home, thank Providence. Beldon said I was a touch feverish, y'know. Went to bed and stayed there all the next day and the next, I was that worn."

"And in your wanderings, did you ever stray up toward the north road?"

"I've no recollection of going that far. If I had, then I might have found my way back without the horse's help."

"Very odd, sir, for some of the soldiers there reported seeing three suspicious-looking men that night. Two took off on a horse and went east on the road and the third ran away inland." Nash had left out one of the chief reasons for our hasty removal from the area, which was that the soldiers had fired upon us. We would have hared off anyway, but flying musket balls had lent additional speed to our exit.

"Three men? Sounds like your escaped prisoners found some help."

"My guess is that they ran into the fellow with the horse and persuaded him to treason."

"Persuaded?"

"That is, if he were a loyal subject. Though a mystery remains as to why he has not yet come forward about the incident. My other best guess is that the fellow was a traitor to begin with and, aware of their escape, took the first available opportunity to step in and help them get clean away."

"Have you taken steps to find him?"

"It did not seem necessary, as I thought that sooner or later he would come to me."

I put on a skeptical face. "Most obliging of him to do so, particularly if he's a traitor."

Nash looked me up and down. "Yes. Most obliging, Mr. Barrett."

"Any idea who he is?"

"A very good idea."

"Why, then, have you waited?"

He took his time before answering, perhaps hoping to make me sweat, but I kept a steady eye and an innocent manner. "Another thought occurred to me that the gentleman"—there was some emphasis on that word—"might find a disclosure of this incident to be not only bad for his health, but of supreme embarrassment to his family. I thought that the gentleman might appreciate an opportunity to avert such a catastrophic scandal."

"That's uncommonly kind of you, Mr. Nash, but might that not be compromising to your duty to the Crown?"

"Only if the gentleman decides to talk about the incident. It has been my experience that given the choice, most men would rather keep silent than put their necks in a noose."

"And silence has a price, does it not?"

"A reasonable one, compared to the alternative," he murmured.

"There's more than one alternative, y'know."

"Indeed?"

I leaned forward into the candlelight and fastened my eyes upon his. Circumstances had changed; I'd misjudged Nash's intelligence and greed. Time to end the bluff for both of us. "Yes, Mr. Nash, and that's for you to forget all about it."

He blinked several times. I worried that he'd had too much beer for my influence to have any effect on him. "Forget?"

"Forget about the gentleman and your suspicions about him. In fact, you have no mind for him at all. The rebels met a stranger on the road and they all escaped. They're someone else's problem now. There will be no bribes given, no further inquiries to other soldiers, to the gentleman, or to his family. It's quite for the best, now, isn't it?"

"Eh . . . yes, I suppose it is," he responded shakily. He seemed a little short of breath. I watched him carefully, worried that he'd been aware of what I'd done to him. After a moment, he appeared to be himself again, if not a touch distracted. I went to the door and called for another flagon of beer. When I came back to the table, Nash had assumed an air of puzzlement, as though trying hard to remember something important. I'd seen that look before on others as well as myself in the past—in the past with Nora. It told me that I'd have no more trouble with the man.

Drink delivered and pot boy gone, I resumed our talk, this time bringing it around to a subject of my choosing.

"I'm sure my father has been to see you more than once about those Hessians that have taken over our old barn," I said, pushing the beer toward him.

Nash eyed it as if undecided about having an additional drink, especially one I'd bought him. "He has, sir. Many others have as well, but I fear I can do nothing for any of them. The troops must be quartered, and better an unused barn than your own house. Everyone else has to put up with it; there can be no exceptions."

As he warmed to something familiar, his confidence returned and he ended with a polite, but uncompromising tone. There'd be no improvement for this situation. I'd expected as much. Besides, if I influenced Nash into ridding us of the men, it might look odd. There'd been enough oddness connected with our family already; I had no wish to augment it. Father and I had done our best. If Mother wanted the Hessians off our land, she could argue with them herself.

"We must all do our duty as the King's loyal subjects, Mr. Nash," I said. "I just hope that the Crown will be equally generous in recompensing us for all our hospitality."

"As do I, Mr. Barrett." Since Nash was into collections, not purchases, he was not responsible for paying people for their lost victuals. In any other time or place he'd be hanged as a thief.

"May I count on you to see that we are not ignored?"

"You may place your every confidence in me, sir," he said heartily. It was a vague enough promise. I trusted him to keep it so long as it did not cause him too great an inconvenience.

"I wanted to consult you about another problem that's come to my attention, sir," I continued.

He made an expansive gesture, certain that my complaint would be within his ability to correct, providing a suitable sum of money changed hands.

"As you've probably heard from both Dr. Beldon and my father, a young girl was outraged by one of the officers in this area—"

"I think not, Mr. Barrett," he said, suddenly cool. "His Majesty's officers are honorable men and not likely to—"

"*Listen to me, Nash!*"

He left his sentence unfinished, mouth agape, and eyes gone wide and dull. I'd had enough of posturing and words with more than one meaning; some of my anger had broken out and threatened to escape entirely. Now that I had a vessel to pour it into, it was extremely difficult to keep it in check. There was a strong temptation boiling up within to let it free, but that, some instinct told me, would not be a good idea. Nora had once lost her temper while influencing someone, and the resulting shock to the other's mind had been most unfortunate.

The memory of that fearful encounter served to calm me. After a moment or so, I was my own master again and able to speak in a civil manner.

"Nash, I don't care about the honor of His Majesty's officers. All I want is redress for that poor girl. The bastard who violated her is to be punished in full, and you will see to it. You've heard his description, you must know who he is."

"Yesss . . ." he said faintly.

"Good. Then you won't waste another minute hunting him down and seeing that you make an example of him for his crime. You'll drum it into the heads of every one of your men, because if this happens again, I'm holding you responsible."

He was trembling. That made two of us, but for very different reasons.

"I want you to treat this business as though that girl were your own dear daughter, understand?"

Eyes blank, body shaking like a leaf in a gale, and brow streaming with sweat, he nodded.

"Then get started." I looked away, glancing back only when his sharp gasp announced that he'd recovered his senses.

He stood, deathly pale, and his eyes did not quite meet mine. "Y—you must excuse me, Mr. Barrett, but I've a most urgent errand to attend to just now." His hands nervously worked one against the other.

When I took a breath to make a reply, I picked up a sudden tang of scent from him and somehow knew what it was: fear. *Well-a-day.*

I could have taken it away from him, but it pleased me that Nash should be afraid. Of me. In my Latin studies I'd read some Machiavelli and made note of his harsh but highly practical recommendation that "it is much safer to be feared than loved," so I left things as they were. The favorable regard of this one soldier was of little value to me; I could live without it as long as he did what was expected of him.

"Of course, Lieutenant. I wish you every success," I muttered to his back as he rushed out the door.

Nash collected all the uniformed men in the common room and left, much to the mystification of the remaining folk. I suppose I could have gone home then, but I was hungry for company. A change of company. He'd given me a sour belly, and unless I found some distraction, I'd likely carry the foul taste of his greedy game playing with me all the rest of what promised to be a long night.

When I emerged in his wake from the private room, questioning eyes focused upon me.

"What 'uz all that about, Mr. Barrett?" someone called.

I hesitated.

They ascribed an ominous meaning to that pause. "What is it, sir? Are there rebels about? They go off t' fight 'em?"

"Rebels? No, nothing like that." I abruptly saw things from their point of view. Having noted my lengthy talk with Nash and his subsequent hasty exit, they might well have thought I'd brought news of some unhappy incursion by members of the rebel forces. "Mr. Nash remembered a duty he'd left undone and went to see about it, that's all he would say to me."

Thus was I able to shrug off their additional questions. I was loath to mention the business about the Bradford girl. The story of her misfortune would carry through the village soon enough.

The coin I'd brought provided the distraction I craved. The price of a few drinks for the other customers guaranteed me all the companionship I could have wished for. Perhaps they weren't as clever or as sophisticated as the friends I'd left behind at Cambridge, but they were solid as the earth itself and honest enough when given the chance. I wondered if any of them had run up against Nash's genteel squeezing, then firmly put it from my mind. Few of them had any money to speak of, unlike me.

Though repeatedly invited to drink with them, I managed to dodge the honor by a solemn invocation of Beldon's name.

"He made my arm better, but tells me it's still mending itself inside. He's particularly strict about my eating and drinking, but never said I couldn't enjoy watching others do it for me."

This brought out an unexpected and extremely ribald comment from Mr. Thayer, an elderly farmer smoking his thin pipe in one corner. What he said and how he said it, combined with the man's age, doubled us over and inspired more talk along similar lines. Because business was so good, Mr. Farr—who usually did not tolerate much rough speech—ignored us and kept the drink flowing.

The ensuing hours passed quickly and pleasantly for us, perhaps more so for them than for me, as most of the jests were improved by the constant ingestion of beer and gin. I laughed along with most of the talk, though, and heard all the gossip to theirs about the progress of the war, such as it was. For us, it was as good as over now that Howe had chased Washington off the Island.

"He'll have to hurry to catch him up," said Mr. Curtis, who had a farm east of the village and was sometimes privy to more recent news than the rest of us. " 'Twill be over soon enough. I heard the whole rebel army was on the run and not planning to stop 'til they reached Connecticut."

"Good riddance to 'em," someone put in. "Connecticut deserves 'em, not us."

"Aye, they do," added another. "Connecticut, bah!" He spat on the floor.

"If you please, Mr. Davis!" protested Farr, preventing the rest of us from following suit.

Davis grinned and drunkenly apologized. "Think I'll take m'self 'ome, gen'lmn." He detached himself from his table and might have fallen flat if Curtis hadn't smoothly grabbed the back of his coat.

"You won't make it home walking on your nose, son," he observed.

"Reckon I won't," said Davis, bent hard over and talking to his shoes.

Since I'd been the direct cause of his drunken state, I thought it only right to see the man to his door. "Come along with you, Mr. Davis. Let's go look for some fresh air. Good night, all."

This time I got a hearty response; even Mr. Farr joined in the chorus of good-byes as I collected Davis and steered him outside.

"No need t' be such trouble o'r me, Mr. Barrett," he said.

"It's no trouble, Mr. Davis."

Weaving, we made our way across the village common. His house wasn't very distant, and he wasn't much of a burden. Had I been in a hurry, I could have easily thrown him over one shoulder, but there was no need for haste or to remove what small dignity remained to him. Besides, the evening air that we sought was pleasant enough now that the wind had died off. It was still cool—as far as I could tell—and the sky yet had a promise of rain in it, but later, probably just before dawn.

Any sentries that were about left us alone. It had long since been determined that the rebel prisoners had made a clean escape, so Nash's unpopular curfew had been lifted. The presence of His Majesty's soldiers in Glenbriar had disrupted things mightily, but life was gradually getting back to normal. Much daily business went on as before and, as evidenced by the carousing at The Oak, the nightly business went on as well.

"Very kind of you, 'm sure," said Davis, mumbling to his shoes again. " 'M in your debt, sir."

"Think nothing of it, Mr. Davis. You and your friends have helped restore my faltering faith in the goodness of man's nature." He couldn't have understood one word in five, but it mattered little to me.

"What about the goodness of woman's nature?" a feminine voice inquired out of nowhere.

I stopped, nearly tripping Davis, who could ill afford a fall. "Who's there?"

She answered with a giggle, no doubt inspired by my startled tone.

Davis swayed in my arms and threatened to topple right over. I peered into the dark doorway of the house we were passing. The voice had come from the shadows within.

"It's Molly Audy, if you're that interested, Mr. Barrett," she said, stepping free of her shelter.

We'd had no formal introduction prior to this encounter, but as Glenbriar was such a small place it wasn't any surprise that she knew who I was, and I certainly had seen her before.

Molly earned her bread by sewing during the day, and the rest of life's necessities were earned on her back at night. She was shunned by the ladies of the village, but not to the point that they could oust her from the community altogether. Molly's behavior and dress were outwardly respectable and modest and she was famous for her discretion, a quality that the men could well appreciate. She'd been the object of much of my study before I'd been sent off to Cambridge, study made at a distance, mind you. She was five years older than I, which had seemed a great gulf of age at the time. I'd been much too nervous to approach her then.

Well, a university education and some spare money can do wonders for a young man's confidence, and, though surprised, I was not reduced to stammering out an awkward greeting as I might have done some three years ago. I wished her a good evening and she returned it to me.

"Looks like your friend's had too much, need some help?" She floated toward us, eyes bright and a smile hovering just behind them. As she came closer, the smile burst forth.

Davis had abruptly turned into a damned nuisance.

"No, uh—that is, yes! I certainly could use some assistance, Miss Audy. I'm not exactly sure which house he belongs to." Oh, dear, but lust does make easy liars of us all.

Molly's raised brows said that she was aware of the lie, but was willing to overlook it while letting me know she was doing just that. She had a remarkable range of expression, I noted.

"It's not far, just come along with me, sir."

At a faster pace than before, I all but dragged Davis along as Molly led the way. She unerringly found and pushed open a door to yet another darkened house. I had little desire to linger in my surroundings and stayed just long enough to drop Davis into a chair before following Molly out again.

"Will he be all right, you think?" she asked.

"I'm sure of it," I said as concern for Davis fairly galloped from my mind. "A good night's sleep is all he wants."

She giggled again. "Don't we all?"

I swept my hat off and bowed, which brought forth another giggle. "I'm deeply in debt for your help, Miss Audy. May I repay you in some small way by safely escorting you home?"

She slipped an arm into mine. "La, Mr. Barrett, but I do like the way you talk."

"I'll be more than happy to continue for as long as you find it entertaining."

"Then maybe you can tell me what you think about 'the goodness of women.' "

"On that subject, I'm sure to turn quite eloquent, given the proper inspiration."

We returned to her dark doorway, and she drew me first inside her house and then inside the reach of her arms. I bent down to give her a proper kiss and got a gratifying response.

"Such a big, strong fellow you are," she said, hands kneading away at my shoulders.

"And you are quite the beautiful lady."

"I try my best, though times are very hard, especially when one is all alone in the world . . ."

Instantly taking the hint, I groped for my money purse and we paused a moment to work out the mundane details of payment for services about to be rendered. Once business was out of the way, we resumed more intimate explorations. Molly, I discovered, very much enjoyed her work.

"Come back this way, Johnny boy," she cooed, slipping some fingers into the waist of my breeches and pulling me along.

To her bedroom, it turned out.

She threw the coverlet to one side and made me sit on the bed. A single candle burned in a holder set in a bowl of water on one table. The room was small but orderly, not that I cared much for her skills at housekeeping. She had other, much more interesting skills to hold my attention.

Like undressing herself.

One by one, she undid the hooks holding the front of her bodice together, playfully slapping my hand away when I offered to help. I gave up, lay back on my elbows, and watched. Free of the bodice, she put it on a chair and next attacked her wide skirts, petticoats, and other complications I couldn't begin to name. It took her some little time, but she finally worked her way down to her corset and shift. She retained her shoes and white silk stockings. I found her red garters to be particularly charming and said as much. For my benefit, she pulled a chair close and put one foot upon it, allowing me to make a closer examination not only of the garter, but the shapely leg it encircled. The lower part of the shift quite naturally fell back a bit owing to this change of position, gifting me with the chance to further my studies.

This time Molly made no objection when I offered assistance in the matter of undoing the lacings of her corset.

"You've done this before, my lad, haven't you?" she commented.

Oh, yes, but Nora was in England and Molly was very much *here*. I zealously plucked at the bow and loosened one loop after another.

"Ah, that does feel good," she said when I got the thing off. Understanding that she'd found its confines rather restricting, I did my best to help restore circulation to her upper body. Perhaps I was a bit too vigorous as she seemed to lose her balance and fell atop me onto the bed. But she was laughing, a laugh that I smothered as I pulled her mouth down to meet mine.

"Your turn," she softly announced a few very active minutes later. One-handed, she discovered the buttons on one side of my breeches and began to undo them.

"Not yet." I was too busy trying to get her shift off to worry about my own clothes. The garment finally flew up over her head and I dragged her close again and kept her fully occupied for awhile.

"Fair's fair, love," she protested. "I've a mind to see those muscles I been feeling." She teased open my neckcloth and began a fast assault on my waistcoat buttons, then my shirt. She was not, I was happy to see, disappointed with what lay beneath. "Now for the best part . . ." Her hand wandered down to my breeches again. I caught it and brought it up to my lips for a kiss, then returned to her mouth.

It's different, I thought. *Very decidedly different than before*.

Instead of a grand stirring of pleasure confined between my legs, I was stirred up, as it were, throughout all my body. It had never been this intense before. My God, if I felt like this now, what would our consummation be like?

There's one way to find out, Johnny boy.

We rolled and tossed around in a most energetic and pleasing way until Molly grew feverish and was impatient for me to finish things off. I kept her away from my breeches, though, for I understood now that their presence or absence would make little difference as to how this event ended for either of us.

She thrashed under me, breathless and calling for me to

hurry. My answer was to seek out the pulse in her taut throat and firmly run my tongue over her smooth skin. Then she went utterly still.

"*Yes*," she whispered.

Teeth and tongue working together, I bit into her neck. Her nails, in turn, bit into my back and her whole body writhed upward against mine. I knew what Molly was going through, having received this kind of kiss myself. Nora had taught me to appreciate every second and to crave the next and that with care, the ecstasy could be drawn out indefinitely.

The red fire of Molly's blood drifted into my mouth a drop at a time, to be savored like the rarest of nectars. She shuddered and moaned and moved under me in such a way as to invite me to drink more deeply from her. The temptation was there; I'd *never* tasted anything so sweet, so perfect.

I drew in a bit more, a whole mouthful.

Swallowed.

It was almost too much to bear. For us both. She cried out and pressed hard on the back of my neck as though she wanted me to empty her to the dregs.

But that would be . . . not right. If I took too much from her, it would somehow be too much for me. For then I would lose myself; I'd be completely overwhelmed and lost.

Ah, but it was so sweet, so good.

Very decidedly different . . .

It was all that I desired and more wonderful than I could have ever imagined.

. . . better. Much, much better.

Except for Molly's heartbeat, all was silent within that room, but within myself I heard her blood roaring throughout my body, my soul. For a time I *was* overwhelmed and lost in the vast pleasure of that hot tide. I floated like a leaf and let it carry me along to . . . I don't know were. Perhaps it was a place where all my happiest dreams lived, safe from the harshness of normal existence, where body, mind, and soul could meld with one another, able to combine all their respective delights into one devastating sharing.

I didn't want to leave, but taking the life from Molly a mouthful, or even a drop, at a time could not last forever, and I would not hurt her for the world . . . or even to maintain this incredible joy. Eventually, after a very long while, I slowly made my way back.

My next clear memory was of kissing away the last traces of blood from her skin. There remained behind two small, angry-looking wounds, but I knew their alarming appearance would pass rapidly. By morning they would be much less noticeable and be completely gone in a day or two.

Unless I decided to return to her.

Molly lay quiet for some time as her breath returned to normal. The orange light from the candle gilded the sheen of sweat covering her. She seemed to glow like an angel in a painting. Propped on one elbow, I ran a hand over her body, taking enormous delight in simply touching all that lovely, lovely flesh.

She turned her face toward me. Her eyes swept me up and down, wide and not a little puzzled.

"What is it?" I asked.

Her mouth opened. She shook her head. "My God . . . is *that* what they teach you in England?"

"You liked it?"

"I didn't have much of a choice, Johnny boy. It sort of grabbed me up and I couldn't stop it—not that I wanted to try."

This wasn't the empty flattery of Molly the experienced prostitute wanting a steady customer; I sensed that right enough. I'd honestly impressed Molly the woman, which made me feel very good, indeed.

She squinted in the dim light. "Your eyes are funny. They've gone all red."

"It'll go away, nothing to worry about. You needn't mention it to anyone." I looked at her closely and ran my hand over the spot on her neck. "You needn't mention any of this to anyone."

But there wasn't enough light for my attempt to influence her to work. Her expression remained unchanged.

"Don't want people to know how you do it? Is that it?" she asked.

Perhaps another candle . . . or if we moved closer to the light . . .

She shrugged. "You've naught to worry about there, Mr. Barrett. Molly the Mum is what they call me, and with good reason. I start passing tales, and gentlemen'll think twice before they come for a visit. I'm like a doctor, I am, and I don't talk about those as come to see me."

"Oh," I said, temporarily nonplussed.

"Anyways, there's stranger things I've done with gentlemen and none of them nowhere as nice as this. God!" She pushed her head back into the pillow and stared at the shadowy ceiling, her eyes shining again.

Well, it looked as though my secret was safe enough without special prompting, though I did feel obligated to offer a caution to her on the subject. "It would not be a good idea for you to try this yourself on anyone, y'know. Or to have them do it to you."

Her voice had grown soft. "I think I figured that out for myself, sir. Besides, without you, it wouldn't be quite the same thing, now, would it?"

"You're uncommonly kind, Miss Audy."

"There you go again with that nice talk," she said, grinning.

"May I take that to mean I might be privileged to enjoy your delightful company in the future?" I asked, playing along with her.

She sat up a little to look right at me. "Lord have mercy, but if you promise to do *this* to me again"—she brushed her neck with her fingertips—"as God is my witness, Johnny boy, I'll be paying *you*!"

CHAPTER
—4—

December 1776

"Then our mother said, 'Anne, we were *so* worried about you, thank heaven you've come at *last!*' and she threw her arms around her like she meant it."

"You think she didn't?"

"Knowing what she's really like?" Elizabeth snorted. "Maybe that's why she hates us so much, because we know the truth about her."

"I don't think she hates us so much as she has no regard for anyone but herself."

"No, little brother. She hates. It's covered up most of the time—that woman seems to have a bottomless supply of pretense—but it is there nonetheless. The fits that overcome her can't excuse it. There's a malignancy in her very soul."

"But not in yours," I said quietly, meaning to reassure.

Elizabeth gave me a sharp look.

"There is none of that in you."

Like a slow fever that refuses to rise high enough to burn itself out, more and more, Mother's dark presence intruded upon every subject, every activity for Elizabeth.

"I think you dwell on her too much."

She looked down, her face going red. "Am I trying your patience with my complaints?"

"No, but Mother is obviously trying yours."

What had begun as a light description of this morning's arrival of Cousin Anne had turned in on itself and soured. My sister, I was grieved to see, was not a happy woman, nor was her mood in danger of leaving.

"Is there no way that you can ignore her?" I asked.

"The way you and Father can? Hardly. It's different for me. Father has his work, and you're gone all the day. I can't leave the house because of those damned soldiers or the weather or some other thing comes up and prevents me from getting away from her. Even my room is no longer a sanctuary—you know how she always pushes in without knocking. You'd think she was trying to catch me out in some devilish crime when she does that. How disappointing it must be for her to find me reading, and when she does, she then criticizes me for wasting my time! *That's* how the Fonteyn madness will come upon me, Jonathan, Mother will drive me to it."

She pounded a fist against the side of her chair several times, then boosted to her feet to pace up and down the library. She wore one of her prettiest dresses, a light blue silk with touches of dark blue in the pattern. The colors were very flattering to her, bringing out her eyes especially, but she might as well have been in rags for all the effect it had on her spirits.

"Perhaps you could go stay with Miss Holland for a while," I suggested.

"I've been thinking of it. If no one else, Hester would welcome my company."

"What do you mean? You've lots of friends who would be delighted for you to visit."

"I know, but the way that woman hammers at me day after day, how I look or walk or questioning the very expression on my face, it makes me feel like no one would want to be seen with me. I'm not like that and I know it!"

"As do I, as does anyone with sense, which utterly excludes Mother."

She paused by the library doors. They were closed that we might enjoy a private talk before the party began, though it was something of a risk with Mother's uncertain temper. She had still not rid herself of her dreadful delusion about her children, and there was always a chance she might burst in and work herself into another fit if she found us alone together. Elizabeth was listening, perhaps, for her step.

"There's no one out there," I said.

"You're sure?"

"One of the maids went by a minute ago, that's all. Sheba, I think."

Her next look was brighter, more like herself. Interest in my improved senses never seemed to flag or lose its delight for her. "You can tell the difference?"

"It's not difficult after a little practice."

The delight faltered as her problems returned once more. "What am I to do? Oh, heavens, I *know* what to do, I just hate that *I* have to do it. She should be the one to leave, not I."

"You'll write Miss Holland, then?"

"After the tea party. I'd start now, but I don't want to risk spotting my fingers up with ink. *She* expects me to perform like some sort of trained monkey, and woe to me if I don't look just right for the show."

"Regardless of Mother's expectations of you, you do look perfect. Besides, the honor of serving the tea always goes to the daughter of the house."

"As I said, a trained monkey could—oh, never mind me, I'll get through it somehow. It's not as if I haven't had the practice." She swept up and down the room, her wide skirts threatening to overtopple a small table as she wasn't paying mind to where she was going.

"What's Cousin Anne like?" I asked, hoping to distract her.

"You can tell she's a Fonteyn with those blue eyes and black hair. She seems nice, but I've had no chance to talk with her or her companions. They've been resting from their journey most of the day."

"We'll get to know them better soon enough."

Perhaps too well, I silently added, having caught some of Elizabeth's pessimism. I was not looking forward to meeting any more relatives from Mother's side of the family. Though Cousin Oliver was a very decent fellow, his mother was a spiritual Gorgon. I worried that Cousin Anne might also carry a similar cruel streak, hopefully not, since it looked like she'd be staying with us awhile.

Sheba presently came and announced that we were wanted in the parlor. Elizabeth gave me a grim smile, set her chin high, and glided ahead like a ship sailing into battle. I followed in her wake, smoothing my own features as I prepared to meet our newly acquired house guests.

• • •

Despite Elizabeth's misgivings, she appeared to find enjoyment in her duties. It was a goodly sized party; several of our neighbors had turned up, and even Lieutenant Nash had gotten an invitation. I suspected Father had extended it, hoping to improve his relations with the commissaries.

Having smoothly taken her place at the tea table, Elizabeth saw to the measuring of tea from its chest and made sure the right amount of hot water was poured into the pot. Soon everyone filed past her accepting the first of many cupfuls for the evening.

Myself included, for I wanted to at least seem to participate with the rest. Father watched with amusement as I pretended to sip at my portion, knowing how difficult it was for me to even bring the cup to my lips. Once a favorite drink, it smelled awful to me now. As soon as he'd emptied his own cup, he took pity and exchanged it for mine at the first opportunity. We'd done this a number of times at other events and had acquired all the practiced ease of stage performers. No one noticed. Into the slop bowl went the dregs from his cup, which I then turned upside down on its saucer, placing the spoon across the bottom. Thus was I able to excuse myself from additional offers without causing offense. As hostess, Elizabeth was bound by courtesy to keep my cup filled, and with Mother watching, she did not dare to "overlook" me.

But tonight even Mother could not find fault with her, for most of her attention was upon her guests and Cousin Anne.

She was certainly worthy of notice.

She did indeed bear the striking Fonteyn features of blue eyes and black hair—though I had to take Elizabeth's word that it was black. It was powdered now and swept up high from her milk-white forehead and elaborately curled in the back. Her movements were polished and full of grace, no doubt part and parcel of the genteel manners practiced in Philadelphia. She wore a splendid dress of some striped stuff that rustled with her every movement and drew many enthusiastic compliments. She lapped them all up as readily as a cat takes to cream. Anne was young and beautiful and enjoyed being reminded of it.

"Yes, it was very fortunate that I was able to bring away most of my things," she said to the crowd of people gathered around her. "There were many, many others who had naught but the clothes on their backs, but then they'd not prepared themselves for an exodus, you see."

"And you've been ready since early in the fall?" asked Father, who seemed to be as taken with her as the other gentlemen.

"Since the summer, Cousin Samuel. We had a horrid time of it for all our readiness. Thank God you and Marie are here and so kind, or I should not have known what to do."

"You are very welcome in my house," said Mother, her face cracking a bit with one of her tight smiles. It did not touch her eyes, but then, none of them ever reached that far. "So you did get my reply to your letter?"

"Indeed, I did not, but then everything is in such a confusion these days."

Mother gave Cousin Anne her wholehearted agreement on that point.

"But with or without an answer from you I had to leave or suffer with the rest of the King's true subjects. I knew if I stayed I'd have no peace in that sad city, for the rebels are horrid in the extreme. Who knows what might have happened to me?"

"Well, you've arrived safely and can put all that behind you," said Mother.

"If I can. It was a horrid time. And so confusing."

Anne garnered much sympathy from her listeners, who begged her for more details about her flight. It took her some while to cover them all, but she eventually concluded that her whole experience was "horrid" and "confusing."

"Had I been on my own, I don't know what I should have done," she went on. "Cousin Roger thought that I should stay, but I just couldn't bear it anymore. Besides," she dropped her eyes and raised her brows, "I'm not all that certain of where he stands on . . . certain things. Political things."

"You mean his sympathies may lie with the rebels?"

"That's it, I just don't know. He won't say one way or another. He's so confusing. Never gives a proper answer, always laughing it off or changing the subject. It's horrid."

"Let's hope he makes up his mind before both sides take it into their heads to hang him," said the tall man standing next to Anne.

His easy remark shocked Mother, but any reproof she might have had for him was left unspoken. The man was no less than Lord James Norwood, younger brother of the Duke of

Norbury, and Mother would have sooner cut her tongue out than say a word against such a jewel of the peerage. Instead, she joined with the others who had found what he said to be amusing. She put some effort into it, and the show looked to be quite convincing—at least to those unfamiliar with her true nature.

Norwood added to his comment, causing more merriment at Cousin Roger's expense. Mother laughed with the rest while I fairly stared, then bent low to whisper into Elizabeth's ear.

"My God, can you believe it? Mother's toad-eating."

"What did you say?"

"Mother's playing toady to Lord James."

But Elizabeth was paying but scant mind to me and none at all to Mother. I might have put it down to her occupation as busy hostess but for the fact that no one was near us.

"Just look at her."

"Yes, I see." Her head was pointed in the right direction, but her eyes were not on Mother. They were locked, instead, upon Lord James Norwood.

Well-a-day, I thought, the dawn figuratively breaking for me. Knowing that any further conversation would be futile, I backed away to watch my sister watching him. If I read the symptoms right, she was well and truly smitten, and no brotherly intervention would be able to penetrate to her just yet. Heavens, had I looked like that the first time I'd seen Nora? Probably, though no doubt I'd possessed considerably less composure and utterly lacked Elizabeth's innate winsomeness.

It struck me just then how vulnerable she had become, and so I also turned my concerned study upon Norwood.

He seemed a well-mannered, gracious sort, but I'd met many at Cambridge who showed one face to the world and revealed quite another in private. I worried that he might be of that number and vowed to get to know him better, although any shortcomings I might discover would make no difference with Elizabeth. Once one is caught up in that peculiar emotional state, one is deaf to all other things.

"Had Lord James and his dear sister not come to my aid when they did, I don't know what might have happened to me," Anne was saying.

The crowd around her turned toward that gentleman, who bowed deeply. "It was my pleasure, Miss Fonteyn, to be of service."

"You're the hero of the day, my lord," said Dr. Beldon, smiling broadly and taking his own turn at toad-eating.

"So brave and kind of you, I'm sure," put in Mrs. Hardinbrook, also smiling.

As he modestly accepted the general praise of the company, I drifted over to Jericho, who was supervising the punch bowl.

"What does his valet have to say about him?" I asked.

"His lordship's valet, Mr. Harridge, does not permit himself to associate with Negro servants," he said with icy dignity.

"Oh, really?"

"Mr. Harridge has informed the servants he does associate with that they may address him as 'my lord' should they need to speak with him."

"He must be jesting."

"Regrettably, he is not."

"I've heard of this happening in England, but not over here."

"It may be described as an importation of questionable value."

"It seems not to sit well with you."

"Mr. Harridge is a great stupid ass, sir."

I had a very hard time of it keeping my face composed. When the threat of laughter had subsided to the point where I could speak again, I asked, "Why should a man like Lord James keep such an insufferable fellow?" I knew Jericho well enough to consider his assessment of Harridge to be highly accurate and was not about to pass it off as anything petty.

"Like often attracts like when it comes to servants and masters," he said.

"Norwood strikes me as being an easy sort of man."

"Agreed, sir, but you've only seen him under these limited circumstances."

"Agreed, though time will remedy that, what with Mother insisting he stay with us."

"And his sister as well."

"I'd forgotten her. Where's she gotten to?"

"Lady Caroline is just over there by the hearth."

"Seems to be by herself, too. Think I'll play host for a bit, then."

Jericho filled a cup with punch and gave it to me. "For Lady Caroline," he explained.

"But this drink's usually for the men."

"A view not held in high esteem by her ladyship. She has had some already and expressed a great liking for it."

"All right. Let's hope she'll like a little more."

Weaving through the guests, I made my way toward Lady Caroline Norwood and put on my best smile when she looked up at me. She'd taken a chair close to the fire and had turned it so her back was to most of the room. It effectively cut her off from any but the most determined approach. I was determined, for she was very pretty.

"Feeling the cold?" I asked. We'd been introduced earlier.

She nodded. "The roads were very rough and the carriage drafty. I don't think I shall ever be warm again."

"Some punch?" I got a sweet thank-you from her as she accepted the cup and drank from it. "Even in good weather the road from Philadelphia is not an easy one. It must have been an especially difficult journey now."

"Indeed it was, Mr. Barrett. I often thought it would never end. Your mother is very kind to invite us to stay here."

"It's our good fortune, Lady Caroline, and our way of thanking you for seeing to the safe arrival of our cousin."

"Poor thing. She was at her wit's end trying to get out of the city."

"How did you meet her?"

Lady Caroline smiled in a most charming way. "At a tea party very similar to this one. Philadelphia may be overrun with seditionists, but the rest of the population tried to maintain civilized habits for as long as they were allowed. Things were going from bad to worse, and several families resolved that they had to leave or be arrested by the rebels."

"I've heard of such foolishness. They've no legal authority to do so."

"Yet arrests have been made. People have been beaten, officials tarred and feathered . . . that was no city of brotherly love that we escaped from, sir."

"Certainly not. What prompted you to travel north, though? Surely a southward road would have been more appealing."

"We had to go with the others—we were with the Allen family and Mr. Galloway—and they were all headed for New York to speak with Lord Howe. They want to persuade him to march to Philadelphia and secure it for the Crown."

"That would be a fearful blow against the rebels."

"Mr. Galloway believes so. Nearly everyone in the city is yet a loyal subject, but the rebels have made them too afraid to do anything."

It had become an old story by now: a small group of knaves holding decent people in thrall with their threats and the frequent fulfillment of those threats.

"I suspect that this wretched trouble has provided you with a poor opinion of our colonies."

"Not at all. I think it is very grand over here. This will die down soon enough, I'm sure."

"How long have you and your brother been in America?"

"At least a year and a half now. James had some land holdings that were being adversely affected by the recent conflicts, and he had a mind to come over and sort things out for himself. I had a mind to see what the colonies were like, so I came with him."

"That's very brave of you."

"So everyone tells me. I did not feel very brave at times, especially when we got to New York. Such a sad place it has become."

"What's it like now?"

"It's terrible and, as I said, sad. There's wreckage everywhere, I don't see how they'll ever be able to clean it up. Wherever you turn are the ruins of buildings with their remains sticking up from the snow like charred bones. So many people were burned out of their homes, and I don't know where or how they keep themselves in this bitter weather. I was very glad when we left."

The burning of New York had been a wonderment and a horror to us all, though for months before the British army arrived there'd been rumors that it would happen. The rebels had threatened to set fires to deny the army sanctuary, and they finally made good their threats one windy night last September.

I'd been out then, testing myself against the strength of the sky. High over the tallest trees, I was doing my best to hover in one spot despite the gustiness of the weather. I chanced to spin toward the west, and it was then that I noticed a lurid glow in the distance so great that it pierced even my fog-clouded sight.

At first I had no understanding of what I'd glimpsed, nor could I gain any better view of it. Each time I grew solid enough to see clearly, I dropped like a stone and had to vanish again lest I come to a hard landing. The vanishing, in its turn, subjected me to the cruelties of the wind, and I had to fight to hold my place.

In spite of these frustrations I finally grasped that I was witnessing a fire of truly awful proportions and that it could only be the city of New York that was aflame. Like others afterward, when they learned the news, I was left stunned, not only by the wanton destruction of such an act, but by the depth of the evil that had inspired it. I was also afraid, for might not the rebels, emboldened by this, do the same for other cities? Worried for the security of my family, I rushed home as quickly as I could.

All was, of course, quiet, but I was so shaken that I had to see Father. I was reminded of those times as a child when I'd waken from a nightmare and rush to his room for comfort. Child no more, but still in need of comfort, it went right to my heart to see the shadow of anguish on his face when I told him the vile news. This was one dark fear that would not go away at a soft word from him.

"It's so much more peaceful here," said Lady Caroline. "Except for all the soldiers, one would never know that anything was amiss."

"But things are amiss, more's the pity. In fact, coming here puts you in more peril than if you'd remained in New York. We're not that far from Suffolk County, which is crawling with rebels, and just across the Sound is Connecticut, another of their lairs."

"You're not trying to frighten me away, are you, Mr. Barrett?"

"Hardly, but I do want you to be aware that though we are reasonably well protected, we are not entirely safe. No one is, these days."

"Now you are frightening me."

"I'm sorry, your ladyship. I mean only to instill caution. I hope that while you stay here you will take care not to wander alone from the house?"

"But surely the soldiers have abrogated any danger from the rebels."

"They have for the most part, but on the other hand, though they serve our King, they are yet men first and thus vulnerable to base temptations . . . if you take my meaning."

She did, and rather sensibly, though I was surprised at how coolly I'd been able to raise the subject to a woman, and a virtual stranger at that. This wasn't the sort of conversation one expects to have during a tea party, but I was finding that I liked her a lot, and with that liking came the desire to protect her.

"Thank you for your warning, Mr. Barrett. I shall certainly be careful in my comings and goings."

"What warning is that?" Lieutenant Nash had come up in time to hear just that much of our talk. He bowed to us both. "If I may be so bold as to intrude upon you?"

"You are most welcome, Mr. Nash," said Lady Caroline, beaming at him like the sun. "Mr. Barrett was explaining to me that there are more perils here than from the rebels alone."

"Really? What perils might they be?"

She went on in a most easy manner and gave Nash the gist of what I'd said.

Nash offered her a glad smile full of confidence. "That danger may have troubled us once, but no more, your ladyship. I can guarantee your safety, indeed, the safety of any woman on this part of the Island."

"That is very good news, then," I said. "Things are much improved, are they not?" There was enough of an edge to my voice to catch Nash's attention. Though he had no solid memory of our interview about the Bradford girl, he still possessed a lingering uneasiness toward me. Here in a comfortable, candle-filled room alive with many friendly faces, he'd forgotten that for the moment. My question served as an excellent reminder. His smile faltered.

"As improved as they can be, given the circumstances, sir. I do my best."

"That's only to be expected from an officer in the King's army," said Lady Caroline. If she noticed our byplay, she pretended not to.

Nash, his eyes tearing away from me and settling upon her, bowed again and thanked her. She gave him another bright smile, her face seeming much more alive than before.

I suddenly felt and consequently knew that I had become superfluous. Excusing myself, I went back toward the tea table. Elizabeth, however, was speaking with Norwood, and it would be as much as my life was worth if I imposed on *that* conversation.

"Never try to compete with a uniform or a title," Beldon advised me.

I gave a slight start at his sudden appearance at my side, and we shared a small laugh. His accurate appraisal was not lost on me. "You've been watching things."

"Only a little. Miss Elizabeth seems quite taken with his lordship, and Mr. Nash has apparently gained the favor of her ladyship."

"He hardly cuts a dashing figure," I said glumly, noting Nash's paunch and the overall stockiness of his body.

"Any man in a uniform is not only dashing but an instant hero in the eyes of a woman. If it's a comfort to you, I doubt if anything serious will come of it. Lady Caroline will hardly squander herself on an aging, penniless lieutenant. She'll enjoy the moment for its own sake, but that's the most of it."

"You sound as though you know Lady Caroline very well. Have you met her before?"

"Sooner or later you'll meet everyone you know a dozen times over, if you live long enough."

"I don't understand."

"It means that most people are the same everywhere. Have you not met someone who instantly reminded you of someone else?"

"Yes."

"And have you then noticed them behaving in a manner similar to that of another acquaintance?"

"I see where you are leading, Doctor. It is an interesting premise. So Lady Caroline reminds you of another lady you've met before?"

"She does. Untitled, but a very nice person, though feckless and fickle. I hope Mr. Nash will not be overly disappointed."

"He may not get that chance. I wonder what this means?"

A Hessian had entered the room, looking quite devilish with his boot-blacked mustaches and face reddened from the cold. He was familiar to me, having been one of the men who'd participated in Jericho's beating months back. I looked across to Jericho and saw that he'd gone quite immobile and his jaw was set and hard. Though he'd recovered completely as Beldon had promised, his spiritual wounds were yet raw.

The Hessian still wore his cloak and hat and seemed in a hurry. Silence fell upon our gathering as everyone stared at this intruder. He paid no heed to any of us, but strode right across to Lieutenant Nash.

Nash scowled and, though he kept his voice low that others might not hear, was obviously demanding an explanation from the man, who leaned close to provide it. Nash soon found his feet, his own expression grim. My father stepped toward him.

"What is amiss, Mr. Nash?"

"An unpleasant incident has occurred, sir, and I must go investigate."

"What sort of incident?" asked Norwood, having abandoned his conversation with Elizabeth.

Had anyone else made such an inquiry, Nash might have been able to ignore him, but he was not without a touch of the toad-eater, himself. "It appears that some rebels have rowed across from Connecticut and made a raid on a house north of here. I must go and see what has happened."

Father went bone-white. "What house?" he asked, in a faint voice.

"The Montagu place."

I caught my breath, my belly dropping to my toes. Father must have been experiencing a similar reaction, but was better at hiding it. Only Elizabeth, Jericho, and I knew what effort he was putting forth to conceal his feelings. Our guests were also shocked by the news and murmured their dismay to one another, for Mrs. Montagu was well liked and respected by all. She had been invited to the tea party, but declined to attend on account of a cough that had been plaguing her for the last week.

Norwood gave Nash a bland smile. "It sounds most interesting. I should wish very much to accompany you."

"This is army business, your lordship, and it could be dangerous."

"Sounds just the thing to do, then. I can't possibly miss this." Norwood did not wait for Nash to offer further objections, but left, presumably to ready himself for his outing.

"I shall come, too," put in Beldon. He'd an inkling about Father's relationship with Mrs. Montagu, but kept it to himself, for at heart he was a decent fellow. "I just need a moment to get my medicines." He bolted out on Norwood's heels.

"And I as well," added Father. "I want to know what's going on."

"As do I," I said, following him. I glanced back once. Nash's mouth was flapping but nothing intelligible spilled out, which was of considerable cost to his dignity. But the ordering of events had been deftly wrested from him, and he had no choice but to accept the help of so many willing volunteers.

Though it took but a moment to arm ourselves—I took my sword cane—and throw on some protection against the winter night, it was somewhat longer before our horses were saddled. The stable lads were by turns sleepy, alarmed, and excited at this excursion, and it took a sharp word from Father to put their minds to their business. I saw to the saddling of Rolly myself. He was restive for want of exercise, shaking his ears and dancing impatiently. I had no choice but to calm him in my special manner. The change from fiery nerve to abrupt docility was noticeable, and Norwood was the one who noticed.

"You've quite a way with horses," he remarked, quirking an eyebrow.

I stroked Rolly's nose and shrugged it off. Norwood continued to throw looks my way as I worked, but was soon distracted by the readying of his own mount.

Nash's man had not come alone; there were five others with him, all on foot. Father cursed under his breath.

"It's taking too long. I'm going ahead, laddie." His face was haggard with new worry. He'd been able to conceal it up to now, but his concern for the well-being of Mrs. Montagu had clawed its way past his self-control.

"Not alone, sir," I said, and we kicked our horses up at the same time.

Nash shouted as we dashed ahead, and the Hessians scattered before us. Norwood called something, and I heard him and Beldon gradually catching us up as we pounded down the lane to the main road.

"We can get there faster over the fields," I called to Father.

"Lead on, then!" He knew I'd be able to see clearly enough to do it.

I urged Rolly onto the road for a time, then cut away to the north, finding a narrow path that marked the informal boundary between our estate and the Montagu property. Sometimes we were at full gallop, but more often than not were reduced to a canter or even a trot depending how bad the footing was. Had I been alone, I might have left Rolly's back and soared ahead, for I could have covered the distance more swiftly, but with Beldon and Norwood along I was forced to limit myself to something less precipitant.

We came in sight of the house soon enough, approaching it from the side. There were no lights showing, not a single sign or sound came to us. Father cursed again and again, fearing the worst. He started to press ahead, but I pleaded with him to wait a moment more.

"Let me go in first and see what awaits. It'll be safer for all."

Torn between fear for Mrs. Montagu and the sense of my request, he hesitated in agony for a few seconds, then finally nodded. I slipped from Rolly and gave Father the reins.

"I'll be right back," I promised, hefting my sword cane.

"Go with God, laddie," he choked out.

"I'm coming, too," said Norwood.

Father told him to hold his place.

Norwood was insulted. "I beg your pardon, sir, but I only wish to help."

"You don't know the land, Lord James. My son does."

This terse statement caused his lordship to subside for now, for Father had all but snarled it. Perhaps it had gotten through to him that this was no adventurous lark, but something far more serious. I had no inclination to waste more time, and walked swiftly and softly over the snow toward the house.

Tracks were all over the yard, but some days had passed since the last fall, and the normal work of the household would account for them. Horses here, boot-shod feet there, I even picked up the faint trails left by small animals, their shallow shadows pressed upon the patches of white. If any of the other markings were caused by rebel raiders, I could not rightly tell. I would find out soon enough.

Reaching the wall of the house, I held hard against it and eased one eye around the corner. The yard on that side was also empty of life, which I found ominous. The icy air was still, nearly windless; the least sound would have carried to me—had there been anyone about to make it.

Another corner, and I saw the barn. Its doors were open. There was no sign of movement within, which meant the horses were gone. I didn't know what to make of that. Moving closer, my eye fell upon a limp pile of brown feathers lying just on the threshold. It was one of the many laying hens that nested in the barn. Some hand had twisted its neck, then cast it away.

I quit the barn and went straight to the house. The doors were wide open there as well. Up the steps, into the entry hall and stop . . . the house had suffered a cruel invasion. Furniture was overturned, ornaments broken, it was a wretched mess. I called out, but received no answer. I listened to silence and felt chilled right through.

Where were they? Mrs. Montagu had several house servants, a coachman, some field laborers; there was no sign of them, not even of the noisy lap dog she doted on. I made my way toward the kitchen, hitting the catch on my cane and drawing the blade free.

It was dim there, but sufficient light from outside seeped in for me to see well enough. To anyone else, it would have been blacker than hell, and, indeed, the mess I found might have been a part of that dread pit.

The fire there had been banked for the night, an indication that the house had been in order as usual before whatever had happened had happened. Order was gone, now, for this place had also been thoroughly ransacked. The smoked hams that should have been hanging from the rafters were gone. They'd been cut down and taken away except for a very large one that might have been too heavy for the thief to carry. He'd dragged it a few feet, then abandoned it.

Other signs of looting presented themselves, but I let them pass, as they were far less important to me than finding out the fate of Mrs. Montagu and her household.

A sound . . . very soft.

It was not repeated and I couldn't really identify it, but it might have come from the cellar. With something like hope I strode toward the door and tried it.

Locked. Most promising. The lock on this side was broken, therefore someone must be on the other side. They'd probably taken shelter there when the thieves had come and didn't know that it was safe to emerge.

I called Mrs. Montagu's name and knocked several times. No answer. Well, they'd have to come out sometime. Perhaps they were too frightened to respond. I banged my fist a few more times, then decided to try forcing the door. Floating through it would have been less destructive, but much too difficult to explain. Besides, I was more than strong enough for the job.

Setting myself, I gripped the handle and slammed a shoulder against the door. It gave a bit, opening a long crack along the point where I'd struck. I put my mouth to it and called again and something staggeringly loud exploded right in front of me. Thrown back with a shout of surprise, I crashed against a large table. My legs abruptly stopped working. The floor came up, faster than lightning, striking hard all over when it hit me.

My ears rang from the blast, making me sick and dizzy; I could not hear anything subtle, but was aware of some sort of commotion going on nearby. People were yelling in fear and alarm, and somewhere a candle wavered and made the shadows dance.

"Oh, my God, it's Jonathan!" someone wailed. The voice was yet muffled by the ringing, but I thought it belonged to Mrs. Montagu.

"Shut yer mouth, ye damned Tory bitch!" a man ordered. The order was punctuated by something that sounded like a slap, and the woman cried out in reaction.

Groaning, I tried to sit up, and that's when a truly terrible pain lanced through my whole body. My groan turned into a gasp and I instantly gave up trying to move.

A large and unkempt man knelt over me. He had a smoking pistol in one hand and wore an expression in which fear and hatred had been fused into a single vile mask. I was already somewhat stunned from being shot; his face completed the work. All I could do was lie on the floor and gape as one of his rough hands probed my chest.

Behind him, Mrs. Montagu was staring at me, her usually pleasant features marred by a look of utter horror.

"This 'un's dead, Nat," said the man. "Or he's a-dyin'. Either way, 'e won't trouble us."

CHAPTER
— 5 —

"You sure?" asked Nat, sounding peevish.

The big man's hand was momentarily heavy on my chest. He was pushing against me to get to his feet. "'E's dead, I say. Let's git 'fore others follow 'im."

"Too late. I see 'em comin'. They heard yer shot."

"I'll give 'em 'nother, then." He drew a second pistol from his belt.

"Right, soon as one's through the door, you take 'im an' I get the next."

"For God's sake, just leave us!" Mrs. Montagu pleaded. I could see her huddled off to one side. Except for a red patch where the bastard had struck her, she seemed unharmed, though very frightened. Gathered around her were several of her servants; they also appeared to be well, but thoroughly cowed by the thieves. None of them were armed.

"Shut yer mouth or I'll cut yer throat," said Nat casually. He had a knife in one hand and a candle in the other. He blew the candle out and left it on the table, then stood with his partner on one side of the door leading to the scullery. Father and the others would most likely use it, as that was the fastest way into the kitchen. After hearing the shot, they'd not wait, but charge right in, and Father would be the first . . .

The pain was still with me, but so was the overwhelming need to get up and do something. Gritting my teeth seemed to help. I was very, very careful not to breathe in. With air in my lungs I might involuntarily vocalize what I felt.

Then Mrs. Montagu gasped when I moved, startled that I *could* move. I was terrified she'd draw the attention of the villains toward me.

"Shut yer face," hissed Nat, and I wholeheartedly agreed with him. He did not, fortunately, turn around, but continued to listen at the door.

Glaring at Mrs. Montagu, I raised one hand in a sharp gesture, hoping she would correctly take it as a sign to be silent. It cost me, for any motion on my right side doubled my pain. I wasn't even sure she could see well enough to know what I wanted until she bit her lips and nodded, her eyes wide and supremely unhappy.

"They're comin'!" whispered the big one gleefully.

Nat slipped back a little so as to be out of the line of fire.

I was on my feet, ready to take them on . . .

. . . weaponless.

The realization hammered home too late. I'd naught but my hands, not even a club. My swordstick . . . God knows where that had dropped when I'd been shot.

Father was almost here; I recognized his step.

Hands. Both of them. Edge of the table.

Push.

It was a very heavy piece of oak, sturdy enough to stand up to decades of abuse from various cooks over the years, but for me it might have been made from paper, as it all but flew across the room. The far end struck the larger of the two men in the back just below the waist with an ugly-sounding thud. He may have made a noise himself, but it was lost in the general scrape, rattle, and bang of the table's swift passage.

His pistol went off toward the ceiling with a flash and a roar, and a cloud of smoke filled the air around him. I saw that much out of the corner of my eye as I lunged forward, reaching for Nat.

Surprised as he must have been, he was fast and whirled to meet me. He made a quick stab at my left side, but I just managed to knock his arm away before our collision. Balance lost, we crashed against a wall and fell. Kicking, beating, biting, and finally flailing at me with his knife, he did me some damage as we rolled over the floor. My fingers found his neck in the confusion and froze around it. He thrashed and gurgled. I squeezed harder and harder. His face went red, then purple, with his tongue bulging out as I squeezed harder and harder and . . .

"*Jonathan!*" Father's voice. Shouting.

I could barely hear him. Didn't want to hear him. Wanted to finish my work.

"Let go of him, laddie!"

He'd never raised his voice to me like that before, not even when he was angry. What was wrong? What had . . . ?

Hands on my arms. Pulling, tugging mine loose from their grip on Nat's throat.

What . . . ?

I let go, and they pulled me from him with a lurch. That's when my strength left me. I went limp, shaken and shaking, and the pain of the shot hit me all over again afresh. There was blood. The smell of it filled the room, mixed with the gunpowder . . . and the scent of death. For one awful moment I seemed to be spinning back in time to that hot August day in the woods, right to the very instant when I'd . . . died.

"*No!*" I said, forcing myself to sit up. I yelped and clutched at my wound.

"Lie back, Jonathan," said Father, kneeling over me.

I tried to push him off. I could bear the pain far easier than the memory. There was no way I could possibly lie still and let death steal up and seize me as it had before.

"Steady, now, it's all right." He stroked my hair as he used to do when I was little. "It's all right."

That calmed me as nothing else would. The panic faded, and I came to see the kitchen was suddenly a crowded, noisy, normal place again; the faces and voices were familiar, reassuring.

Beldon appeared. He was pale, but in control, and issued a few quiet commands. Someone lighted candles; another went to find brandy. Before I knew it the stuff had been poured into a cup and was being pressed to my lips. I sputtered and turned my head away.

"Don't force him, Doctor. Let him catch his breath," said Father. He turned to Mrs. Montagu. "Mattie? How is it with you?"

She grasped his extended hand, her eyes all but lost for the tears. "I'll be fine, but for God's sake, see to Jonathan. The poor child was shot."

"Shot?" exclaimed Beldon, who was just starting a closer examination of my wound. "Come, gentlemen, help me with him. Quickly, please."

"I'm fine," I whispered.

They paid me no mind. Beldon, Father, and Norwood all lifted me onto the table. Orders were given to fetch water and bandaging.

"No, wait! Father . . . I'm—"

"Be still, laddie."

"But I'm—"

He bent over me. "Hush, laddie, let Beldon have a look at you."

"Remember my *arm*!"

"What?"

Beldon pulled open my bloodied coat and unbuttoned an equally stained waistcoat. This hurt like hell, as it pulled at something that seemed to be attached to my flesh. When I protested, he asked Norwood to hold my hands out of the way. He thoroughly ruined both waistcoat and shirt by cutting them to get to the source of all the bleeding.

"My arm!" I repeated, trying to fight off the well-intentioned Norwood.

Then Father remembered, but I could tell that he had no idea what to do next. To be fair, there wasn't much that he *could* do, but no matter; it was a relief that he finally understood me.

"What do you want?"

That was when I realized I had no idea, either. In the meanwhile, Beldon went on with his grim examination.

"That's odd," he said, sounding mightily puzzled.

Damnation. "Father? Get the others away, please?"

He instantly saw the wisdom in that and took steps to clear the kitchen. Mrs. Montagu was in a bad state, as might be expected of a woman whose home had been invaded and herself so ill-treated. Father took her hand and guided her out, murmuring that everything was going to be all right. He herded the other servants before them, then called for Norwood.

"Directly, sir. I want to make sure these rebels are no more threat to us." He was by the scullery door, checking the fallen men. His inspection did not take long, and he soon joined the others.

Distractions removed, I was better able to order my thoughts; however, I possessed far more questions than

I had ready answers. Foremost in my mind was why I had not vanished. The last time I'd been shot, I had disappeared without any conscious effort, and upon my return had been fully healed of all wounds, old and new. What was different about now? I squirmed to try to see what had happened.

"Be still, Mr. Barrett," Beldon cautioned.

"Then tell me what's wrong."

His eyes rolled over to meet mine, but I exercised no influence on him. His puzzlement was firmly in place, and mixed with it was a touch of fear.

"Tell me!"

He jumped, for my voice was rapidly regaining its old strength. "You . . . there's . . . that is . . ."

Impatient, I nudged things the tiniest bit. "Tell me, Doctor."

His eyes wavered, then steadied. "The ball seems to have passed right through you, but the damage is . . . not as I expected. Perhaps I am mistaken. The bleeding makes it difficult to see very clearly."

I lay back and tried to vanish. No matter if Beldon saw, I'd deal with his memory later. I tried . . . and failed. The pain flared and flashed along my side.

"How bad?" I demanded through my teeth.

He was at a loss to answer. I pressed him again. More firmly. Face slack, he said, "There is no wound from the pistol ball. You've some wood splinters embedded in your flesh. They'll have to come out. That's where all the blood is coming from."

It occurred to me that I could ill afford to lose much of that precious substance.

"Then see to your work, if you please," I said through my teeth.

"I'll need help."

"Get my father."

Dear God, but the next quarter-hour was the longest I'd ever endured. Father was not an ideal doctor's assistant, either. He was more than willing to help, but it was difficult for him as a parent to bear the sight of his child's discomfort. Too late I thought of this as I watched him go from white to pale green as Beldon got on with the wretched business of drawing out the splinters.

"I'll be fine, sir," I promised him, then immediately followed this with a sharp grunt that could not have inspired him with any sort of confidence in my promise.

Beldon discarded a nasty-looking shard of wood and asked for Father to hold the candle closer and with more steadiness. He brought it close, but was unable to completely keep from trembling. As the splinters came out, though, my pain lessened, and with it, much of Father's anxiety melted away.

"The bleeding's stopped," Beldon announced, amazed.

"That's good, isn't it?" asked Father, though he was looking at me for an answer. For the moment, I was just too weary to provide one, not that I had any.

"But don't you see? The punctures have closed right up!"

Father could not help but share in his amazement, but he was more restrained in his reaction.

"It's *unnatural*, sir," Beldon went on, with emphasis. His voice rose a little.

Damnation. Tired as I was, something would have to be done. I glanced at Father, questioning. He frowned slightly, but nodded.

"Doctor . . ." I touched Beldon's hand and got his attention.

A few minutes later Beldon had finished winding a bandage around my middle. It was for show only, for with the splinters gone, my skin had knitted itself up again, leaving behind some red scars that were rapidly fading. Of the stabbings from Nat's knife, there were no signs, though there were plenty of holes in my clothes to mark where the blade had gone in. I dimly recalled those cuts, but had been too immersed in the madness of the fight to notice them at the time.

Finished, Beldon went out with Father to tell the others that I was not seriously hurt at all and that a full recovery was inevitable.

From the kitchen I heard Mrs. Montagu release a sob of relief and Father telling her to be of good cheer.

"Samuel, I am so sorry," she was saying.

"There's no need."

"But he might have been killed. I can hardly believe his escape even now."

"Tell us what happened, madam," suggested Norwood.

Manners and social customs will out under the most extraordinary circumstances. Father introduced Lord James

Norwood to her, touching off a considerable reaction and flurry.

As they talked, their voices faded briefly for me. I found I could vanish again, for which I felt an absurd relief. Gone for a moment and then back, the lingering fire in my side completely abated. I offered heartfelt thanks to my Maker and decided that a little more rest would not be amiss.

Mrs. Montagu had some idea that she should play the hostess for Norwood, but he managed to steer her away from that and repeated his question.

The story gradually came out. One of the stablemen had been the first to give the alarm. He'd shouted a warning to the house and, after narrowly eluding capture, had run off in the direction of the old barn on our property where the Hessians were quartered.

"It's not far from here," she explained. "I'd told all the servants that if there was any trouble to either go there or to Mr. Barrett's house for help."

The rebels had not known about the closeness of the troops. They became so engrossed in their thievery that no one noticed the new arrivals until it was nearly too late. All but two fled, carrying what they could.

"We were hiding in the cellar and heard the row, and then it became quiet. I thought they were gone, but when I opened the door, those awful men pushed their way in. They were going to wait, thinking to let the soldiers get well ahead before making their own escape. They thought they could find help by going to Suffolk County."

"The only place they'll be going is a burying ground," said Norwood.

"What?"

Beldon murmured agreement. "Yes. One of them has a broken back and the other a broken neck. Young Mr. Barrett seems to have defended himself rather ably."

Young Mr. Barrett sat up on the table, all thoughts of rest vanquished. My mouth was like dust. Death. I had smelled death in this room.

Could still smell it. Could see it now.

The big fellow, the one I'd rammed with the table, was on his side, bent backward at the hips. Bent very sharply. Nat lay nearby, his head twisted over farther than what might have been considered comfortable to a living man. His face was suffused with blood; his black tongue thrust past his lips. The marks of my fingers were clear on his throat.

I stared at them and felt sick.

Beldon returned. "Mr. Barrett?" He saw the look on my face and came over, standing between me and the bodies.

"I killed them," I said. I'd lost much of my breath and not replaced it, so what came out was barely a sound at all.

He pursed his lips. "Yes."

"Oh, God."

"As a soldier in battle must kill," he added. "Think of it that way, and it may be easier to bear."

I swallowed with difficulty. Though there was nothing like food in my belly, it still wanted to turn itself inside out. "Was . . . was Father the first through the door?"

"Yes, and I was just behind him. Why?"

I motioned for him to stand away. Reluctantly, he did so. I looked at the dead men in their final, undignified poses; looked until the sickness in me passed.

"And you're both all right?" I asked.

"Perfectly."

Nodding, I managed a smile, though it must have been a ghastly one. "*That* makes it easier to bear, Doctor," I told him, as though it were a profound confidence.

He did not ask for any explanation.

Beldon decided that my removal from the kitchen would be of more benefit than risk to my health and helped guide my steps into the next room. I was well able to walk, but saw the need to maintain the pretense of still being hurt. Too quick a recovery would invite comment. Norwood found a chair and dragged it over, and Beldon made me sit.

"You're staying the night, Jonathan," said Mrs. Montagu. "You're dreadfully pale."

"It's but a scratch or two, madam, I've had worse falling from my horse," I responded in a stout tone. As for my lack of color . . . well, I had an easy enough remedy for that. "A little rest and I'll be able to travel, but I think that you should not be left alone here."

"Certainly not," said Father, smoothly stepping into the opening I'd given him. "I'd be honored to remain and make sure of your security, madam." He'd assumed a more formal manner of address to her, and she echoed it.

"If it would not be too much trouble, Mr. Barrett."

"None at all."

Such was the resumption of their gentle pretense that they were no more than good neighbors to one another, not mistress and lover. Only their eyes betrayed the real feelings beneath the innocent words, and for the thousandth time I regretted the circumstances that prevented them from freely uniting as man and wife.

While the servants tried to wrest some order from the wreckage, Lieutenant Nash and his troop of Hessians finally arrived. They charged into the house as though it were a battleground and halted, disappointed, perhaps, that there were no rebels to attack.

Nash stared at the lot of us in wonder, then his eye finally fell hard upon me. "What the devil's going on here?"

His greeting pushed home the fact that I was quite the terrifying spectacle with my bandaging and my torn and bloody shirt hanging from my shoulders.

"Things got a bit warm here, Lieutenant," said Norwood. "Some of your lads missed a couple of the rebels and it was left to Mr. Barrett to deal with 'em."

He'd said just the right thing at the right time, sparing us from any bullying Nash might have been prepared to deliver to us presumptuous civilians. The lieutenant was only too happy to listen to his lordship, and after inspecting the corpses commended me for my bravery and quick thinking.

"Thank you, sir, but had I been thinking quickly from the start I might have avoided this and somehow spared those men."

"They'd have hanged anyway, Mr. Barrett. I found no papers on them, which means they were mere looters, and part of no man's army. We've dropped more than a few from the gibbet over the months, and if this continues, we'll have others joining them, you mark me."

Cold comfort, I thought, but better than none at all.

Nash was of a mind to go track down the troops who had given chase to the other thieves. When Mrs. Montagu expressed concern for the servant who had run for help, he opined that the fellow was likely to be found with them. "Once a man gets the blood up for a hunt, there's no stopping him." He grimaced at Father, Beldon, Norwood, and finally at me. "If he's still in one piece, I'll see that he's escorted home again, madam."

With this reassurance, he left behind one of his clerks—an Englishman attached to the commissary office—to get a more detailed account of the raid and left with the rest. Norwood watched them go, unable to refrain from showing a resigned wistfulness. He turned away and looked at me and assumed a more neutral expression. It came to me that from his point of view I'd had all the "adventure" that evening. I looked him over anew and tried to understand why I'd come to that conclusion.

He was a solid, muscular man with a back like a ramrod, yet exuded a kind of restless energy. He had quick dark eyes and I hadn't noticed much expression in them, but put that down to the class he'd been born into. Such constant self-restraint must have been instilled into him from the cradle, if his raising proved to be similar to that of other duke's sons I'd met at Cambridge. His interest in the doings of Nash's men touched me, though, for his chances of participation in something more interesting than a tea party must have been rare to nonexistent for him.

"Why don't you go along?" I asked.

My question did not seem to startle him; he smoothly supplied the excuse I expected. "My duty lies here, Mr. Barrett, to lend what aid I may to the wounded son of my host."

"Not at all, Lord James," I said. "I am quite able to manage, and Dr. Beldon is here, after all. Go along with them, if you can talk Nash into it, then come back to the house and tell us all that happened."

His face lighted up, but he wavered, compelling me to urge him a bit more until he finally accepted the idea. He promised to provide a full account upon his return. So saying, he left, apparently seeing any objections Nash might have as being entirely surmountable.

"He maneuvered you into that, laddie," Father observed, speaking to me quietly from one side of his mouth.

"I know, sir. It doesn't matter."

"Doesn't it?"

"Not this time, anyway. Besides, I'm curious to know what's going on as well. Nash might be able to prevent you or Beldon from tagging along to see things, but he shan't turn down his lordship."

"By God, I wonder who's doing the maneuvering here?"

"I'm just taking advantage of what's been offered," I said modestly.

He smiled, a small one, with his lips tight together, and looked me over narrowly. "How are you?"

He was not asking after my wounds. "I don't know yet. I feel numb."

"When the numbness wears off, you come talk to me, y'hear?"

"Yes, sir."

Then he enfolded me in a brief, hard embrace.

Beldon and I got back well after midnight, but found the house still awake and ourselves the objects of excess worry. I kept my cloak tight about me at first, so as not to frighten Elizabeth, and told her and all the others that Father and Norwood were unharmed.

"And Mrs. Montagu?" my sister anxiously demanded, for like me, she also had a deep affection for the woman.

"Frightened and dismayed, but unhurt. Father and Lord James are staying there to reassure her and help better secure her home."

Without difficulty, Elizabeth took my real meaning.

"How is it with my brother?" asked Lady Caroline, also anxious. She was pale, except for two spots of color high on her cheeks, and I thought she looked very pretty, indeed.

Prompted by that and further questions, I shared all that I knew with them, with some exceptions. On the ride home I'd asked Beldon to say nothing of the men I'd killed, and so he'd remained silent as I skipped over the unpleasantness; with that omission, I was also able to leave out the business of my wounding. Beldon had taken my insistence on that point to be a combination of wanting to avoid excessive fuss and a desire to spare the ladies further worry, for which he was entirely correct. Later, I would tell Elizabeth the whole story, but I was exhausted now. It could wait until tomorrow.

Surrounded as I was by Elizabeth, Lady Caroline, Cousin Anne, Mrs. Hardinbrook, and—unfortunately—Mother, not to mention a dozen servants watching close by, I suddenly became aware of a desire to be alone that was as great as my weariness. I wanted time to myself, to touch and find assurance amongst the familiar treasures of my own room . . . to change

from my wretchedly used clothes. With a deep bow, I begged
leave to be excused and was able to escape for the most part.
Elizabeth and Jericho went ahead of me, Jericho to prepare my
room and Elizabeth because she saw there was more to things
than had been said. Well, I wouldn't mind talking to them, but
Mother . . .

"You could have been killed, Jonathan Fonteyn," she said,
as we all took the stairs. She was just behind me; Beldon,
box of medicines in one hand, hat in the other, came last. I
glanced back at her, surprised by this show of concern, but
came to a disheartening conclusion: Mother's words might
have the show of worry, but their substance indicated that
her worry was for herself. Had I been killed, how might she,
herself, be inconvenienced? As that question had already been
answered for me last August, I should not have felt such bitter
disappointment now, but did, anyway.

Once at my room, Beldon invoked his authority as a doctor
and requested everyone to leave, saying that I was in need of
rest. For various reasons, no one was inclined to listen to him.
Jericho busied himself pulling out my nightclothes, and Mother
and Elizabeth stood just inside the doorway.

"There will be no more of this foolish running off with
soldiers, Jonathan Fonteyn," Mother stated, arms crossed and
head high. She didn't seem to be looking at me so much as
at something just over my left shoulder. I knew nothing was
there, it was just her way. It suited me, as I had little stomach
for looking at her, either. "You're a gentleman, not some kind
of idiotic camp hanger-on for those soldiers. They don't need
your help to do their duty."

"No, Mother," I said meekly, hoping she'd finish soon and
get out.

"And don't use that long-suffering tone with me, young
man. You're far too impertinent."

"Forgive me, Mother. My fatigue troubles me and makes
me short."

"Fatigue," she spat. "I wonder how long it will take you to
recover from this? You tell me that. You're far too lazy as it
is, sleeping all day and not lifting a finger to help your father
even when you do manage to dislodge yourself from bed."

Each of her words beat against my head like some awful
hammer. Bang, bang, bang. I'd been through enough disruption
for one evening, but it appeared that more was waiting in store.

When Mother paused for breath to continue her tirade, Elizabeth stepped forward. "He's very tired, Mother, can you not see that? Please let him rest."

Mother, her mouth slightly open as she started to speak, stopped. She was still looking past me, but now seemed to see nothing. Her eyes . . . there was something dreadfully wrong there.

And without word, without warning, Mother raised her hand and swung her whole body around. Her palm struck Elizabeth's face with a resounding *crack* and my poor sister was knocked right off her feet. It was so swift that I was unable to take it in for the first few seconds, not until I heard Elizabeth's sobbing gasp of pain, and then I was moving toward her, arms out to help.

"I didn't send you to Cambridge for you to sleep your life away—" Mother continued, as though nothing had happened.

"Mrs. Barrett!" cried Beldon from where he stood flatfooted in a corner, utterly shocked.

But before I could get to Elizabeth, she'd surged right back up again, swift as thought. She had the beginnings of a red mark on her face oddly similar to the one Mrs. Montagu had received; beyond that the resemblance ceased. Elizabeth's expression, indeed, her whole body, was suffused with it: blind fury. While Mother still babbled on, heaping more reproach upon me, Elizabeth launched herself at her.

Mother's speech abruptly stopped, replaced by a snarl of surprise and followed by thumps, howls, and thuds. They were on the floor, skirts flying and fabric ripping as they rolled on the floor and tore at each other like cats.

"You bitch!" bellowed my sister, landing one solid blow after another. "Bitch, bitch, *bitch*!"

Beldon joined me quickly enough, but it was hard going to find an opening. He and I finally managed to make a lucky grab each and pulled them apart. I had Mother, and he got Elizabeth out into the hall, perhaps with the idea of taking her to her room. He'd need help there, for Elizabeth was still cursing and crying and fighting him, her face contorted and looking uncomfortably like Mother's.

That lady was moaning in my arms, groggy, for she'd received the worst of it in the brief fight. Elizabeth had put all her rage-driven strength into it. Mother's face was bloodied, her hair all in disarray, and her gown in tatters. Any stranger seeing her in such a plight might have been moved to instant pity and an offer of immediate succor. But I was no stranger. I was her much disliked, if not despised, son, and hadn't the vaguest notion of what to do with her.

Jericho had frozen in place during all this and now looked torn between going after Elizabeth and remaining with me. He'd also noticed something.

"Mr. Jonathan . . . your clothes . . ."

My cloak had fallen open, revealing the—literally—bloody mess it had so handily concealed. "Oh, God." I pulled the edges together to cover it all again.

"But, sir—?"

"Jericho, I promise you that I am unhurt, but please, don't ask about it just now. Beldon can tell you—"

Beldon returned before I could further confuse things. With him came our guests and servants, drawn by the commotion. My room and the hall grew noisy with all the questions, all called at the same time, making it impossible for them to hear any answers, had we been of a mind to give any. Then Beldon shouted for silence, shoved back those nearest, and slammed my door in their faces. It was the only impolite action I'd ever seen him take.

"Up there," he said briskly, returning to his patient and kneeling.

We lifted Mother to my bed. Beldon had his box of medicines open and was reaching for the laudanum bottle. He measured out and prepared a dose—quickly, as he'd had much practice—and got Mother to drink it. He then checked over her other injuries.

"She'll be all right," he stated hollowly.

I accepted the news without a single flicker of emotion. I was dead inside. She was nothing to me. An irritant at the most, like a speck of dust in the eye that's washed away by a few tears and then forgotten. Except that I had no tears in me. Not for her, at least.

"I'm very sorry, Mr. Barrett," he murmured.

"Thank you." Other replies had come to me, but I'd ultimately settled upon the simplest as being the best.

"Do you wish your father to know what's happened?"

That one required thought. On one hand, Father would want to know; on the other, he had enough worries for the moment. "Yes . . . but there's no hurry. You can send a messenger to the

Montagu house at first light tomorrow. Despite the presence of Mr. Nash's men, I don't think it wise for anyone to be traveling alone tonight."

"I agree. I shall see to your mother's needs, then write him a note. What about Miss Barrett? She was very shaken, if you want my help . . ."

"Thank you, but I'll talk to her myself."

I backed away, found the door, and let myself out. The people waiting there with their questions drew back from me and went silent, then obligingly parted as I stalked down the hall to see Elizabeth.

She was lying on her bed, turned away, hunched around a pillow, and sobbing into it. She hated to cry.

Young Sheba was with her, but the situation was beyond her ability. I wasn't so sure of myself, either, when I dismissed her to fetch hot tea and some brandy from downstairs.

I sat on the bed and put my arm around Elizabeth and told her it was over and that things were going to be all right. It was nonsense, but the object was to let her know she wasn't alone. By the time Sheba returned with her tray, the worst of the storm, I hoped, had passed, and Elizabeth was sitting up and making thorough use of a handkerchief.

Pouring the brandy myself, I signed to Sheba to close the door. Both Anne and Lady Caroline had hesitantly come forward to offer assistance, and I'd thought it best to politely refuse. They knew nothing of the situation; Elizabeth and I knew it all too well. The door bumped shut, affording us some much needed privacy.

I felt cold. And distant. From myself, strangely, but not from Elizabeth. And my feeling for her was sorrow that she was having to experience such pain in both body and soul. On her cheek was the red mark of Mother's hand; it would turn into a nasty bruise soon enough. I urged her to take some brandy. She offered no argument against it.

"Oh, Jonathan, how could I have done such a thing?"

I had no real answer for her. "You should ask yourself how could she have done such a thing."

But she wasn't listening. "Was it the Fonteyn blood showing through at last? Is that it?"

"It was *you*, not your blood. You, Elizabeth, who had been sorely provoked beyond all patience."

"Provoked or not, I shouldn't have done it. Something just came over me. It's as though I suddenly don't know myself."

"Oh, yes, you do. We all lose control now and then." My voice caught as I thought of Nat and his big companion. But a few hours earlier, these same hands holding Elizabeth's had squeezed and snapped the life from two of God's creatures. "It's not always good . . . b-but it is understandable. You've nothing to reproach yourself for."

"But I do. To have done such a thing . . ."

"Is understandable," I emphasized. "Even if you don't understand it, others will."

"I don't want others to know about this."

"Very well." It seemed pointless to mention that others did, already. Cousin Anne had been flighty and mystified in the glimpse I'd had of her, but Lady Caroline looked to have drawn some perceptive conclusions. It wouldn't take much for her to decide Mrs. Hardinbrook would be her best source of information on what was going on in this house. And that gossipy lady would certainly be more than happy to supply a few dramatic details to the sister of a duke. Not that any of it mattered.

"I feel awful," Elizabeth muttered.

"Sleep will cure that."

"And what about *her*?"

Mother. "Beldon's with her. I expect she'll recover. If it's like the other times, she won't remember a thing."

"How nice for her."

"I think it's a pity."

She sat up to stare. "What?"

"For her to not remember is a great pity."

"Why is that?"

"Because if she did, then she might think twice before losing control herself again. The sad part is, she probably won't, therefore you need to be careful around her. We all do."

"It's not fair."

"No."

Another idea sprang into her mind. "What about Father? Oh, God, what shall I tell him?"

"The truth, as always."

"How can I face him?"

"I think he will have the same concern for you as I do now. You needn't worry. Just remember how dearly he loves you.

Nothing you've done will ever endanger that."

More protests, more assurances from me. In the end, though, she settled down, and I called Sheba in to help her get ready for bed. I left quietly and was surprised to find the hall clear. Beldon must have taken charge and sorted things out, God bless him.

Order had been restored to my room: Mother was gone, the bed's coverlet smoothed again and turned down that I might occupy it, which was all sham. As ever, I would sleep in the cellar.

I stripped out of my clothes. Perhaps Jericho could find someone in the servant's hall able to repair the cuts and tears, though I could take it all to Molly Audy some night. The thought of her warmed me up enough to draw out a faint smile. She and I had become very good friends over the last few months.

But the smile faded as other thoughts crowded Molly's pleasant company from my mind. Poor Elizabeth. Poor me. Poor Barrett family.

I washed my face and hands. Several times. What I really wanted was a scalding hot bath, but that was impractical at such a late hour. Pity.

It was all so absurd. There I'd been, trying to comfort her for having lost control when I was far more seriously guilty of it myself. Absurd.

And hypocritical, at least where my sister was concerned.

For in my heart of hearts, I was glad that Elizabeth had done it.

CHAPTER

— 6 —

January 1777

"A letter for you, Jonathan . . . I think it's from Cousin Oliver!"

I'd barely emerged from my cellar sanctuary when Elizabeth all but pounced on me, waving her packet. She usually reserved her greeting for later, after I'd had a chance to change clothes for the evening. Then we would sit in the library and she'd catch me up on the day's events. I was startled by this abrupt assault of news, but instantly recovered and eagerly accepted when she shoved it into my hands. The address was written in Oliver's sprawling scrawl and I wasted no more time before tearing it open.

"What does he say?"

I plowed through the first few lines. "All is well with him."

"What about Nora?"

"No mention of her yet. God, what writing the man has! I can barely make out . . . there's her name, let me see . . ."

I read on and my heart fell right into my shoes. It was readily apparent to Elizabeth, who insisted that I share my knowledge.

"Nora's no longer in England," I announced mournfully. "She's gone away and Oliver doesn't know exactly where."

"Gone? What's happened?"

I read a little more and shook my head. "Oliver thinks she may have followed the Warburton family to Italy sometime last

November. He knows where they are staying, so he's written to them asking if they can find Nora for him. She was a regular visitor to Tony Warburton, y'know. Oliver thinks they might be able to get my letter to her."

"That's something, at least."

"Yes. More waiting for me. Probably months more."

"I'm sorry."

I shrugged. "It hardly matters now. Most of the questions I'd asked Nora have found their own answers after all this time."

"But some have not."

"True, but there's nothing I can really do about that. Thank you for bringing me this, though. What other news is there tonight?"

"Not much. It's just been one more dreary winter day."

"Did Lord James go with Father to Hempstead?" Last night he'd expressed a keen curiosity about Father's work and gotten an invitation to come and observe legal procedures.

"Just after breakfast."

"Lucky man." I should have been the one to go with Father, as I'd studied hard for just that purpose, but my condition utterly precluded it. Travel was no problem, so long as it was at night, but I'd never see the inside of a courtroom again, nor ever have the chance to practice law.

Elizabeth knew what I was thinking, for I'd made enough complaint about it over the months. "Father's left a huge stack of papers for you in the library."

More copy work, I thought. "Clerking, not real law. I'm like an artist who's forbidden to paint. The desire and talent are there, but the execution . . ." I flapped my hand in a throwing-away gesture.

"We're in like situations, so I understand what you mean."

"In what way are they like? You're able to stay awake while the sun's up."

"And do what? Housewifery? Needlework? Gossip?"

"Missing him, aren't you?" I asked, with sudden inspiration coupled to a desire to change the subject.

That delayed further speech from her as we left the kitchen and climbed the stairs. She made no inquiry about whom I was referring to, there being no need. Elizabeth blushed for a portion of the trip and opened her mouth several times to reply, then snapped it shut again every time she caught my grin. The topic of Lord James Norwood was a tender one with her.

"And he's been gone only a day?" I added.

She looked ready to explode for a moment, then abruptly gave it up. "Yes," came her rueful admission. "All bloody day and probably tomorrow as well."

"It will pass soon enough."

"It's forever," she grumbled.

"Does he know how you feel?" I paused at the door to my room.

"Sometimes I think he does. I wish I knew how *he* felt about me."

"You can't tell?"

She looked entirely helpless. "No."

"I could talk to him . . ."

"*No!* Don't you dare!"

"But if it will end your uncertainty—"

"*No!* I absolutely forbid it, Jonathan! Don't! Please promise me you won't!"

"All right, all right. I just wanted to help."

"I'll do my own helping, thank you very much. You promise not to say anything to him?"

"I promise, though if you should change your mind . . . ?"

Brows high, eyes wide, and teeth bared, she shook her fists at me in mock rage. I pretended to cower away from her and, laughing, took shelter in my room.

Things had been easier in the house in the last few weeks as evidenced by our play and the shared laughter. Against all my expectations, it appeared that Mother had not conveniently "forgotten" the fight that had taken place between her and Elizabeth, after all. She never spoke of it, but since that time there was a marked change in her behavior toward us, particularly toward Elizabeth. So far there had been no more reproaches, no scoldings, no adverse attention or pointing out of our shortcomings. Instead, she utterly ignored us.

The first day or so of this was puzzling, as we anticipated her to return to her old pattern of behavior once she had recovered from her bruises. But as the days (or for me, the nights) followed one another we saw that she was either purposely or accidentally overlooking us in all things. She never addressed us directly and should we be in a room with her, her eyes simply skipped over us as though we were invisible.

The puzzlement was soon replaced by a grateful relief as we saw how things stood. We found it infinitely preferable to be ignored by her than to be subjected to her constant abuse. Even Father was benefiting from it as some of her more acidic commentary concerning him dropped off. She had become polite without the usual underlying tone of sarcasm.

Of course, he had not been pleased about what had happened, but his interview with Elizabeth on the incident had been a gentle one. He advised her to exercise more self-control, but so far she had been spared from testing herself further.

Another expectation of mine that had gone unfulfilled was the speedy exit of our guests. It had been a highly embarrassing episode and I'd thought that the Norwoods would soon invent an excuse and leave, but they stayed on. Lady Caroline was most gracious about the business and chose to regard Mother in the same way as Father did: that the woman suffered from bouts of illness over which she had no control. Norwood had missed it all, so any impression it might have made on him when he heard of it from others was negligible.

Cousin Anne was a bit less charitable, deciding that it was all "horrid" and "confusing," but she, too, stayed on, for she had nowhere else to go. As for Mrs. Hardinbrook, it was just another in a long series of unpleasantries that she found easy to dismiss after so much skillful practice.

I'd asked Dr. Beldon for his opinion about the change in Mother, but he was not as candid as he might have been. "It seems to be for the good," he said, "but I won't hazard to say how long it might go on. Mrs. Barrett's condition has ever been an erratic one in the past."

"But she's always been consistent in her poor behavior," I pointed out.

"Ah, yes. One could say that. She has displayed a certain nervousness in her temperament." He was trying so hard to be tactful.

"Let's be honest, Doctor, her temper has been consistently bad, especially toward her family. Now she's become almost congenial. Without making comment on how it was brought about, I'd just like to know how it may be continued."

Beldon, so used to social pretense, floundered on that one. "I have no answer for you, Mr. Barrett. And as a physician I can hardly prescribe a reenactment of what happened between your mother and Miss Barrett as a course to take should the . . . nervousness return."

I winked at him. "Still, it's something to think about, isn't it?"

He covered his mouth with his fist and coughed trying to hide the smile there, but I'd seen it and thus did he confirm what Elizabeth and I had earlier determined: that a firm hand was needed with Mother. In other words, those few seconds of knocking about had done her (and the rest of us) more good than three years of constant placation and submission. Not that either of us planned to repeat the violence, but because of its occurrence it may have gotten through to Mother that she was immune to the consequences of her actions no longer.

I had come to like the winter, even as the worst of it settled upon us like a vast white bird with icy wings. With the nights so closely following the short days, my time and enjoyment of the society of our guests was happily increased. With Father's permission, I'd worked my influence upon them, ensuring that they found nothing unusual in my daytime sleep in the cellar or avoidance of the supper table. And so when I came down after changing into more suitable clothes for the evening, no one remarked upon it, or even thought to try.

I went straight to the library, planning to answer Oliver's letter right away and then get started on the work Father had left for me. However dull it might prove to be, I would do my best to help him in all things.

"Hallo, Cousin," said Anne, who was standing by the book-case when I came in.

"Hallo," I returned. "Finished with my Gibbon already?"

"Hardly. He's very interesting, but I wanted something different tonight. Something a bit lighter than history."

"Hmm. Let's see, what about this one?" I plucked down a volume of Shakespeare.

"A play?"

"A comedy. It's about twins, a boy and a girl who are separated by misadventure, so to make her way in the world the girl disguises herself as a boy."

"You're jesting!" Anne found the idea to be a bit of a shock.

"Then she falls in love with a nobleman, but can't reveal it to him, and then a lady, also fooled into thinking she's a young man, falls in love with her and so on. Elizabeth found it all very amusing and so might you."

"But a girl dressing as a boy? It's so immodest!"

I shrugged. "There are even a couple engravings in there showing it."

Her jaw dropped, but curiosity won out over her objections. She seized the book and scurried off to explore its apparently vulgar pleasures, tossing a hurried "thank you" to me over her shoulder. I smiled after her and realized that I quite liked my cousin.

Anne had a sweetness in her nature at odds with her Fonteyn blood, so presumably she'd escaped its dire effects. However, she was not an especially clever woman, and much of her conversation was of a repetitious nature. She was pretty, though, and at her best when singing, for she had a lovely voice. As there was nothing to dislike about her, she was generally liked by others as well, so long as the conversation was not too intellectually taxing.

I thought that she might have a working mind hidden away somewhere; it just wanted a little encouragement to emerge. From what I gathered in listening to talk about what things were like in Philadelphia, a girl was not expected to have much of an intellect, nor was one needed. Pouring tea correctly, wearing a pleasant face no matter what, and keeping the servants in line was all that was expected of one; that, and being a good listener when a man was talking to you. I could see why Elizabeth had such a low opinion about what polite society thought desirable in women.

"You're very kind to her." A woman's voice. Lady Caroline.

I turned from the bookcase to find her at ease in Father's big chair by the fire. She had a book in one hand, her finger marking the place where she'd left off reading. I gave a little bow.

"It's nothing."

"Oh, but it is. I tried to interest her in Shakespeare ages ago and she wouldn't even touch it. Thought it might be too confusing. I admire the way you tempted her into it."

"Thank you," I said, with happy sincerity.

Where Anne was lacking was made up for by Lady Caroline, and I found myself rather strongly drawn to her. She was also very pretty and easy to talk to on many different subjects.

"What book have you found?" I asked.

"It's one I brought with me. It's music." She opened it to show the pages, which were indeed covered with bars and notes, all unintelligible to me. I left such art to Elizabeth, who had a natural talent for it.

"You're reading music? How can you do that without playing it?"

"I just can. It's no more difficult than reading words, I assure you."

"For you perhaps. Is there a story buried somewhere in your tune, then?"

She laughed very charmingly. "I think it would be easier for me to play it for you so you can work out your own story." Lady Caroline was accomplished at the spinet and attributed her skill from having taken lessons from Joseph Haydn during the years prior to his entering the service of the great and wealthy Esterhazy family where he was finding some fame these days. His name meant little enough here in the Colonies, but I'd heard it often while in England and was impressed.

"I should like that very much," I said.

"Your sister and I could take turns. She has an excellent ear and eye, I've noticed."

"She will be delighted to know you think so, Lady Caroline."

"I think quite a lot of your sister, you know . . . and so does my brother."

Well-a-day. "Indeed?" I nodded and raised my brows to indicate I was an interested listener.

"He's given me to understand that he has a very high and respectful regard in his heart for her."

Though Elizabeth had extracted my strict promise not to talk to Norwood about her, she'd made no mention about avoiding the subject with his sister. "Then his lordship will be pleased to hear—if he doesn't know already—that Elizabeth also has a very high and respectful regard for him."

"That is good news, as far as it goes, but what shall be done about it?"

"I believe that once the principals understand things, the situation will likely take care of itself."

"Ah, but there are other matters to consider, Mr. Barrett. Practical matters."

"What might those be?"

"Money, for instance, should it come to pass that my brother wishes to propose marriage to Miss Barrett. From the first when he began to confide his feelings to me about her, I could see that he would probably be too occupied with those feelings to even think about the dowry. I don't know if there are different customs over here, but in England, the bride is expected to bring a suitable sum into the marriage."

"There's naught to worry about there, Lady Caroline, for the custom holds here as well. In fact, upon marrying, Elizabeth comes into her full inheritance from her maternal grandfather's estate. It is a sizable sum with a very comfortable yearly income attached. Of course, any marriage she seeks must have the approval of her parents, or she forfeits everything." Such was Grandfather's hold from the grave on his female descendants. I had not been so restricted and had come into everything on my twenty-first birthday last summer.

"That requirement for approval must lessen the chance for any hasty elopements," she said.

"I believe that was the idea behind it." Though I knew Elizabeth was headstrong enough to ignore it if she felt she had to; in this case it was irrelevant and I said as much.

"Do you think your parents might bestow their approval on such a match?"

"That is something that Lord James will have to take up with them, though I can say that in my opinion I doubt they will have any objections." Father would not forbid Elizabeth any chance at happiness, and Mother would positively dote on the idea of having a duke's brother for a son-in-law. She would, of course, have to abandon her policy of ignoring Elizabeth. Or not. Well, we'd get 'round her somehow.

"That's good. Then I shall pass the good news on to James. It seems he gets all tongue-tied when in the presence of your dear sister and has been unable to speak to her of those things of the heart which most concern him."

We both took amusement from that picture, but it was somewhat at odds with my memory. Norwood had ever been smoothly articulate at all times. My guess was that he was genuinely interested in Elizabeth, but testing the waters via his sister. If he planned to press his suit, he'd want to be sure it was worth his while. This might be considered cynical, but it was the way things were done. Most marriages dealt with the issues of property and money before anything else, including love. But in this case, there seemed to be no problem over any of those concerns.

Lady Caroline, her questions answered, made leave to excuse herself. "I should like a chance to practice," she replied against my objection. "Then I shall be able to give you a proper recital. Who knows, but I might even have the honor of playing for a wedding party soon."

I bowed deeply as she left and smiled after her. She was a lovely, graceful young woman and understandably, my thoughts of her drifted along some pleasantly carnal lines for many moments. I entertained also the thought of entering marriage with her. Though I had no title to offer, I did have money, and that counted for much in these troubled times. She would still retain her title, after all.

No, I told myself gently. It was not for me. Then that gentle negative grew in strength as it came to me that marriage to any woman was certainly a much more serious consideration for one such as I than it would be for an ordinary man. Firstly, any proposal would also have to entail a confession about my particular condition . . . and how I had come to acquire it. Very risky to the relationship, that, but the only honorable course to take in order to be fair to the lady. It wasn't the sort of revelation one reserves for the wedding night.

My God, *why* had Nora always refused my many proposals? For all the intimacy of our relationship, we might as well have been married. And I had known all about her condition. Did she think I might reproach her for the other men she knew, the ones who willingly supplied her with money . . . and blood?

She would not have wanted for money with me, and I knew from experience that human blood was not her only source of food. Why, then, had she—?

The hurt washed over me like a cold sea wave, but dear God, how I missed her. Lady Caroline vanished from my thoughts, replaced by the shining image of Nora. How could I think of anyone else, think of marrying anyone else, even in play?

I'd write another letter to her, to follow the other and hope that they would reach her soon.

But first I would have to write to Oliver.

I settled in at Father's desk and put aside the work he'd left for me for the time being. There was a long night ahead, with little else to do; I'd get to it. For now I plucked up a pen, charged it with ink, and began a serious address of my cousin, thanking him for his efforts on my behalf and encouraging him to continue, if he wouldn't mind.

That business covered, I undertook to catch him up on the events of the last few months since my previous writing. Much was the same, yet much had changed, something of a mirror of my own condition. I included a guarded account of the incident at Mrs. Montagu's house, mentioning that I'd been wounded, but only slightly and was all better now. I said little about Nat and his large companion, only that they'd been killed, not a word on who had done the killing. I'd almost omitted the business altogether, but went ahead and put it down, anyway.

Father and I had had a long talk about it, or perhaps I should say he listened while I talked. It had not been easy to admit to that fatal loss of control, but to hold it tight within would have been worse. For several nights after I was bothered by the memory of Nat's red face and the feel of his flesh between my fingers as I squeezed the life from him. Like some latter-day Pilate, I found myself washing my hands every time the image turned up before my mind's eye. Thank God I was no longer troubled by bad dreams.

Perhaps because Nat's death was so vivid, I did not dwell as much on how I'd killed his friend. I thought this was because he'd been so eager to murder my father. It might be easier to bear such a burden when one is defending for another rather than attacking for oneself, but now and then, I could still imagine feeling the shock of the table edge as it slammed into the man's spine traveling up my arms. When that happened, I washed my hands.

Much to my disgust, Nash and others were hailing me as the hero of the hour, an honor I'd have been pleased to do without. I wearily maintained that my heroism was due to poor judgment and worse luck and asked that no more be said of the affair. It was then thought that I was being too modest. The story got out regardless and grew in the telling, much to my chagrin. Only Father and Beldon, both veterans of war, seemed to understand. At home the subject was hardly raised. I went on as usual, pretending to recover from my wounds, and gradually time worked its magic as present concerns supplanted past woes.

Most of them. That blooding often puzzled me. Why had I not disappeared for a swift healing when I'd taken the shot? Though the pistol ball had passed right through me as before, this time I'd been left with a bleeding wound. In discussions with Father and Elizabeth about it, we quickly concluded that the foreign matter of the wood splinters in my body had somehow prevented it, this theory confirmed by the fact that I'd been able to vanish again upon their removal. Why this should be escaped us, but I was not of a mind to further any researches and, much to their relief, had promised to do my best to avoid any situations of peril in the future.

The Montagu household had also come to settle down as the days passed by without further invasions, but they had lost quite a bit of property including two fine carriage horses, some cattle, and whatever food had been lying about, such as those missing hams. Their losses were not important when compared to the fact that no one had been hurt. Other houses similarly ransacked had not been so lucky, as the rebels had not hesitated to assault and even murder people in their quest for booty.

Norwood, upon his return from hunting the thieves with Nash, had reported the sad fact that everything had apparently been loaded into whaleboats and carried off to Connecticut.

"Don't know how they managed it with the horses and cattle, but their greed must have given them heart and ingenuity for the task," he said. "We found the spot on the beach where they loaded them in and pushed off. The water was like glass, so they must have made swift time getting home again. There was no other sign of them when we arrived, more's the pity."

"What about the other soldiers tracking them?" I asked.

He laughed. "Almost no sign of them, either. They'd gone about their duty with much enthusiasm, but little direction, and got lost in the dark. Poor fellows were so cold and tired from chasing after shadows all night they looked like a pack of stray dogs when we found 'em. Uniforms wet through and muddy, polish of sweat on their faces and the bootblacking smeared from their mustaches, I think they were more unhappy at not maintaining a smart turnout than in losing their quarry."

Nash had been just as disappointed as well as angry at the escape, for it reflected badly upon his ability to keep the peace in his allotted area. Not that his commissary duties called for him to do much soldiering, but the rebel actions did directly threaten his source of supply. In the end, despite Mrs. Montagu's objections (and Father's), a half-dozen of his men were detailed to be quartered in the emptied stables.

Unhappy that his proposal was met with such a cool reception, Nash bulled ahead regardless, pointing out that the people and property would be safer for the presence of troops. He pledged his word on the integrity of their behavior, and so far there had been no trouble from them. Apparently my past visit concerning that poor Bradford girl had put the fear of God into him, and he'd passed that fear on to his men. Father had heard later that the guilty man had been punished, though privately, as the army was reluctant to show its dirty laundry to civilians. It was not a wise policy, as those outraged civilians could only conclude that nothing was being done on their behalf. But in this case, at least, we knew better and trusted that things would remain relatively peaceful.

Despite this settlement, Father began making a point of going over for a short visit nearly every day to see how things were for his lady, a courtesy that was much appreciated by her. He extended other favors, like the "loan" of two of our horses and a milk cow, that she might not be left stranded or without a source of butter and other necessities. Nash, for all his rapaciousness, made not the slightest move toward collecting the stock for his own people. I'd been there at the time, and though Nash's eyes had sharpened, they grew dull enough again when they chanced to meet mine. Since that last interview we seemed to have developed an unspoken understanding, so influencing the man into charity was unnecessary. He'd come to his own conclusion as to how I might view any requisitions made from her and decided to save himself the bother.

Not all of this was passed on to Oliver, of course, but I did fill up a page or two with news I hoped he might find of interest. On a lighter note, I told him all about our house guests at length, including the interview I'd just had with Lady Caroline. If things proceeded as I thought, we would soon have Lord James Norwood as a relative. I asked Oliver if he had any opinion on the Duke of Norbury and his family and closed with a wish for a speedy reply to my inquiry about Miss Nora Jones, no matter what the news might be.

This done, I took out more paper and began my salutation to Nora. What followed was brief, but from my heart as I poured it out to her. I had many new questions about myself and many more about her, and included my hopes and prayers for her well-being. It didn't seem enough, but it was all I had until I heard from her once more.

And a long wait that would be, unless she'd received my first letter by now. The reply might be on its way to me, or even arrive tomorrow. Hope was ever with me, but often a bitter companion for every day that it went unfulfilled.

Addressed, sealed, and ready to go out in the morning, or whenever the next post finally came, I placed my latest packet under the cup of lead shot as usual and, with a sigh, began examining the top paper on the stack Father had left.

Father and Norwood returned the next day, though I was unable to celebrate their arrival until my evening awakening. It was determined that another tea party should take place, though this one was on a smaller scale than that which had been interrupted by the rebel raid. As more and more supplies were being drained away by the British and Hessian armies, it was not considered wise to be too ostentatious in one's entertaining. If this limitation on our hospitality grated at Mother in any way, she did not show it.

There was only one other change besides the size of the party. This time Elizabeth was not pouring; that honor went to Cousin Anne. Elizabeth offered no objections. We'd discussed it and decided that it was one more way in which Mother maintained her new routine of ignoring her daughter. The usual custom was that if no daughter of the house were available, the task went to another unmarried lady. Lady Caroline might have taken it, but Anne was younger.

As it turned out, Elizabeth's not too convincing chagrin at losing the post was disguised delight, since it gave her a better opportunity to see Norwood. I'd repeated my conversation with Lady Caroline to her and apparently the lady had done the same with her brother. Norwood and Elizabeth had found a corner that afforded some slight privacy and the two of them were smiling at each other in a manner that could only be described as soppy.

"It looks as though the fever is sorely afflicting them," Beldon remarked to me, but with vast good humor.

"'Tis a painless complaint, I hope."

"For now, certainly, and for evermore, God willing."

"You think they'll make a match for themselves, then?"

"I certainly hope so."

"Indeed?"

He pursed his lips. "Well, you are aware that my sister has ever entertained certain hopes. It will be of considerable relief to me if things arrange themselves so that she can gracefully abandon those hopes."

Perhaps not gracefully, but at least in silence, I thought. From the first day they'd descended upon our house Mrs. Hardinbrook had been badgering her brother to woo Elizabeth for his bride. As Beldon had no interest in women for matrimonial or any other purposes, the situation often became awkward for him. I could well understand that Elizabeth's marriage to another would provide him with a long desired ease from her nagging . . . until Mrs. Hardinbrook picked out a new prospect for him, anyway.

That lady was even now eyeing Elizabeth and Norwood and drawing some deadly accurate conclusions about the glowing, besotted looks passing between them. She glanced at her brother, scowled, then forced her eyes down into her tea cup as though it might provide her with either inspiration or consolation.

My former tutor, Rapelji, came over. A short man with amazing energy, he had finished his tea but not yet turned the cup over.

"Would you like some more, sir?" I asked. "Or perhaps some punch instead?"

"Tea will do, but I'm enjoying this too much." He nodded at Elizabeth, his eyes shining with good-natured amusement. "Well, well, now I'm wondering if I should pass any of the news on to the girls."

"The girls" were his elderly housekeepers, Rachel and Sarah. They were known for their exhaustive herb lore, good cooking, and choice gossip.

"It might be a bit premature, yet," I said. "They've only just gotten to talking with one another."

"They seem to be talking remarkably well. I've never seen your sister looking prettier, and I daresay Lord James would agree with me."

"I think any man would agree with you on that point, Mr. Rapelji," said Beldon. Though indifferent to women, his nature was flexible enough to allow him to have an aesthetic appreciation of them.

"I shall not debate with you, sir. What do you think of it, Jonathan?"

"Think of what, exactly?"

"A match between those two, of course."

"I shall support whatever decision my sister is pleased to make."

"What? That almost smacks of disapproval."

"Or a trust in my sister's judgment."

"Ho-ho, sir, I wish I'd thought of that one."

Now Father came over to our group and some of our informality faded. "Good evening, gentlemen. Anything of interest?"

"We were just remarking on the beauty of the ladies, sir," I said, uncertain whether Elizabeth's occupation with Norwood was the right subject to bring up with him at this time.

"There is much to remark upon," he agreed. Then I saw his eyes light upon the couple in the corner and twinkle. They shifted to mine, and he winked. After passing some time with Beldon and Rapelji, he leaned in close to me. "I wondered when he'd work up the courage to finally approach her."

"For how long?" I asked.

"Since the morning we left for Hempstead. His mind was on Elizabeth for the whole trip, I think, as he was ever eager to talk about her. Can't say that I'm exactly pleased, though."

"Have you anything against Norwood?"

"No, he seems pleasant enough, but by God, I hate the thought of him taking away my little girl."

On that I could sincerely commiserate, for I hated the thought of losing my sister to . . . well, he was a lord, but still a virtual stranger to us. I'd have to try to get to know him better.

"Are you done with your tea, Father?"

"What? Oh, yes, sorry."

We quietly exchanged cups as usual and he drained away some of mine.

"Got it just right this time, laddie," he said with a grateful smile. Father enjoyed lots of sugar in his tea, a habit I'd learned to imitate for his sake.

"Did Cousin Anne make it strong enough for you as well?"

"Yes, but she's let it steep too long. It's been very bitter."

"She may be distracted tonight."

"Oh? She taken with you, then?"

"Ahh . . ."

"Or is it the other way around to cause such distraction?"

"Really, sir!" And then I saw that he was only playing.

"She's a pretty enough girl, long as she doesn't talk too much," he said. "I heard her mentioning Shakespeare with some enthusiasm, though, so maybe there's hope for her."

"Hope for what?"

"That she might get that mind of hers into some kind of activity. I also hate seeing waste, and a pretty girl not given the chance to think is a terrible waste, or so it seems to me. To other men, too, I've seen on occasion. Having a beautiful but empty-headed woman for a wife can be an altogether wretched existence."

He was looking at Anne in an absent sort of way, his words running on lightly as though there were not much thought behind them. Tea party conversation, nothing more.

Or was there? Then, with a bitter shock, I realized he was thinking of Mother. She had certainly been beautiful once, if that portrait in the library was anything to go by. What had he been like himself? Young, about my age now, good prospects ahead, and then he falls in love with the stunning Marie Fonteyn. Had he been so wrapped in its fever that he'd not noted the flaws amid the virtues? Possibly. It ran in the family, too, if my feelings for Nora were anything to go by. Perhaps it ran in the whole human race.

Mother had looks—once upon a time—but she was not especially clever. She got on well within the rules imposed by society and custom, but her intelligence was more of a kind of instinctual cunning than anything else. No wonder she worried so much over what people thought. They, all unknowing, essentially did her thinking for her, telling her what was right and proper to do and say. All that she did and said did not come from her own desires, but were a mirror of theirs.

I fairly gaped at my mother, feeling shock, horror, and pity swirling up through me in one uneasy swell. That was bad enough, but to look on Father and feel the same but more of it . . . God have pity on us all.

"Something wrong, Mr. Barrett?" inquired Beldon, who had returned to stand next to me. Father had gone off to the library with Rapelji. "You seem a little—"

Haunted?

"—pale."

"I think I should like some air, Doctor."

He stepped back to give me room to pass. "But it's very cold out."

"Good."

I left my upended cup and saucer on a table and quietly left, not wishing to draw any attention to myself. Going out the front door, I picked up my stride until I was safe from sight behind one of our larger trees. The snow was not so deep on this side of it, barely coming up over my shoes. Not that I was worried about that or much of anything for a time. I breathed in and out, as if to clear myself of the dusty taste of that suddenly stifling room.

"Mr. Jonathan?"

Bloody hell, I wanted to be *alone*.

Jericho came up, wearing a worried face.

"What is it?"

One of his eyebrows quirked. "I'm aware of what passed between you and Mr. Barrett."

Yes, he'd been standing right behind us, busy as usual with the punch bowl. Of course, he'd have heard everything. But could he have heard my very thoughts? He had a reputation for such in the servant's hall.

"Your father is a very great man," he stated.

More thought divination? No, but Jericho had correctly read my reactions. Having known me since birth, he'd instantly understood what had been set off by Father's most casual remark.

"He is a wise man, too."

"I'm glad you think it," I said roughly.

"But a wise man only becomes so after making mistakes."

"So Father marrying Mother was a mistake?"

"Your judgment of him is."

As soon as his words were out, I was flooded with shame and dropped my head. "I'm sorry."

"Your father is human, Mr. Jonathan. As is mine. As are all fathers, all parents."

"Yes, I know that. I've always known that, but tonight it just seemed to hit me all at once, all over."

"No children are ever happy to learn about the true vulnerability of their parents. It shakes their world up too much."

That's what had happened, I thought. "You're exactly right. I've been very stupid about the whole business."

This time Jericho remained diplomatically silent. For a while. "It is rather cold, sir."

"So Beldon said to me a moment ago. Very well." I let him lead the way back to the house. We stamped the snow from our feet.

"Will I look at him the same as before, though, I wonder."

He shook his head. "Never. But this time it will be with more understanding."

He returned to his duties as I eventually did to mine.

No one had missed us, apparently. The party was going well. Beldon was with Mother and Lady Caroline and saying something amusing. Both were smiling, though Mother's smile, as ever, was a brittle one. I don't think she had any kind of a sense of humor, but at least Beldon was trying. Elizabeth and Norwood were still in the corner, discussing all kinds of things, probably. Cousin Anne was alone at the tea table, so I went to her for a bit of company.

She reached for the teapot, but faltered, seeing that I had no cup.

"Had my fill ages ago," I told her, "but thank you very kindly."

"A single cup fills you?"

I shrugged amiably and changed the subject. "Enjoying that play, I hope?"

Her eyes glazed as she searched her memory, then brightened. "Oh, the one you gave me? Yes, very much. Some of the language was *very* antique, but it was quite interesting. I went back the next day and got another one to read. He's a bit confusing in language until one gets used to it, and then it abruptly makes sense. I seem to know exactly what he means, once I've worked things out. But people didn't *really* talk like that then, did they?"

I thought that Rapelji might provide her with a better answer and looked around for him before recalling that he was probably still in the library with Father. As I started to form my own opinion for her, the gentleman himself came into the room. The energy that constantly propelled him through months of rigorous labor pounding knowledge into stubborn skulls had suddenly deserted him. He seemed to have just enough strength to totter a few steps in and then had to grab the back of a chair to support himself. He was very white.

He'd been so quiet that no one had noticed but me as I just happened to be facing in the right direction. The dreadful expression on his face went straight to my heart. Something was wrong, wrong, *wrong*.

"The doctor," he whispered. "Where's Beldon?"

Now others stirred and looked over, but I paid them no mind as I was rushing out the door for the library. Had I been breathing regularly, I'd have been choked with terror. Instead, clawing and clutching, the stuff invaded my brain and body like a swift, icy fever.

CHAPTER
— 7 —

The fever did not abate, but increased its numbing effect on my mind, as I strode into the library and found Father stretched out on the settee. I called to him, but, disturbingly, he did not respond. He might have been taking a nap, but he was much too still and slack. His mouth was open, but his lips and skin had a blue cast to them that turned my cold fear into frosty panic. I was unable to move, and barely heard or felt Beldon pushing past me to get to him.

He loosened Father's neckcloth immediately, then pressed an ear to his chest to listen to his heart. I could hear its slow beat, noted his deep, slow breathing, but combined with his stillness, neither seemed . . . right.

Beldon shook Father's shoulders, trying to wake him, shouting his name as though the man were across an open field, not right in front of him. The others coming up behind me were greeted by this row, and worried questions began to be whispered in tight little voices. "What's going on? What has happened?"

"Jonathan?" Elizabeth's voice managed to penetrate to me. She put a hand on my arm.

I looked at her and saw a reflection of my own white and hollow-eyed face. I turned and hugged her close for a moment, and that seemed to help.

"Someone get my box," Beldon ordered.

From the corner of my eye I saw Jericho sprint off, taking the stairs three at a time.

Other orders were given and various servants rushed to obey him.

"Mr. Barrett."

This time he addressed me, not Father. I stepped forward.

"Help me get him to his feet."

"Is that wise, sir?"

"Just do it," he snapped. He was already trying to lift Father to a sitting position. I helped him complete the job, and between us we got him standing. Father mumbled a protest at this liberty and tried to push us away. "We must wake him up and keep him awake."

The three of us moved from the library into the larger hall like drunken sailors stumbling home from a debauch. The others parted out of our way, scuttling off and collecting in corners like dust. Jericho hastily came downstairs again with the box of medicines clutched in his arms. Beldon told him to put it in the library and then return. When he did, Beldon had him take his place helping me with Father.

"What is wrong with Mr. Barrett?" Jericho whispered.

"I don't know," I whispered back, unable to trust myself to speak with a full voice.

Back and forth we went, encouraging Father to walk and to wake up for us. He shook his head at this, whether in denial or in an effort to comply, I could not tell. His face was slack, but now and then a beatific smile spasmed over it and he mumbled unintelligibly. Most of the time he was unaware of us, virtually asleep on his feet.

Beldon, who had gone to the library, called Elizabeth in with him. She'd been watching our progress, in agony over the driving need to do something and the utter lack of anything to do, and now fairly jumped at this chance to help. They reappeared again, Beldon with a cup of something in his hand and Elizabeth carrying a cloth and a basin one of the maids had been ordered to bring. We stopped pacing a moment and Beldon managed to get Father to drink what was in the cup.

We resumed walking, with Elizabeth standing nearby. Not much time passed before Father's body gave a frightening, uncontrolled jerk and he doubled over. Biting her lips and with tears streaming unnoticed down her cheeks, Elizabeth held the basin for him as he vomited into it. When he was finished, Jericho and I had to support him completely. He groaned, head drooping. Elizabeth tenderly wiped his mouth with the cloth, then draped it over the noisome contents and took it back to the library.

Beldon lifted Father's head and pried open his eyes. They were like solid blue buttons, with hardly any pupil showing. A madman's eyes, I thought, a chill stabbing right through me to the bone.

"Doctor . . ." I couldn't bring myself to say more, but he heard the pleading tone and put a reassuring hand on my shoulder.

"He'll be all right, I'm sure. Just keep walking him up and down. I have Mrs. Nooth making some very strong cafe noir and he is to drink all of it."

"But what is it? What sort of attack has he had?"

"I'm still working that out, sir. For now, keep him moving. No rest, no matter how much he may protest."

At this point Father was incapable of protesting, period. His skin was dreadfully gray, but it looked marginally better than that unhealthy blue tint. When the coffee arrived, I held him steady while Jericho persuaded him to drink some. The first cup did not stay down, no doubt because of the purgative he'd taken earlier. Beldon had anticipated this, though, for another vessel had been brought in to catch it. The second cup stayed in him, and a third, and so on until the pot was empty. It took a while, but eventually Father was walking on his own, though he still needed help and looked far from well.

"There's something wrong, Jonathan," he murmured, over and over. "What's wrong? Please tell me, laddie."

"Would that I could, sir," I said, hardly able to hold back my tears.

"It will be all right, sir," said Jericho. I could not tell which of us he was trying to comfort.

After a brief word from Beldon, Norwood took charge of the others and urged them to all wait in the music room. Mother objected to this and demanded a proper explanation for Father's condition. There was no tremor in her voice, though it was respectfully lowered. I got the strong impression that she thought Father was himself responsible for his wretched state.

Beldon put on his best doctor's manner. "It's a bit early to tell, but I believe Mr. Barrett has had an attack of the flying gout."

"Gout? He's never had gout in his life."

"That's most fortunate, but this is the flying gout, with diverse symptoms and diverse manifestations . . ."

I felt a fist closing hard around my throat. Oliver had studied medicine and had shared many observations with me on the subject. Whenever a doctor mentioned flying gout, it almost always meant he did not know what was wrong. I glared at Beldon but did not question him or his medical judgment just then. That would come later, in private, and he'd damn well better be able to account for himself.

Mother was finally persuaded to retire with the others to wait and distract themselves with futile speculation. Elizabeth remained by the open door of the library, ready to rush forward if needed again. Archimedes had taken up a post at the parlor door and watched everything with a dour face. Only Beldon dared to pass him, and did, spending some time in that room before emerging to go to the library again.

More coffee was brought in and Beldon saw to it that Father had an ample sampling. The poor man was awash with it by now, and after Beldon called for a chamber pot we retired elsewhere to allow him a chance to relieve himself. Beldon took that pot away rather than turning it over to a servant, which I thought odd.

Up and down we walked, and Father ceased to ask me his heartbreaking and unanswerable questions. He was silent now, his eyes looking more normal but still dimmed and groggy despite the coffee and activity.

"Something's afoot," he said in a soft but clear voice. We'd just passed the library and seen Beldon within, though we couldn't make out what he was doing.

I said nothing, but silently agreed with him.

"And keep that lot away from me," he muttered.

We'd passed the music room and caught the combined stares of the others. I couldn't blame him for any shred of reluctance about talking to them. My heart lifted an inch or two. Father was sounding more like himself.

"God, I'm tired. I want to sit down."

I called Beldon, who came out and looked at Father's eyes again and listened to his heart. "Very well, but no brandy. Coffee only."

Father made a sound to indicate that he was sick of coffee, but he obediently drank more when it was offered.

"Can you tell me what happened, Mr. Barrett?" Beldon asked when Father was seated. Jericho had brought a chair out from the parlor.

"What d'you mean?"

"When did you start to feel sleepy?"

Father shook his head. "I'm not sure. I was at the gathering . . . talking . . . Mr. Rapelji and I came away to talk about his school . . . perhaps then."

"What did you eat and drink tonight?"

"Same as the others, I think. Ask them."

"No medicines?"

"No, I'm not ill, or at least I wasn't. What's this about, sir? Explain yourself."

Beldon looked to be in difficulties. He sucked in his lips.

"Yes, Doctor," I put in. "I know enough of medicine to understand about the 'flying gout.' What's really wrong with Father?"

He glanced around at us all. Elizabeth and Archimedes had both drifted closer; Jericho stood on one side of Father, I knelt on the other. The five of us looked back, each with the same intense need to know his mind.

"I really hope I am wrong," he began hesitantly. "If I am not, then we have a most unpleasant situation to deal with."

"Out with it, sir," said Elizabeth, her eyes fairly burning through him. "What is it?"

His expression was such as to make it clear he would have preferred to be very much elsewhere. "I've made a thorough examination of . . . things and—"

"What things?" I asked, sensing he was trying to be delicate.

"The—ah—contents of the basins and chamberpot."

I wrinkled my nose in reflex.

"I've also checked my medicine box and found . . . a notable discrepancy in the contents of the laudanum bottle."

No one spoke. The silence was that awful, brittle, waiting kind that happens when something terrible is about to crash into your life and it's impossible to leap out of the way.

Father was the first to break it. "You mean I've taken laudanum, Doctor?"

"Yes, sir. Quite a lot of it."

"Please clarify that," said Elizabeth.

"The dose was probably sufficient to have very serious consequences."

"How serious?"

Beldon's answer got stuck somewhere in his throat.

"*That* serious," stated Father in a very dry whisper. He rubbed his face and sighed heavily, unhappily. "How?"

"It would have to have been in your tea, the taste disguised by plenty of sugar."

At this, Father's weary eyes suddenly sharpened. His hand had been resting on my shoulder; its grip tightened.

"Tea? How might it have gotten into just one cup, then?"

"That is something that we shall have to ask Miss Fonteyn."

"You think that girl tired to—"

Beldon shrugged. "I don't know, sir. It hardly seems likely. People were milling about at one time or another during the party, especially when the first cups were being poured. Anyone could have made an opportunity for themselves. Questions must be asked . . . and answered, for there is a chance this could happen again."

"Again?"

"The amount of laudanum that was taken was more than enough to . . . well, not all of it may have been used tonight."

Elizabeth put a hand to her mouth and drew in a sharp breath. She looked as gray as Father, and for a moment I thought she might faint. I knew that because I felt the same way.

"Everyone must be questioned," Beldon insisted, pushing on, though he could see what it was doing to us, but the alternative was worse. The implications of what might happen should there be a yet unused portion of laudanum waiting in our future were frighteningly clear to us. "I said it would be unpleasant," he added forlornly.

Father made a soft, contemptuous snort at Beldon's understatement. "Yes . . . no . . . oh, how my head buzzes. I need rest. No questions tonight, Doctor. I'm not up to it."

"I can do that, sir."

"No."

"But, Mr. Barrett . . . ?"

Father gently waved him down. "No, sir. If any questions are to be asked, then I shall ask them. If someone in this house played a careless joke on me, then I shall face them myself. I'll not leave it to another to do my business for me."

His face went first pale, then red with outrage and fear;
Beldon stared down at his patient. "Sir, you could have *died*
tonight! This was not any kind of a joke, but a most serious
and considered attempt on your life. I will not allow you to
delude yourself into thinking otherwise."

"Nor have I. But I am asking you to be silent over it."

"But, *why*?"

"As you said, this promises to be a most unpleasant situation. Would you really care to question the entire household?"

"It's necessary in order to find out who's responsible."

"I believe I already know, sir."

That silenced Beldon. It silenced the whole room.

"Archimedes."

He straightened a little. "Sir?"

Father swallowed. With difficulty, as though ready to vomit
again. "I want . . . want you to discreetly go through Mrs.
Barrett's room. You'll be looking for . . . what? A twist of
paper or a small bottle?"

Beldon murmured agreement.

"The doctor will show you what the stuff looks like. If you
find nothing, then you'll look again tomorrow. Pay special
attention to the pockets of the garments she's worn tonight.
Jericho, I want you to check the parlor right now for the same
thing, and the music room later after they're all out of there.
Go through the drawers, check under the furniture, the whole
room, every corner."

"Sir."

"And both of you . . . don't let yourselves be seen by anybody. What you've heard here, stays here."

Both nodded with grim faces and waited impatiently as
Beldon went to the library for the bottle of laudanum to show
them what they'd be hunting.

"What happens should they find it?" I asked.

Father let his head fall against the back of the chair and
shut his eyes. "They give it to Beldon, who will lock it in his
medicine box, once he has a lock put on the thing."

"What about Mother, though?"

"Nothing."

Elizabeth shot me an anguished look over him. "We can't
do nothing."

Father was quiet. Thinking, or tired beyond thought.

"She tried to poison you!"

"It failed, by the grace of God. I have my warning and I shall be more alert now."

"No, Father! You can't live in a house with that woman, day after day knowing that the next bite of food you take could be your death. I won't have it!" Her voice had dropped to a shaken whisper, but was as forceful as a shriek.

Father made no response, but the lines on his forehead deepened as his brows came together.

"This has gone too far. You *must* do something about her."

"I will, but in my own way."

"But—"

He raised one hand slightly from the chair arm. "In my own way."

This did not sit well with Elizabeth, not at all well. Her eyes were burning red from tears shed and tears yet to come. "What is that, then?" she asked, her voice thin as she tried to maintain control.

"We'll take steps to see that the opportunity Dr. Beldon referred to has no chance to repeat itself."

"That hardly seems enough," she objected.

Father was still ill and greatly weakened or he might have chided her for that. All he could do was shake his head, reminding me that now was not the time for such discussions. Later, when he was well again, not now.

"We're worried for you, Father," I said unnecessarily, using it to cover a warning look thrown at Elizabeth. It got through and she shut her mouth, though her jaw worked dangerously.

"I'm worried for all of us. This was unexpected, but it can be dealt with. Actually, I'm not too terribly surprised that something's happened, I just didn't anticipate it would happen in quite this manner."

"What do you mean?"

"I've been careless, laddie. About . . . Mrs. Montagu. Your mother's finally found out and this"—he indicated himself—"is her reaction. I'd thought that should the day come, she'd fall into one of her fits, but she's changed lately. She's gotten more subtle."

"Suppose it wasn't Mother?" I asked uneasily.

His eyes opened. "Who else would want to?"

The names of all those people living with us tumbled through my mind. Long-time servants, guests old and new.

None of them could possibly have any quarrel with Father. None. He was a well-loved, well-respected man. The only person in the house who did not love or respect him was Mother. She had had access to Beldon's medicines and was certainly familiar enough with the use of laudanum by now. The more I thought about it, the likelier it seemed.

She was a strong woman, but not stronger than Father, so a physical attack against him would ultimately be futile. But poison . . . now that would equalize things nicely. There was a horrid, repulsive coldness to poisoning, but also an ugly fascination in the process. To stand by and pretend concern while watching with secret interest as the stuff gradually carries away a life—that was of a kind of wickedness so alien that I could hardly credit its existence. But here it was, right in my own house.

"What will you do?" My voice was thin, ghostly.

"Take more care," came his simple reply.

You'll need more than that, I thought, my heart filled with leaden sickness.

Elizabeth made a choking sound and turned away to hide her tears.

Much more than that.

Archimedes and Jericho found no laudanum that night or in the days to follow. They had been uncommonly diligent in their searches, but we were left with the uncomfortable conclusion that either nothing was there to be found, or that Mother had been more clever at hiding it. Beldon offered the slim hope that the amount taken from his box had all been used that same night. No one was too eager to trust in that, though.

Beldon saw to it that a stout lock was attached to his medicine case and began to lock his room whenever he left it. He kept both keys on his person and soon developed a habit of now and then tapping the pocket they occupied to make sure they were there. Their soft clink was a source of great reassurance to him, it seemed.

He also continued—at Father's firm request—to perpetuate the fiction about the attack of flying gout. It was bad enough for us to know the truth behind his illness, but it would have been much worse for the others to know as well. For all to suffer with such knowledge . . . well, the strain and worry would have made the place impossible to live in.

The story also served well enough to cover the reason why Beldon demanded Mrs. Nooth's close supervision of Father's meals. As for drink, the cabinet in the library holding a small stock of wines and spirits also quietly acquired a lock. Father hinted to the locksmith about petty thievery of his stock and rather than confront the tippler, he preferred to confound him. The tale was so common that it would hardly be worth repeating, which was what Father hoped for and likely got.

Father was shaky the next day, his body still busy trying to recover from the aftereffects of too much laudanum and coffee, but he was more himself on the next, and out doing his usual business after that. He made one very brief visit to Mrs. Montagu, mentioning it to me later.

"I told her that things were becoming difficult here, requiring my presence, so she mightn't see me as often. I did not tell her what happened, nor do I wish her to know."

"Hasn't she the right?" I asked.

"Yes, but she's burdens of her own to bear at this time. Later, when I'm ready, she'll hear it all, but not just yet. In the meanwhile, I'd appreciate it if you'd look in on her now and then when you're . . . out and about. See that things are quiet. You know."

"I'll be happy to do so." He knew all about my flying adventures, such as they were. The winter nights were perfect for this activity, at least when the winds were not too fierce. The cold weather drove people indoors and kept them there, allowing me considerable freedom to enjoy the open sky without fear of being seen. More than once I'd let myself drift all the way into Glenbriar to socialize at The Oak or visit Molly Audy or both. Molly's fortune improved for all my extra business, and at the inn I was able to expand my knowledge of the German language by talking some of the night away with the Hessians there. Would that things were as amicable at home.

The evening following the tea party was a quiet one, though. Father was up in his room, the rest were downstairs pursuing cards or music. Beldon had gone so far as to tune up his fiddle and was attempting a duet with Lady Caroline. Norwood and Elizabeth managed to place themselves on the same settee, ostensibly to listen. Mother, Mrs. Hardinbrook, and Anne were attempting some sort of three-handed card game I couldn't readily identify. All appeared peaceful and normal. Perhaps it was, but my perceptions had been so altered that I was seeing things in a skewed manner.

Studying Mother's every movement and expression, I tried to read the truth within, if any could be discerned. I saw a middle-aged woman, her once beautiful face marred by years of unhappy passions and futile and frustrated goals. This was not a contented soul. Any peace in her life came from moments like this, where distraction from her own inner demons might be found in the company of her friends.

That was interesting. I'd always known it, but only now did the realization come to me: Mother was rarely ever alone. Mrs. Hardinbrook was with her most of the time, Beldon as well, then there were all those tea parties and making calls on others. For all the acid of her personality, she always managed to have some company around her. I wondered why. Was she so afraid of those demons she could not face them?

Having faced down a few myself, I couldn't blame her for that.

Elizabeth rose and excused herself during a break in the playing and walked unhurriedly out to the hall. As she passed me she raised her brows and gave a very small movement of her head to indicate she wanted to talk. Anything more open might draw unwelcome attention from Mother. After a moment or two, I unobtrusively followed.

She was not waiting in the hall as I'd expected, but there was a faint glow of candlelight coming from the open door of the library.

"This is hard, Jonathan," she said just as I came in.

"Tell me what it is first and I might agree with you."

She was blank for a moment, then waved her hand in a gesture of irritation. "*This*. Not being able to talk about last night or at least about the real truth of it. To pretend that nothing happened when all I want to do is scream about it to the heavens."

"I know you do."

"To sit in the same room as that woman . . . full of acting and pretense over something this serious. If we do much more of it I'll burst."

"You won't."

She snorted. "I shouldn't like to wager on that."

"Father will take care of everything."

"We can hope so, but . . . I don't trust that blind spot he has for her. Yes, he feels honor bound by an oath to care for her, but cannot that oath be broken or at least bent by this change of circumstances?"

"He'll think of something, I'm sure." My responses were easy and without much thought behind them. She mostly wanted someone to talk to, a chance to air her complaints and fears. As she was unable to speak to Father about it, I was now her only confidant, aside from Jericho and Archimedes. But they were servants and I was her brother. I accepted her fears and kept my own in check for the moment.

"You're wanting to tell Lord James?" I asked, prompted by an unexpected insight.

Her teeth were showing, but in a grimace, not a smile. "I don't know what I want. Yes, I do . . . oh, damnation!"

I couldn't help but laugh at her, but quietly. "You are in love, aren't you?"

Now she flushed red and paced up and down, wringing her hands together. "I think so. I don't know. I've never felt like this before. I can't see straight or think about anything but him or do anything for myself. Am I ill?"

"Definitely, and I hope you'll treasure that illness."

"But, it's frightening, too. Is that how you felt about Nora?"

"It depends on what sort of fear you mean." Nora had inspired several kinds in me during our relationship.

"I mean the sort of fear that comes when you stand on the edge of what you know to be a cliff. You have to step off, not knowing whether you'll fall into a stack of straw or dash to pieces on a pile of rocks."

"Yes," I said with a sigh of remembrance. "I've been through that."

"What did you do?"

"I stepped off, of course. I didn't have much choice. I just went, because any other choice would have hurt worse than landing on the rocks."

"That's what I want to do, but how can I do it without being truthful to him about things?"

"You really think it's necessary to tell him about last night?"

"It's . . . been preying on my mind. Coming between us. I want to tell him, but I'm not sure. He'll probably tell his sister and she might mention it to Anne or—"

"Just ask him to pledge on his honor to keep it to himself."

"Is it just that simple? I hate secrets unless they're happy ones, like a surprise present. Those are the only ones I'm comfortable keeping."

"A man like Lord James would probably be delighted to have your confidence and a pledge on his honor would be safe with him. It would make him feel quite the hero with you confiding such privileged knowledge to him."

"The point is not to impress him, but to be honest."

"He will be impressed, anyway."

"But the knowledge itself is so sordid. It might put him off me."

"I can't advise you on what to do in this, or how he might react, but if he really loves you, nothing will keep him from you."

"I suppose I'll have to think about it some more. It's just that sitting there with Mother behind us and playing cards as though nothing were wrong . . . my God, if Rapelji hadn't been with Father we might be weeping around a coffin right now."

Time to give her a hug. Past time. I put my arms around her and told her everything was all right. I'd been saying that a lot lately. I hoped with all my heart that it was true.

Footsteps. I recognized their purposeful clack and broke away from Elizabeth.

"What is it?" she asked.

I put a finger to my lips and faded away as fast as I could. And that was very fast. Elizabeth gave out with a little "oh" of surprise as she suddenly found herself alone in the room.

The steps, muffled for me by my present condition, halted, probably at the doorway.

"What are you doing here?" Mother demanded.

The reply was slow in coming. It might have been caused by my disappearance or by the fact this was the first time in ages that Mother had directly spoken to her, or by both.

"Nothing. I just wanted to find a book to show to Lord James."

"Where's your brother?"

"I last saw him in the music room."

"He's not there now." Mother stepped forward and around and circled the library. Assuring herself that Elizabeth was indeed alone and that I wasn't hiding behind a curtain or crouched under the desk.

Elizabeth remained silent. So did Mother. Eventually, she left. When I was sure she was far enough along not to hear, I returned.

My sister jumped when she saw me.

"Sorry. I thought it would avoid trouble if I—"

"My God." She put her hand to her heart and breathed out a laughing sigh of relief. "My God."

"I'm *sorry*."

"Don't be. I was just wishing that *I* could do that, too." She went to the door and looked out. "Gone back to her game, I think. You saved us from considerable unpleasantness just now."

"That was the idea."

"And a good one. Thank you, little brother."

I bowed good-naturedly. "She spoke to you."

She'd been smiling; now it faded. "Yes. I hope she won't make a habit of it. I . . . don't think so."

"Why is that?"

"Just a feeling. In the past she's never failed to find some fault with me and make some kind of disparaging comment over it. She had the opportunity now and did not use it."

"Perhaps she wants to maintain as much distance from you as you do from her and knows that talking to you would diminish it."

" 'Though this be madness' . . . ?"

"She knows 'a hawk from a handsaw.' "

We fell silent a moment and stared out the empty door. Distantly, Beldon drew a few notes from his fiddle, then sawed out a few others, but with more confidence. The spinet followed his lead, then passed him.

"Lord James will be missing you," I said.

"I'm missing him."

"What will you tell him?"

"I'm not sure. Talking to you about it . . . well . . . I have to think some more."

"Will you tell him about me?"

She was startled. "Why should I?"

"In the interest of honesty. Why not? It's a secret as well."

"But not an awful one. It's not the same."

"It's been pretty awful to me, at times."

"This must not have been one of them. You should have seen your face when you came back after she left."

"I wish I could."

Elizabeth knew all about my problem with mirrors. "Feeling sorry for yourself?"

I made myself smile and shook my head.

I wandered back into the music room some while later. Lady Caroline had relinquished the spinet to Elizabeth and was now sitting next to Norwood, but nothing else had changed. I listened as she and Beldon played through a few songs they both liked, nodded at anyone looking my way, and eventually wandered out again.

The mood was a familiar one: I was too restless to sit, or read, or do much of anything. I hated this kind of waiting, of not knowing exactly when it would end.

It was very cold when I finally thought to go outside. I had no cloak or hat, but the chill would not affect me for a goodly time, despite the high wind. The noise of it bothered me more than the low temperature. It hissed and snarled through the bare tree branches and sent loose crystals of snow skittering over the drifts. I plunged my bare hands into a thick white pile and dug out the makings of a sizable snowball. Packing it down solidly, I smoothed it, rounded it, slapped more snow in where it lacked.

There was ice mixed in and it cut me. I regarded the stinging slice in my finger for a moment, vanished, and returned. The cut was gone.

I liked that, and laughed at myself. Then I hefted my snow-ball and threw it as high and as far as I could over the trees. Couldn't tell where it landed. Couldn't hear. The wind carried the sound away.

Elizabeth had been right to question whether I was feeling sorry for myself, but my pity was for our family in general, not just for me.

Well . . . maybe *some* of it was for me . . . but I wasn't giving in to it, not for now.

I made more snowballs and threw them out into the pale winter night until my fingers grew stiff and blue, then went inside to thaw them by the library fire. Around me the house was gradually settling down for the evening. The last bit of cleaning was being seen to in the kitchen, along with preparations for tomorrow's cooking tasks. I heard Archimedes's stately tread going up the stairs to see if Father wanted anything more before retiring. Jericho made a last round to see that the doors and windows were locked, then went up to my room to set out my things as usual. He and his father came down together, their voices soft in the liquid sound of some African tongue. Jericho understood his father's language, but rarely spoke it where a white person might hear. He said it made them nervous.

The music had stopped and conversation had ceased. Norwood escorted his sister to her room. Beldon saw to the other ladies, then came to the library.

He did not see me as he cast about for a book for this evening's reading. I made sure of that. Only when he was gone did I return. I didn't usually vanish to avoid people, but tonight I didn't feel like having further conversation.

Beldon trudged up to his room, and one by one people upstairs and down retired to their beds. If I listened very carefully, I could just hear Mrs. Hardinbrook's first snores.

Other than that and the wind outside, all was quiet. When I was busy with clerking for Father or absorbed in a book, I hardly paid mind to any of it; now it all seemed to shout at me, "You're alone, alone, *alone*."

Indeed, I was. More so than most. Even Mother.

When the silence went on for an hour, I shifted myself from before the dying fire and quietly padded upstairs, carrying a candle. My shoes were on the hearth, still drying out from the snow, but I'd have left them off anyway.

On the landing I went left instead of right and paused outside Mother's door to listen. She was asleep. My hand dropped lightly on the handle and pushed, and I slipped inside.

In all her time here, I'd never been in her room. I'd never had an interest in seeing it since she'd moved back with us, nor had she ever invited her children to visit. Only Mrs. Hardinbrook had been welcomed here, and Beldon, when a doctor was needed. It had all the usual furnishings, including a very large mirror. I could ignore that for now.

She was buried under a thick layer of coverlets, the sheets made comfortable when one of the maids had passed a bed warmer between them earlier. Mother lay on her back, her

carefully dressed hair wrapped up for protection against disarray in her sleep. Her face was thick with powder and paint,
the feeble tools used to retain some ghost of her former beauty.
She looked like a ghost, a very still one, with its mouth slightly open.

My throat was tinder dry and I knew I was afraid. I could
back out even now and no one would be the wiser.

Mother grumbled uneasily and turned a little. The lines on
her face that should have been smoothed by sleep deepened
into a scowl. If she dreamed, then it was an uneasy one.

Elizabeth was right, there was hatred in this woman, but was
it enough to inspire her to poison a husband she had ceased to
love decades ago? The more I looked at her the more likely
it seemed. And the more pressing my need to do something
about it.

I glided to a bedside table and lighted the candle there from
the one in my hand. The room had been too dark for what
I needed to do. I found another candle and brought it over.
Their three lights still seemed too feeble, that, or my fear was
making them so. It was that skewed perception again.

Unhappily giving in to it, I turned up one more candle, just
to be sure. Plenty of light now, no chance for failure . . .
unless someone walking past in the hall noticed the golden
gleam escaping under the door and . . .

No. None of that. I'd hear anyone walking past first. With
my hearing, I'd know when they first set foot to floor from
their beds.

Get on with it.

I had to work my mouth a bit to get enough spit in it to talk.
Then I wavered and cursed myself for my hesitation.

Taking a deep breath, I leaned over Mother and gently shook
her shoulder. It felt strange to touch her. She never encouraged
it. The last time I'd touched her had been at my homecoming
from England. It had been a very perfunctory embrace, no
more than what was needed for show. After that, nothing.

I expected iron, or something equally hard and cold, but
this shoulder was soft and flaccid under my fingers and I
drew them back as soon as she stirred. She mumbled and
shifted.

"Wake up," I whispered. I could barely hear myself.

Have to do better than this.

I shook her again, more firmly. "Wake up, now."

Her mumble turned into a whimper. I worried that she might have taken one of Beldon's sleeping draughts. Damnation if she had.

"*Wake up!*" A more fierce whisper.

"No," she moaned, drawing it out into a near whine. "No, Papa."

"Come on." I shook her again, trying to break her from her dream.

"Please, no, Papa. Don't."

"Mother . . . wake up!"

Her eyes flew wide and she gasped and shrank from me. I hadn't known what to expect when I woke her, but not this. Not this kind of shock, not this kind of naked fear. My God, what had she been dreaming about?

"What?" The last shreds of sleep tore away from her puffy eyes. They sharpened, cutting into me. "What are you doing here?"

Such was the force of her question and my ingrained habit of obedience that I nearly wasted time answering her. But I caught myself and said, "Quiet. You will be quiet, Mother."

Our eyes were locked together. That was what was important.

"You—"

"Quiet . . . and listen to me. You will *listen* to me . . ."

The fear, anger, hatred, outrage—whatever it was that drove her—eased instantly. It was frightening to see just how swiftly the change came over her, almost like one of her fits, but reversed.

No wonder Father had thought of this acquired talent of mine as both a gift and a curse and had asked me to use it sparingly, and so I had. For the most part. Nora had used it often enough to protect herself, letting her conscience guide her, and I'd taken that as a wise example to follow. Bullying Nash into a more compassionate behavior did not seem to be an abuse of power, after all, but what I was about to try now might be thought . . .

No. I would not start worrying about what people might think. Do that, and I'd end up like Mother.

I'd once agreed with Father that to enforce my will and thoughts upon others was not only ungentlemanly, but dishonorable. It had seemed so simple then to do so. The right thing. One of the first ideas to occur to him was that I might

be tempted to influence Mother into better behavior, and I'd
all but given him my word that I would take no such action.
Now as I stood here and stared down at her empty eyes I felt
shamed over having to betray his trust.

But what I was doing was right. It *had* to be right.

The agreement we'd made so easily last summer did not
cover this threat, had never even considered it. I wasn't doing
this for any other reason than to protect him, but then I wasn't
planning to tell him about it, either. Out of considerations of
honor, he might forbid me to do anything.

Damnation, again. I *was* becoming like Mother: for I was
doing this for Father's own good, without his permission.

So be it, I thought wearily. For peace in the family and out
of love for my father, so be it.

I straightened, resumed looking into Mother's eyes, and
began to speak.

CHAPTER

— 8 —

Days—and nights—passed and nothing happened, thank God. Responding unknowingly to my influence, Mother did what was asked of her, which was to do nothing.

I'd kept it to the absolute minimum, making the brief and simple request that she should not attempt to hurt or harm Father ever again. Once assured that she understood completely, I suggested that she forget my intrusion, but not her promise, and to go to back to sleep. After a moment, when I stopped feeling so unsettled, I put out the candles, carefully returned them to where I'd found them, picked up the one I'd brought, and left.

Without, the hall, rooms, the whole house had been as silent after as before. A listening silence, said my guilty fancy, but I was safe enough from discovery.

Depending on one's conscience, guilt can be eased by the passage of time, and to my surprise, I found my conscience to be rather more flexible than I'd thought—at least in this matter. As one night succeeded another without further incident, I began to see that what I'd done had been the right action to take. The only drawback was not being able to speak of it to the others.

It would have helped them to know that their worries were over, but it seemed best to let things run on as usual. Not that I was indifferent to their concern; I offered reassurance when it was needed, but kept my mouth shut the rest of the time. After a while, life gradually relaxed back to normal. Or something close to it. Father resumed taking tea with us and ceased looking so dubious when presented with his evening meal. Elizabeth, distracted by Norwood, left off drifting along in Mother's wake whenever the woman left a room alone. Jericho and Archimedes stopped their searches for laudanum, though they continued to keep a sharp eye on Mother during any gatherings with food or drink.

Beldon remained watchful, though. Frustrated perhaps by Father forbidding him to ask questions, he'd continued to keep an eye on Mother as much as he could.

"I feel badly about this, Mr. Barrett," he confided to me one night not long after. "My carelessness was inexcusable. It shall not be repeated."

"Hardly your fault, sir. How could you have known? Or even anticipated?"

"But I should have." He touched the pocket where he kept the new keys to his medicine box and room. "Nevermore."

"Then surely there's no reason to feel bad."

He offered me a bleak look. "There is should your Mother decide to make another attempt, by another means."

I retained my serious face. "What is open to her, then?"

"There are a number of hunting arms in the house, some pistols, and you know that Lord James has quite a little collection of his own."

"You hardly need worry over that. Mother knows nothing about the loading or shooting of firearms. You have to know what you're doing to get them to work properly, and she doesn't."

That brought him a measure of solace, for it was entirely true. We had the arms and powder and shot at hand and ready to use because of the roughness of the times. With rebel raiders threatening to swoop upon us ready to commit common robbery under the thin guise of patriotism, Father had taken pains to augment his cache of guns over the months. However, it was impractical to leave them lying around loaded, as the powder might become too damp to fire. He did make certain that everyone in the house from Elizabeth to the scullery boy knew how to load and shoot, though. Everyone but Mother, who claimed to despise the noise and mess, and did her best to make a virtue of her willful ignorance. I think she may have regretted her attitude, for Lady Caroline turned out to be a most enthusiastic shootist, setting a good example for the rest of the ladies to follow.

"What other means of mayhem might she turn to?" I asked Beldon.

"A push down the stairs?" he hazarded, then shrugged sheepishly. "I know, I'm probably worried over nothing, but I am very fond of your family and should bitterly regret any harm that might come to them. Your father was uncommonly generous in taking my sister and me in and allowing us to stay."

That, of course, had been Mother's idea, for this was her house, not Father's, but in truth, Father had come to welcome their company, Mrs. Hardinbrook as a buffer against Mother, and Beldon as a physician . . . and friend. I was reluctant to admit that, unwilling to relinquish my first impression of the man: that of a self-serving toad-eater. But though he often fell into that habit, especially around people like Norwood, he'd ceased to do so with our family. Perhaps some of our own honesty with one another (with the exception of Mother) had made a favorable impression upon him.

"We're all grateful for your presence, Doctor, and for your concern, but things are well in hand now."

He looked skeptical.

"I don't mean that we should not be vigilant to potential trouble, but I think things are safe enough that we may be at ease most of the time." There, that was as much as I would tell anyone and much more than I'd wanted. Father and Elizabeth would certainly have been able to discern what was behind my words and to correctly guess what I'd done to be filled with such confidence. Beldon, though, did not. From his wan smile I got the impression he was putting it down to youthful optimism. I hoped he would choose not to quote me before others. That might prove to be rather awkward.

But this night, like the last few, was quiet. The usual game of cards went on; they might have had enough for a second table of play, but I had no desire to join them and Norwood was gone. Some business in Hempstead claimed his attention and he'd left at dawn that morning. Poor Elizabeth had had a dull time of it waiting for him, or so I gathered when she greeted me earlier. Now she poked glumly at the keys of the spinet, her eyes starting up every time she fancied hearing a noise that might be the announcement of his arrival home.

Lady Caroline was busy with some delicate needlework, and Anne was reading another of Shakespeare's works. They sat on either side of the table, close enough to share the candlelight. The flames lent a golden tone to their high-dressed and powdered hair that was soothing to behold. I had a book of my own, but my attention kept wandering from it to them, particularly Anne. Her brow was deeply furrowed in concentration, but it was not unattractive on her. I quite liked the effect, as it gave a more serious air to her pretty, but usually blank face.

Then she must have sensed me watching her. She looked up to meet my eyes. I smiled politely and got one in return. She tried to continue reading, but I'd spoiled it for her. After a few more efforts, she gave up and smiled at me again.

Well-a-day. I'd seen that expression more than once on others and recognized it, or thought I did. The question to face now was what to do about it. Possessing a healthy portion of curiosity, I decided to find out if I was mistaken. I nodded back to her with a friendly expression. Hers was also friendly . . . and maybe a bit more.

She quietly folded her book and left the room in such a way as to bring no notice to herself. That usually requires either talent or raw instinct to do well, and Anne apparently possessed both those qualities. As she passed me, I got another look from her. No, I had not been at all mistaken, so after an interval, I followed. I wasn't sure about my ability to be as quiet as she, but I tried.

She was in the parlor. The fire was out and the only light came from the single candle she'd taken with her. She put it on a table.

"Hallo," I said.

Anne briefly pulled her lips into a thin line, then said, "You seem to like me."

"Yes, I suppose I do."

"As a cousin, or as something more?"

"Ahh . . . well . . ."

"Is that why you were looking at me? Were you trying to decide?"

I laughed a little. "Maybe I was. I'm sorry if I've given you any offense."

She shook her head. "I'm not offended, but I am curious."

What a coincidence.

"I know we are blood cousins, but I . . . think you're very handsome . . . and kind."

"Thank you. I think you're very pretty and sweet."

She swallowed. "That's good."

I moved fractionally closer. "Perhaps it's just that we're both curious."

"Yes, I'm sure of it. But I . . ." Now she looked rather helpless and lost. Was she standing on the edge of that cliff Elizabeth had spoken about? What lay below, a soft landing or something painful?

"Do you think you might be in love?"

Her lips thinned again as she bit the lower one. "I don't know what answer to give you."

"What answer do you give yourself?"

"That I'm not."

"But you're still curious?"

"Yes."

"Then perhaps we should simply attempt to satisfy our mutual curiosity and leave it at that."

She thought it over and her face lightened. "What shall we do?"

"Yes, well, there are any number of things that may be tried."

"I'd like to kiss you."

"That's a good start."

"But I don't know how. You won't laugh at me, will you?"

"My word of honor," I said solemnly, which seemed to give her some comfort. And I was not playing with her, for I knew just how difficult and frightening total inexperience can be.

She straightened and composed herself. "Will you show me?"

Now I had a moment of difficulty, not from inexperience, but from the responsibility I was about to take on. I vividly recalled how Nora had been aware of it for herself. With her example in mind, I knew then that I wanted Anne's first kiss to be just as happy a memory as mine was.

"All right. Stand close."

She did so.

"Relax a bit." I placed my hands lightly on either side of her face, then bent a little and kissed her, just like that. Softly. Gently. "There now," I whispered. "It's very easy. Want to try another?"

"Mm-mmm."

I took that to mean that she did and so obliged her, taking more time. She seemed to enjoy it, but had a puzzled look when I pulled away.

"Is that all there is? Not that it wasn't nice, but I thought—"

"Actually, yes, there is more. Quite a lot."

"Oh, that's good. Will you show me that as well?"

"If you wish, but not everything. Don't want to overdo it the first time out, y'know."

I put my arms around her and she followed suit. She was on the small side, but we managed to put our lips together again. I slowly opened mine and after a pause she did the same, catching her breath as I tried a more intimate touch with my tongue. That woke her up.

"Oh, dear," she gasped when I paused.

I didn't ask whether she liked it or not; it was obvious that she did, but had only been surprised.

"Does everyone do it like this?"

"Perhaps not as well," I answered, eschewing modesty. I felt there was no need for such. Nora had, after all, been an excellent teacher.

"Again, please?"

Explorations proceeded on both sides. Her breath came faster and deeper and I could feel her heart pounding throughout her whole body. I was subject to some extremely pleasant reactions of my own, the most noticeable of which forced me to draw away before she discovered anything odd about my mouth. I began kissing her cheeks, forehead, temples, ears, and finally dropped as far as her throat.

And there . . . I had to reluctantly stop. My corner teeth were out and I was more than ready to put them to use, but that wouldn't have been right. Not for either of us.

"Are you—are you finished?" she asked shakily.

"I think it might be a good idea to leave off here," I murmured somewhat indistinctly.

"Do other people not continue . . . to other things?"

"Yes, but I'm not prepared to do so. That is for another person to do."

"Who?"

"The man you'll fall in love with someday."

"What if I changed my mind? What if I'm in love with you?"

"That would make me a most fortunate fellow, but you're not."

"How do you know?"

"I just do."

Her hands fluttered over her lips, paused at her breast an instant, and then clasped one another determinedly. She breathed in and out once. "Then what am I feeling?"

"The normal kind of lust that is often generated by bit of healthy kissing."

"Lust?"

"Yes."

"That's a bad thing, though. Isn't it?"

"You do have to be careful around it, but under the right circumstances it can be very good indeed."

"And these aren't the right circumstances?"

"And I'm not the right person."

"You're sure?"

"I'm afraid so."

Her eyes were sharp and guarded. "How do you know that?"

"Because if it were otherwise, you and I would be feeling far more than just curiosity for ourselves."

She thought that over for a time. "Or lust?"

"Exactly."

More thought. Her hands unclasped. She took one of mine and went on tiptoe. I leaned down once more and we kissed once more. Rather chastely. She was smiling afterward. "Well . . . Cousin, if and when I should fall in love with a man, thanks to you, I shall be better prepared to deal with him."

"I'm happy to have been of assistance."

"But he will have to be someone very exceptional, I think."

I bowed gravely. "You are most kind, Cousin."

Her eyes were playful again. "Do you still like me?"

"More than ever."

"But not enough to be that person?"

"No. You see, I've . . . been in love . . . still am in love."

"Who is she?"

"It doesn't matter."

"Why don't you marry her?"

"I really couldn't explain."

"And I am prying too much," she concluded.

"Not at all, I'd just rather not speak of it."

That should have put an end to things, but she made no move to leave. "I don't feel like going back to the others yet," she said shyly.

"Neither do I. Would you like to sit and talk awhile?"

For an answer she glided to one of the chairs, sat, and smiled up at me. "About what?"

For anyone else it might have been affectation, but Anne was blessedly free of such encumbrances. I laughed a little and decided that I liked her very much indeed. There was not any great depth to her yet, but she was quite charming in her own way. Innocence has its own strong appeal, either for corruption or for appreciation. I had a mind to be appreciative.

I took a chair opposite her. "Whatever comes to mind. How do you like living here, for instance?"

"Oh, it's very grand. Much better than Philadelphia. If Cousin Roger knew how nice it was here, he'd have forgotten his politics and come along with us. Your mother has been most generous to take us all in as she has."

That was almost what Beldon had said, although he'd ascribed the generosity to Father. The similarity was enough to start a line of thought for me. Questions that had hovered half-formed on the edges of my mind now bloomed forth.

"What do you think of Mother?"

Her brow creased once more. "She's a very great lady, but . . . nervous, I believe."

The memory of her first night here and the altercation between Mother and Elizabeth must have been before her. Like Beldon, she leaned on the side of diplomacy over honesty.

"Yes, she is very nervous," I agreed, hoping to make her comfortable. "I think you understand that I don't know her very well. She lived away from home for most of my life, y'see."

"That's very sad, I'm sure."

A blessing, more like, I thought. "And because of her nervous temperament, she's not very easy to get to know. I thought that you might be able to tell me more about her."

"I could try." She did not betray any great enthusiasm for that pursuit.

"Was Mother very nervous when she lived in Philadelphia?"

"Not that I noticed."

Probably not. Without her family there to bother her and—family—those odd things she'd mumbled when I'd awakened her . . . "What do you know about her as a girl?"

"Before she married, you mean? Oh, hardly anything. She often speaks proudly of her father, Judge Fonteyn, and shares news about her sister in England, but that's all. It's rather odd, to think on it. Most people like to tell stories about themselves now and then, things that happened when they were young, but . . ."

"Mother never does?" With her mention of it, I knew this to be true. In her time with us she'd been strangely reticent about her past.

"Yes. One would think that she never had been a young girl."

"I wonder why she is so silent. Did your father ever speak of his brother?" If I could get no information about my mother, then I'd settle for knowledge of my grandfather, though trying to find it out via my granduncle's daughter seemed a rather roundabout way of accomplishing it.

"He talked about his life at school, the little adventures he had there, but he never spoke about his home life—how odd."

"Perhaps life was very hard for them."

"Oh, but the Fonteyns are very rich."

"I meant that—"

"Oh, I see, that they might have had a strict upbringing? Yes . . . now that you call it to mind, I remember Father saying he was glad to leave home and go to school, which made him very different from the other little boys." She gave a sudden little shiver.

"So he never talked about his oldest brother?"

"No . . ."

"What, then?"

She shrugged, using her hands. "I'm not sure, but I got the impression that Father didn't like him much. His own brother. It's horrid, isn't it?"

"Very." But not too surprising. My father also didn't like the man, and from the scarce information he'd shared about him, I would have probably followed his suit. My grandfather had been a most disagreeable fellow, according to Father, a foul-tempered tyrant subject to fits of rage, which would certainly account for Mother's behavior toward us, since she seemed to have taken that as a proper example of how to treat one's family. That was what Elizabeth and I had come to call "the

Fonteyn blood" and regard with dread lest we succumb to it ourselves.

But it did not explain why Mother had been afraid in her dream, the one I'd interrupted when I'd gone to see her that night. She'd been pleading like a frightened child. Her voice might well have been a child's voice, and I was forced to admit to myself that it had shaken me to hear it. At the time I'd been too preoccupied with what I'd been doing, but later that voice had come to haunt and worry me. And instead of looking upon Mother with my usual unhappy tolerance, I'd allowed a small piece of compassion to enter into my regard of her. It made her seem less of a barely controlled monster and more like . . . what? A lost and wounded child? Dear God, I could understand that, having been there myself. Perhaps Father was not the one in the family with the blind spot.

"Was your father a strict man?" I asked almost absently, for the silence had stretched long between us. I needed fresh conversation between me and my thoughts.

Anne smiled. "Mother sometimes accused him of not being strict enough."

"He was a loving man, then."

The smile thinned and faded altogether. "No, not really. He cared for me, but I . . ."

"If this is painful for you—"

"No, really, I've just never thought of it before. I see it now. He never allowed himself to get close to anyone. How sad. I wonder why?"

"He may not have known how. Or been afraid to try."

"Father afraid?" She shook her head, then spread her hands, smoothly retreating into her most common defense against the harshness of life. "It's all too confusing for me."

Or too close to the heart. "Quite so. Besides, I was trying to learn about my mother."

"And I haven't been of much help."

"But you have . . . and I'm grateful for it."

Anne and I made an amicable parting and I trotted up to my room only to come down again soon after, garbed for the outdoors. I passed Jericho in the hall and told him I was going to take the air. He nodded, reminded me to put on some gloves, and resumed whatever errand I'd interrupted.

Gloves . . . yes, in the pocket of my cloak as usual. With my indifference to the cold weather, I sometimes forgot them.

A spare handkerchief was there as well, wrapped around two lumps of sugar. Good. Jericho was uncommonly efficient in anticipating my needs. I was hungry tonight and would find those items very useful.

I let myself out by the side door as usual and trudged over my own footprints toward the stables. The wind was high and the ground hard from the cold. My boots crunched and cracked against the frozen mud and snow. I paused outside the far end of the building away from the house and glanced around to be sure no one was watching, then vanished and pushed my way through the wall to get in. It was strange to feel the texture of the barrier, but not the solidity as I flowed through the minute cracks in the boards like so much water. Not exactly unpleasant, but not really enjoyable either. Using the door would have been better, but not as quiet. When on this business, I wanted to be very quiet indeed.

All was dim and dark within when I reassumed my form. Bereft of any outside light, my eyes were no better than anyone else's now, but I knew the way. Ahead on my right were the stalls, and one or two of their occupants sensed my presence and stirred slightly, dark shapes against a dark background. The familiar scents of horse, straw, and manure filled my head. I felt my way toward the first stall, then passed the second, and on to the third. Though the great animals could easily part with a sizable quantity of blood before feeling it—more than I could drink in one night—I took care not to feed from any single one more than once in a week. Since we had a number of horses and I needed to sup only every other night or so, their health remained blessedly robust.

My eyes had adjusted somewhat to the dark, and I found that Desdemona was in this stall. She turned her head 'round to get a better look at me. Like the others, she'd come to associate my late visits with some form of reward and may have already smelled out the sugar in my pocket. I decided to leave her alone, though, as she would be foaling in the spring. We'd mated her to Rolly and had high hopes for what was to come, and it seemed best not to require any more from her than to continue to quietly gestate, undisturbed by my hunger.

She gave a decidedly human-sounding snort of disgust when I moved to the next stall and began patting down Belle, who happily consumed the sugar and stood rock-still while I fed from her. As always, the taste was rich with life and entirely good to me. I had all but forgotten what other, more solid—more normal—food had been like. I did know that it had never imparted such a feeling of completion to me as the blood did now.

The second lump of sugar followed the first and I wiped my mouth clean with the handkerchief. Within my body I felt the red warmth flush throughout my vitals and spread to my limbs. It was like feeling summer sun soaking my soul from the inside out. No yearning existed in me to see that fiery orb again. There was no need to; I carried it in my veins.

I quit the stables by the same path and set out once more into the night.

The wind was a nuisance, but not unbearable, and the walking itself would keep me warm should the cold finally overcome my resistance to it. I pulled my cloak close and marched down the lane to the main road. Once I was out of sight from the house, though, I grew too impatient to stay on my feet and so took to the air.

It was hard going with the wind against me, but I relished the struggle. At least it was something simple and straightforward. I made most of the trip blind or half blind, being unable to retain much solidity as I moved low over the ground, but it was a familiar trip and did not take long. Just before reaching the first buildings of Glenbriar, I went solid again and walked the rest of the way.

As I'd expected, there were lights showing at The Oak. Freezing and windy or no, the soldiers here would not be kept from their drink, nor the locals, either. Some horses harnessed to a wagon were tethered outside, huddling miserably together and unable to put their backs to the wind. If the riders were too drunk and irresponsible to take care of their mounts, then I'd have to have a word with the landlord about them. No sense in letting the beasts suffer for their master's lack of concern.

I pushed through the door and called a general greeting to the company within. It was a mixed lot, uniforms, homespun, and fair to fine tailoring, each in their own groups, though there was some tentative mixing. One of the Hessian officers who had rather good English was holding forth about his war experiences to a spellbound crew. He could tell a good tale; I'd listened to enough of them myself on previous visits. His name was Eichelburger, and he'd been of great help to me in improving my knowledge of German. I waved over their heads to him and got a wave in return, all without interrupting his narration.

Mr. Farr had by now long adjusted himself to my return and came over to offer a glad greeting. His acceptance of me may have been tempered by my free-spending habits. I always bought an ale for myself and hardly ever failed to invite a few others to join me. Surrounded by a crowd, I could more easily get away with not drinking it, and if I wanted to empty my tankard, all I had to do was leave it unwatched for a moment by Noddy Milverton and he'd swiftly dispatch it for me. Not that we'd made any arrangements; Noddy just had an insatiable thirst and not much money. He was a bit simple, so few of his victims objected, least of all myself.

"There's some horses out front that are feeling the weather," I told Farr.

"I'll have someone see to 'em," he said, and signed to one of his pot boys. As it was so common an occurrence, no further instructions were needed; the lad nodded and went out. "They always come in for just a moment, then stay all night. Thankee for tellin'."

"Any news?" Again, there was no need to be detailed, as there was only one kind of news anyone was interested in.

He shook his head. "Soldiers all gone to ground for the winter. All's been quiet as far as I know, and I'm pleased for it to stay that way. The Suffolk County lads 'ave been restive, though. Stole some sheep t'other day."

"I s'pects we knows what they stole 'em *for*!" put in the ribald and unrepentant Mr. Thayer. He was in his usual corner, puffing on his pipe. I wondered if he had grown roots to that chair yet.

"Now, now, sir," cautioned Farr, but he was chuckling, too.

"Any more thieves from Connecticut?" I asked.

Farr shrugged. "Not in my hearing. There's plenty of tales if you want to hear 'em, but nothing I'd put my trust in. I've heard talk from the soldiers that the whaleboat boys sometimes shelter in Suffolk, but it don't seem too sensible. The rebels in Suffolk are more like to thieve for themselves, not be sharin' the pickin's with others. Same goes for Connecticut."

"And either way honest, loyal folk take the loss."

"Some of 'em, but not all. Gunsmiths 'ave been busy. Nothing like a few musket balls for helping a rebel to change his mind about taking your livestock."

I could appreciate that well enough. It was reassuring to know that things had been quiet elsewhere. The weather had been none too good lately, either full of wind or sleet or snow or a combination of the three. Hardly encouraging to an enterprising thief looking for booty. We'd all learned to dread quiet nights, especially when there was little or no moon.

We talked a bit more, and others joined in or moved off. Noddy took care of two other tankards besides my own, all without being noticed. I said good evening and made my way out. Mr. Thayer's seamed face cracked as he gave me a comically broad wink. He was used to seeing me leaving early, and his long experience told him why.

"Gi' my regards to Molly Audy, will ye?" he bellowed across the room. This raised a tidal rush of laughter that swept me right outside. I wasn't so sophisticated yet that I couldn't blush, but I may have escaped into the dark before anyone saw it.

Most of the villagers were indoors and either in bed or getting ready for it; of course, that meant something different to a woman like Molly. Going to bed and going to sleep were often mutually exclusive, depending on the success of her business. She was apparently doing well enough tonight. Lights were burning in her front room and bedroom. I quietly let myself in the door to wait until she was finished with this other customer. There were some interesting sounds issuing from beyond the closed door in the back, but I could not judge just how far along they were to concluding things.

Hat in hand, I paced a little. Friendly curiosity aside, my experience with Cousin Anne had provided me with sufficient inspiration to want to carry what she'd initiated forward to a more satisfactory conclusion. Further inspiration was this time provided by the noise Molly and her friend were making, and I was growing naturally impatient for my turn to come. After what seemed like an indecently lengthy interval, the bed and its occupants finally made their last groans together. The voices resumed normal speech, Molly murmuring admiration and the man making similar responses.

Oh, dear. Sudden recognition of the man's voice flooded me. My mouth went dry as sand. All the enthusiasm that had been building in me abruptly fled. Molly's customer . . . *damnation.*

Flat-footed as I was with surprise, I had enough time to recover and completely vanish before they emerged. I stayed that way until he was well and truly gone and even then waited long before returning.

Molly had gone back to the bedroom again and so I found myself alone in her "parlor" where she conducted her sewing business during the day. Bits of fabric, thread, and pins littered the place, adding a legitimacy to this half of her livelihood; as for the other half . . .

Well, she was the favorite of some of the more moneyed gentlemen of the village, so I needn't have been so startled by this latest visitor. The way things were, especially in the more civilized parts of the world, it was fairly common for a man to seek a degree of physical satisfaction with any lady who might take his fancy. Whether she was his mistress or a paid prostitute depended on his situation in life and the depth of his pockets.

But in this case I was so deeply disturbed because this particular fellow was paying suit to my dearly beloved sister.

Visions of rushing after Lord James Norwood and demanding an explanation or wrenching a promise from him to cease and desist clouded my eyes. Other visions also intruded, including a rather tempting one of caning him to within an inch of his life. Oh, but *that* would have brought such a lovely and wicked fulfillment to my baser nature: to thump him about the shoulders and finally smash his handsome face to a pulp for this insult to Elizabeth. How *dare* he pay honorable court to her one day and then—literally—pay out to Molly the next?

He'd be on the road back to the house for certain, easy enough for me to find him and then provide him a very solid lesson in polite behavior toward one's . . .

Damnation.

Elizabeth.

My anger leached from my heart as I thought of her. Certainly I could think of ways to deal with the man, but that would hardly change his status in her eyes. In fact, if he turned up in a less than perfect condition, it would certainly bring about a great flow of sympathy from Elizabeth. And if she demanded why I'd misused the fellow so, then I'd have to tell her the extremely painful truth and . . .

Damnation. Again.

Of course, Norwood was perfectly within his right to do what he liked. He and Elizabeth were not really engaged, after all, but this discovery was a singularly unpleasant one for me, made the more so because I didn't know what to do about it.

Several questions began to tumble through my mind as I wondered if he still planned to pursue his courtship of my sister. If so, and they were married, would he continue to improve the trade for women like Molly? That was enough to set my jaw to grinding and turn my hands into destructive fists.

If he caused Elizabeth the *least* unhappiness, by God, he *would* answer to me.

Molly emerged, saw me, gasped, and gave a jump. "Goodness, Johnny boy! I never heard you coming in. Why didn't you call out?"

I was almost as surprised as she, so involved was I in my speculations. Shoving them forcibly to one side, I pasted what I hoped to be a pleasing expression over my true feelings and went to kiss her hand. "I'm sorry, but I didn't want to disturb you if you had company."

"Oh, my company's been and gone. I was just starting to feel lonesome again. Glad I am that you happened by." She wriggled into my arms and made a good-natured inquiry on whether I planned to stay awhile.

"For as long as you'll have me," I replied.

"Then that depends on how long *you* plan to have *me*," she returned. "It's been much too long since I've seen you. Whatever have you been doing with yourself? Or is that it? Have you been doing it with yourself?" She ground her body against mine in a delightfully suggestive way.

"Never," I said with utter sincerity. Since my change, that was one form of carnal pleasure denied to me. But though my body's expression had altered, the appetite for it remained, and so Molly and I did share company fairly often. I had an idea that my maternal grandfather would have been rolling in his grave if he knew where a fraction of my inheritance from him had ended up over the last few months. That idea added a certain . . . piquant flavor to my frequent beddings with Molly.

The memory of Cousin Anne's curiosity reasserted itself and combined with the actuality of Molly; I found myself easily sweeping the latter up for a sound kissing. Her laughter—somewhat smothered by my lips—was genuine and I was once more pleased to realize that I was certainly her favorite customer. What matter to her if I kept my breeches up and drank her blood? She seemed not to mind those differences, but relished them as much as I, since it never failed to impress a lengthy and highly satisfying climax upon her. So when it came down to it, I was essentially paying her to have a good time. She'd once joked about paying me, but I never took her up on it. Thanks to Grandfather Fonteyn, I could afford to be generous.

She finally pushed me away, puffing for air. "This is lovely, Johnny boy, but it's drafty out here. Wouldn't you like to find a warmer place to finish things?"

"Indeed, yes."

It didn't take long for us to settle ourselves into her bed. She'd been wearing a thick wrapper of some kind and shed it quickly, throwing it atop the coverlet for extra warmth before diving into the sheets. She had good cause to complain of the cold, since the only thing she'd been wearing under the wrap were a number of goosebumps. I liked to think that some of them were due to my actions rather than the chill of the outer room. Perhaps so, as she was most eager and called for me to hurry myself.

I took off my cloak and spread it on the bed as well. My coat and boots went on a chair, but I kept the rest of my clothes on, as part of Molly's own pleasure included a great fondness for unbuttoning things. I slipped into the sheets with her. They smelled of her . . . and others. It had not bothered me before. Which of those musky scents had been left behind by Norwood?

"Was that Lord James I spied leaving here a bit ago?" I asked.

She'd just started to work on my waistcoat. "Mayhap it was, but then lots of gentlemen come here. You know that."

This, I remembered, was "Molly the Mum" talking. She never gave away names or told tales. Any other time I'd have applauded her discretion, but not now. "Decent fellow, I hope?"

"Very decent . . . but you're better."

"Tell me about him, Molly."

She finished the last button and paused. "Now, Johnny boy, that wouldn't be right. You know I don't gossip about any of my gentlemen. 'S not nice to gossip."

"I've a special reason, though."

"What's that?"

"He's courting my sister."

"Lucky girl, then."

"He's likely to marry her, too, so I'm curious—"

"What, you want to know what he's like with me so you can tell your sister?"

"Ahh, no! I mean, that's not—good God!"

Molly's giggles for my shock finally subsided. "Oh, I do like you, Mr. Barrett, and I understand why you want to look out for your sister, but I can't just tell tales whenever a gentleman gets curious."

"Perhaps I've not been as liberal with you as I should be . . ." I dug into a pocket with some spare coins in it.

She gave a firm shake with her head, eyes briefly shutting while she did so. "It's not that at all. I have my rules and I stick to 'em." She was being nice about it, but her manner indicated she would not be moved on the subject.

But there were ways around this. At least for me.

I looked right into her eyes. There was enough light for it this time. "That's very good of you, but I think you can make an exception this time."

And she did. Not that I gave her a choice in the matter. But now that she was willing to answer my questions, I wasn't sure what to ask her. Her thought that I might inquire about Norwood's habits in bed struck me as being far too personal, though I wouldn't deny the temptation was there. No . . . I'd let that one go. Better to find something else to talk about.

"Molly, tell me what you think of Lord James." That was the way to do it: ask her for an opinion she might have offered anyway if not for her damned rules.

"He's a nice enough sort," she intoned, a little flat, slurring her words.

"Do you like him?"

"Well enough."

"Anything bother you about him?"

She made a face. "'E does like to haggle the price. Spends more effort trying to save a penny than 'e puts into 'is bedding. Must think I don't 'ave to work 'ard for it, but I do. 'E won't find no better than me for the price. Skinflint."

That was interesting. From this I might deduce that Elizabeth need not worry about him squandering her dowry, though too much thrift can be just as burdensome.

"How does he treat you, Molly?"

"Well enough," she repeated. "'E's nice as it suits 'im. Not as nice as my Johnny boy, but all right."

"Thank you. Do you like him?"

"'E's a nice sort . . ."

"Do you like him?"

Her answer was long in coming. "Not really," she said with some reluctance.

"Why not?"

She shrugged.

"Then why see him?"

"I need the money, love."

A foolish question, that. Like any person in trade, Molly would have to deal with all sorts of customers and be polite no matter what. I could certainly admire and respect her dedication to her work. "Think he'll be coming back to you?"

"S'pose 'e will when 'e's a mind for it."

"Think he'd have a mind for it were he married?"

Another shrug. "Won't be able to tell that 'til it 'appens. Wouldn't be the first time, nor the last."

I wasn't about to question her experience there.

Molly woke out of things gradually, unaware of what had happened, ready to pick up where we'd left off as if no time had passed. My influence on her had put her into an even more receptive mood than before, but my own was considerably dampened. I'd fed heavily and had a lot on my mind. It took a bit more effort on her part to drag me back to the business at hand, but we eventually made a consummation that suited us both. She'd had a long day, though, and the extended pleasure my nature provided for us only added to her exhaustion. She was asleep almost as soon as I pulled my lips away from her firm, sweet throat. I dressed quietly, made sure the covers were pulled up and tucked about her, put out the candles, and left.

Late. Or early, since it was well past midnight. High clouds obscured the stars, but I could sense the hour more or less. No need to hurry, but no need to tarry, either.

The wind was worse than before, very hard, very gusty. Better not to vanish and travel on the air in these conditions. I'd tried often enough before and found myself being carried along out of control, which is a very vile feeling. I got my flapping cloak wrapped tight around me, held my hat in place, and started down the road leading home.

Miserable stuff, wind. It roars in your ears, deafening you to all other sounds. If cold, it cuts through your clothes with more surety than the sharpest knife. It buffets the body, stealing your balance, and it makes harmless things like trees and grass seem more alive than they should be. When it's really strong it makes them whisper and laugh to one another, mocking and vindictive to all who pass them.

I felt their rancor, or fancied I did, while trudging along. The road was full of ruts and icy, but it was easier than facing the banks of snow on either side. There was no point in complaining to myself about any of it, but I did so, since it kept my mind off the larger problem of Norwood. I grumbled and mumbled, though my voice was a small and fragile distraction.

Then another sound intruded upon me, at first so faint and uneven that I wasn't sure I heard anything. It was behind me, that was for certain, the wind saw to that. I waited, listening, and finally caught the jingle of bits and the crunch of wheels going over the frozen ground. There was a slight bend in the road, and soon a wagon came around it into sight.

There were no lanterns showing, which was odd but understandable. As unsettled as things were in the area, it was a wise course not to draw attention to oneself. I would have—had my eyes been normal—preferred to take a chance and had some light with me in case of trouble.

Though going at a good pace, I thought it might stop long enough for me to get a ride to my gate. It would be a poor Christian indeed who would deny so small a favor to another soul on such a night. I walked a little more, but slowly, and let it catch me up.

The driver crouched over his reins, urging his horses forward. He was not much more than a shape to me even as he came closer. He wore a heavy coat and his hat was tied to his head by a rag of a scarf, the ends of which snapped in the wind like some tattered banner.

"Hallo!" I called, when he was near enough to see me.

He must have understood what I might ask of him, for he pulled on the reins.

"Commun over," he called back, when they'd stopped.

I wasted no more time and scrambled up next to him. "Very kind of you, sir."

"Aye. M'name's Ash. Who're you?"

"Jonathan Barrett."

"Y'sure o' that?"

I thought it a strange question to ask, but made no comment since he was being kind enough to give me a ride. However, we were not moving yet, as he seemed far more concerned with introductions than anything else. "Yes, I'm quite sure."

"Barrett as lives down the road? This road?"

"Yes—"

His face split in a big grin and he made a sudden move with one hand. Before I knew it the muzzle of a pistol was in it and the business end was shoved into my belly.

CHAPTER
—9—

"My God, man, what are you about?" My outrage was genuine. I was too surprised to be afraid.

He ignored me. "Now, boys!" he shouted in my face.

When reason fails, instinct takes over, if you're lucky. I ducked blindly, but a fraction too late. Dark shapes, I don't know how many, erupted up from the back of the wagon, hands reaching for me. One of them caught me by the hair and strongly dragged me backward and down. My head cracked far too solidly against the wagon seat, and for the first time in months I saw the sun. It seared right through my skull and out the other side in an instant and was gone, leaving behind the most horrendous pain I'd ever felt in my life. It crowded out all thought, all motion, all sound. Nothing else was in my world but the hideous, explosive agony clamoring between my ears.

"Ye've killed 'im!" someone cried.

"Nay, 'e's but stunned. Git 'im in so we can go."

Helpless, I felt myself being hauled up into the back of the wagon; at least, that's what I worked out somewhat later. At the moment I was too stunned to know what was happening or to care anything about it.

"I got me a fine new 'at!" one of them sang out.

"Cloak too," added another. "See what's in 'is pockets."

Hands, prodding and rough, made a thorough search of me and grabbed away prizes, winners crowing in triumph. I didn't care, didn't have enough awareness to care. I wanted only to scream out from the pain, but was too paralyzed to do it.

Ash whipped up the horses. The wagon lurched forward.

If I could have moved, I'd have probably been sick, but nothing was moving, nothing at all. I might as well have been a corpse, but being drearily and inescapably shackled to my body, I knew I hadn't died.

Not yet.

We rattled quickly over the ruts. I lost track of time, drifting in and out of consciousness, perhaps. There was no way to tell. Some things were clear, others less so. The clear bits hurt.

"Easy now," said Ash. "Hessians quartered in a barn hereabouts, remember? Keep 'im quiet."

"'E ain't movin'."

"Good."

Barn? Our barn. We'd passed my gate. I was being carried right away from my home . . . safety . . . help.

The wagon rumbled on, the men heedless of my silent objections.

Why? The question bobbed up in my mind like a piece of cork. *Why had they done this to me?*

The answer took a bit longer, for I'd faded out again, or so I assumed, since I was all too aware of waking up. The pain had dampened enough that I was better able to think, but only in a disjointed sort of way. I understood that I'd been attacked and had been robbed and was in the process of being kidnapped.

Why?

They'd been after *me*, not just any unlucky traveler on the road, but me.

Wh—

Then I didn't care why, couldn't think why. All I could do was . . .

. . . wake up again, some long time later. How long . . . ?

My eyes were open. They'd been shut before. I could blink. But not much else. Fingers were cold. Couldn't move them. I'd forgotten to put on gloves again. Jericho would have something to say about that. No matter. The fellows here would have probably stripped them from me by now.

Now. *What* now? What was the time? I tried desperately to read the sky. It seemed lighter, but that might have been a normal reflection of the snowy fields on the low clouds. I didn't know the time, which was almost as hard to bear as my injury. Maybe they were linked. Whatever clock I had inside me had been thoroughly shattered when my head struck the wooden bench of the wagon.

Head. I could have done without the reminder. It ached abominably and I felt sick all over again, hot and cold at the same time. There was salty bile pooling at the back of my mouth, but I couldn't spit it out. Couldn't move yet.

Why . . . hadn't I vanished?

This hurt far worse than getting shot. I should have disappeared at the first shock. Were there splinters in my head where I'd . . . no, it didn't feel like that. This was different, duller, but no less forceful when it came to discomfort.

I tried to . . . vanish.

Nothing.

The effort left me shivering. And sicker than before. Overwhelmingly so. I lost track of time again, finding it I don't know how long later when the wagon gave an especially sharp jolt. This waking was a little better than the others. I knew what had happened, but still not why or . . .

Where were we?

Couldn't see anything but the sky and skeletal branches now and then when we passed under an occasional tree growing by the road. Couldn't tell if we were even on the same road. If we were, then I was being taken to Suffolk County. Despite the presence of all the troops, the place was crawling with rebels, absolutely the last spot on earth one of His Majesty's loyal subjects would want to be. I couldn't think of a worse place, unless it was in the middle of General Washington's camp.

Raving. Get hold of yourself.

Not raving. Righteously scared.

Get hold of yourself anyway.

Not being able to move my head yet, I couldn't see much of the others. The first heady feeling of victory had passed and now they were hunched against one another, probably feeling the cold. No one spoke or paid much notice to me. Only one face was visible, familiar, but still a stranger. I'd seen him . . . at The Oak . . . one of the other patrons.

Not that that was much help.

He continued to ignore me and remained silent.

Who were the others? Or did it matter? Perhaps not. They'd all be strangers to me, or else they'd wouldn't have had to be so sure of my name before attacking.

Why? What had I done? Why should these strangers . . .

Oh, God.

Now I did become sick. The pool in the back of my mouth filled and thickened into a foul mass. My guts were all watery as the realization seized me like a giant's hand. A nasty, bubbling sound issued from my throat like a death rattle. I shut my eyes tight and let the first wave of panic rush over and drown my thoughts. Fighting it wouldn't have done any good; better to let the body finish with its reactions, then let the mind take charge.

The wave passed. Slowly. It left me weak and worried, but not utterly frozen with terror. I swallowed and was surprised that the bile went down. And stayed there.

Better. I was feeling—very marginally—better. The pain was slightly less crippling than before. I could move my fingers; that was something.

I had also, with this small recovery, grown very angry. Instead of the burning heat or frosty chill running over my skin, it was simply warming. Comforting, like the taste of blood.

Blood . . . I could smell it. My own, of course. There was a cold patch on my head where the skin must have broken and bled when that fool had smashed my skull. The blood was cooling and drying in the harsh air. God, they might have killed me with that blow, though maybe it wasn't as bad as I . . . no. It was bad. Bad enough as I found when I tried to move more than my fingers.

"'E's come 'round," said one of the men, having noticed my feeble attempts to master my body again.

"Just keep 'im quiet," said Ash.

"Drummond got 'im good. Thumped 'is 'ead like a summer melon. 'E ain't goin' to make no trouble."

The big fellow closest to me laughed at the compliment. Drummond. He would pay for this, I thought.

"When do we get there?" whined another man from the back.

"Soon, Tully," came the weary reply. From that brief intonation I got the impression that Tully whined rather a lot.

"It's been hours. I'm freezin' sittin' 'ere like this."

"Then get out and walk."

The suggestion was not received very well, but it shut Tully up for the time being.

Arms. I could shift my arms a little. Legs, too, after a moment of concentration. Didn't want to try vanishing just yet. Too weak. Better to wait.

As some of the pain receded, other discomforts cried out for attention, like the ride itself. I was on the unprotected wood bottom of the wagon and its hard, harsh surface bumped and jolted me with every uneven turn of all four wheels. No wonder I was so sick. My head was bad enough, but combine that with the motion of our travel . . . ugh.

I gulped again and tried to think of something else.

Like the cold. Apart with the other discomforts, I was finally beginning to feel its bite. Even the warmth derived from my anger wasn't up to fighting it off now. The damnable wind clawed at my exposed skin and seeped beneath all my clothes. I wanted my heavy cloak back. Which one of the bastards had taken it? Couldn't see him from this angle.

I silently cursed them and prayed to God for an ending to our journey. The answer came surprisingly soon when Ash turned the horses off to the left. The clouds spun over me and my stomach objected until I shut my eyes. The road became much worse than before and I had to hold my teeth hard together to keep from crying out at the change. Pity I couldn't have slept through it all; I wouldn't have minded missing this part.

We creaked to a halt and the men stiffly crawled from the back of the wagon. I had another instant of panic, thinking they'd leave me to die out in the cold until someone grabbed my ankles and pulled. All in all, I'd have preferred freezing to death. I was just able to lift my head to spare it from scraping over the worn boards, but that was the extent of my control. The same hands that had thrown me in now carried me out, this time with much grunting and complaint.

I briefly saw the walls of a poor-looking house, then we squeezed through a door and there was some general activity as they sorted and settled themselves. A big grumbling man was sent to take care of the horses and wagon. I was hauled over to a rough bed and dropped into it. The mattress was sparsely stuffed and so thin that I felt the supporting rope lattice beneath. My captors would get no objections from me; it was heavenly compared to the wagon. I was out of the wind and though the house was cold, it was not numbing.

A wretched place it was, to be sure. It seemed to have but one room and the fireplace could have been larger. Tully was busy there with a tinderbox, muttering to himself while another man offered unwanted suggestions. A table teetered in the middle of the dusty floor, surrounded by a long bench and some crude chairs. Those things and the bed were the only furnishings. The walls were stripped of any decoration or tools, indication that no one actually lived here. My guess was that these men had simply found the place and taken it over.

Ash had been more successful with his tinderbox and had lighted two lamps. He brought one over to have a better look at me. I took the opportunity to have a better look at him. I'd want to remember his face, all their faces. His was hardened by both the weather and a difficult life and possibly an even more difficult temperament. He grinned down at me with an evil satisfaction that might have been comical but for the grimness of my situation. I did not find him remotely amusing.

"'E's a soft'un, I'll warrant. Ye din't 'ave to crack 'im so 'ard, Drummond. We coulda tied 'im up wi' a piece o' string 'n' led 'im 'ere like a lamb."

"Hah!" said Drummond.

"Pasty-faced Tory bastard," Ash went on. "'E's soft as a slug from 'igh livin' on 'is pap's gold, that 'n' all 'is drinkin' 'n' whorin'."

"Where am I?" I asked, wishing to change the subject. My voice was thin, little more than a whisper. A stranger's voice. The fear that I'd managed to shove away for a time began to seep back at this lack of recognition for myself. I tried to pretend it wasn't there and concentrated on gaining useful knowledge.

"Yer with us, that's a' you needs t' know."

"Must still be in Nassau County," I remarked faintly.

"Hah!" said Drummond.

"We've got us a right stupid Tory bastard, don't we, boys?" said Ash, enlarging upon Drummond's short but informative comment. So I was in Suffolk County, miles from home. How many?

"I *have* to be there," I insisted. "We couldn't have traveled all that far."

"Fifteen mile, if it were an inch. Maybe more." He was proud of the accomplishment and contemptuous of my disbelief.

"Ridiculous." But I didn't press further, lest they catch on to what I was doing. "What do you want of me? Why did you bring me here?"

"What we want is fer ye to do what yer told, then Drummond won't be 'aving to cut yer heart out 'n' 'andin' it to ye."

"Hah!" said Drummond.

Not too reassuring, but at least they weren't planning to kill me right off. On the other hand, if I didn't get away from here before dawn, they wouldn't have to trouble themselves.

"I like them ridin' boots," said a thin fellow, talking through his hatchety nose.

"Be off with ye, Abel, I already claimed 'em 'n' everyone knows it," said another man who was homely enough to have been his brother.

"Yer feet is too big fer 'em!"

"Are not! You've got 'is cloak, I git 'is boots!" This declaration was followed by a noisy tussle. Ash watched the combatants with disgust.

"Those two should be Cain and Abel, not Abel and Seth," he growled to Drummond, who for once did not say "hah!" but did step in and roughly part the two. He lifted each by the collar, shook them soundly, then let them fall. The argument was over for the moment and I consciously relaxed my tightly curled toes. I had no desire to be hiking home in stocking feet.

The door opened and the other fellow who was almost as big as Drummond came in. I wondered if he was in charge of this lot, as none of them appeared to be impressively gifted with intelligence. He gruffly announced that the horses were bedded, then went to warm his hands by Tully's fledgling fire.

Six of them. Daunting even with my full strength, quite impossible now.

"What's the time?"

My question amused them. There was no clock in the hovel and probably never had been.

"Gittin' on to dawn in a couple hours, I should think," said Ash.

"I'm hungry," whined Tully.

"Then fix somethin'!"

Tully subsided and poked about in whatever supplies they had.

"Why am I here?"

Ash's grin, a singularly unpleasant one, returned. "Yer a prisoner o' war, that's why."

"I'm no soldier—"

"Aye, but yer mighty good at killin', ain't ye?" he sneered.

There it was, the confirmation of my worst fears. My heart sank and they could see it on my face. No need or point in pretense.

Ash leaned close. I could smell his rotten teeth. "Ye murdered two fine men, ye Tory bastard. Cut 'em down cold 'n' yer goin' t' pay fer it."

I snapped my mouth shut. There was also no need or point in arguing my side of it with them; I'd made that conclusion earlier when I'd guessed who they were. The panic threatened to return, but I couldn't afford it this time. I had to keep my mind free of it. Free . . . and thinking.

"You want something more, though, don't you? Or else you wouldn't have brought me here."

"Aye, we do. Yer rich pap's goin' to pay t' git you back, ain't he? We reckon 'e can spare the gold 'f he wants to see 'is brat again, right?"

I reluctantly nodded. For all the house and fine clothes, my father was not a wealthy man; Mother had all the money. I wondered if she would pay a ransom for me, then decided it didn't matter. These men were not going to let me live whatever happened. I kept those thoughts to myself and tried to look anxiously cooperative. "Yes. My father will do anything you say. Just name your price and he'll pay it."

It was exactly what they wanted to hear.

"Right!" Ash produced a dirty sheet of paper. One side was some kind of obsolete handbill, all patriotism and high emotion, and the other blank. "Put down what we tell ye."

"If I can." And I sincerely meant that, for I was going all weak again.

Drummond picked me up and dragged me to the table. I was dropped onto a chair, but he had to hold me up. Dizzy and suddenly shivering, I eased forward and tenderly cushioned my cruelly aching head on my folded arms.

"What wrong with 'im?" asked Tully.

"Got no belly fer man's work," said Ash, but he sounded worried.

I ground my teeth together to keep from sobbing from the pain. Very gently, I felt around the side of my skull where it was the worst. Dried blood matted my hair, but there seemed to be no fresh bleeding. There was a soft spot there . . . bruised and swollen skin, perhaps. I hoped that was all. Pain flared, threatening to blaze up into something truly unbearable if the tentative exploration continued. I moaned and shook involuntarily, hating my show of weakness, but unable to stop it.

My hosts were silent except for some hard breathing as they looked on. No one offered to help.

"Drummond hit 'im too hard," Tully stated mournfully. He was the youngest of the group, not much more than a boy, and an unhappy one at that. "'E's gonna die on us. Did ye see 'is face?"

Ash snorted. "Not before 'e does us some good. Straighten up, you. Yer gonna write yer pap."

"Give me a minute," I pleaded, still gasping from it.

It came in waves, a relatively pain-free period followed by nausea, and I was going through a bad spot of the latter. Drummond's tossing me about like a rag toy hadn't helped. I wanted desperately to try vanishing again in the hope of healing, but my last attempt had knocked me out. It would have to be later, when I was stronger and not so hideously ill. As for these louts seeing it, I didn't care.

Ash snarled more frustrated threats, but did nothing. Someone found a bit of charcoal and pushed it into my slack right hand.

In a few minutes the worst of it passed and I found I could see once more. Not well. The lantern lights seemed unbearably bright to me. I could hardly open my eyes. Ash impatiently urged me to work. I felt for the sheet of paper. The charcoal slipped from my fingers and I had trouble trying to pick it up.

"I'm sorry," I whispered. "I can't. It's too much."

"You'll write it, I say." Ash again. God, what a miserable, scratching voice the man had.

"I can't. One of you will have to. I'm too badly hurt."

"But not so hurt ye can't talk? Write, damn ye, or Drummond'll start 'is cuttin'."

I groaned and managed to hold the charcoal. Despite all the discomfort, there was a warm and tight feeling of triumph in me. Ash's insistence that I do the writing meant that none of them could. Not one of them had made the least move to take over in response to my pitiful act.

Not that I was acting.

"What do you want to say?" I asked, barely audible.

"This is to yer pap. Tell 'im you've been captured."

Easy enough. *Dear Father, I've been kidnapped . . .*

I laboriously scraped the charcoal over the paper, trying to make clean, legible script and finding it difficult. The paper was cheap and rough; even if I'd had a proper quill and ink it would not have been any too easy. I took my time, the others staring at my every move as though I were performing some magical rite. Meaningless symbols to them, possible help for me.

"Yes . . . what else?"

"If 'e wants you back alive, 'e's to give six 'undred pounds in silver or gold to the man giving 'im this note."

I formed letters. *Being held about 15 miles from home in Suffolk by Montagu house thieves . . .*

Paused.

"Don't follow the man or we'll cut yer throat."

. . . will try to escape. Hold and question this man.

"Sign it."

Jonathan.

Ash took the paper up and looked it over with smug pleasure. "There it is, lads, a tidy 'undred fer each of us."

I buried my face in my arms lest I betray myself, though I really hurt too much to smile.

"Aye, but will we get it? What if Knox don't come back?"

"Y'sayin' I'm a thief, Abel?" Knox, the big fellow who'd tended the horses, had an ominous growl.

Abel backed down. "Not 'xactly, jus' what if somethin' should 'appen to ye?"

"Nothin' will. I'll be back with the money 'n' don't ye be thinkin' otherwise or I'll fold you in two the wrong way." His size made him more than capable of carrying out that threat.

"Abel, go saddle a horse for 'im," said Ash. "A fresh 'un, mind you."

Wrapped snuggly in my cloak, Abel went out.

"'Ow long'll it take ye?" he asked Knox.

"Travelin', not long. Waitin' fer the money, I dunno. Ye'll 'ave to wait 'til I get back. Keep a sharp eye on the road. If you see soldiers, git to the boat 'n' git out. I'll catch up with ye later. With the money," he pointedly added for the benefit of any other doubters.

He left soon after. I kept my head down and rested.

The length of time between bouts of nausea was increasing and the sickness passed off a little faster, but I gave no sign of recovery, continuing to show them the worst possible side of it. A man in my poor condition would be seen as no threat, and I hoped they might get lax in their watch.

Indeed, it already seemed so. Food and drink were traded around and they did a fine job pretending I wasn't there while seeing to their own best comfort. None was offered to me. In fact, no one bothered to address me at all. That alone would have informed me of my eventual fate, had I not already figured it out. They weren't about to make friends with someone who was going to die.

An hour crept past, or more. It was hard to tell. I never moved, nor was invited to move. Tully took over the bed and began snoring. The others found spots to rest and talk amongst themselves before drowsing off. A natural topic was what they'd be doing with the money from this endeavor; they then warmed to other jobs, comparing them in terms of profit and effort. They'd stolen all manner of things, beaten and even killed people who attempted to resist them and one and all considered it work well done since—profit aside—they were doing it in a good cause. Any and all harm done to one of the King's loyal subjects was seen as a righteous blow for liberty, and the more harm inflicted the better.

I hadn't exactly hidden myself away from the war going on in the broader world beyond my own little piece of it, but it had not been very real to me for the most part. I had other concerns to keep me occupied, and the conflict was something that was happening to other people miles in the distance. These men were forcing me to see it as something much closer and consequently much more immediately threatening. Our big house with all its people, shuttered windows, and firmly locked doors was no safe fortress against such brutes. If they wanted what we had, they would simply take it. They weren't smart, but they did have a base, instinctual cunning that chilled me to the bone.

I raised my head, blinking, cautious of pain. It was there, drumming like thunder during a storm, but not as bad as it had been. I didn't want to push myself, but with the coming dawn I might not be left with any choice. Vanishing was first and foremost on my mind. If I was strong enough for that, then my greatest worries would be over. Then I could just float outside amid their confusion and get myself well away from here.

"Be light soon," said Ash. He and Drummond had shared the table with me, though neither of them had paid much notice of me once I'd finished writing the note.

"Aye." Drummond looked at me, cool and uncaring. I didn't like the possibilities that that implied, preferring Ash's raw hatred to this utter lack of regard. "Shouldn't we wait fer Knox?"

"That's been talked out. No matter if 'e gits the money 'r not, this 'un's got to go, we all agreed to it."

My belly turned over. Violently.

Drummond sighed. "'Tis better to do it now, then, while the others are asleep."

I'd been expecting such talk, but that didn't make it any easier to hear.

"They need to git used to it," countered Ash. "This's a war on, not a damned tea party for fancy Tory bitches 'n their silks 'n' velvets."

Not now, not yet, I cried in my mind. I was still too weak and nearly frozen with alarm.

I looked back at them, trying to summon enough concentration to influence them. Which one? I couldn't do both. Too late I picked on Ash, but he was already up and moving. Drummond followed.

Too late . . .

"Up with ye," said Ash.

"Wait—I can pay you more money."

"Oh, aye?"

"I've money of my own, separate from my father's. You can make twice as much."

"An' run twice the risk. No thankee. What we'll be gittin' 'll more'n do fer us." He pulled out his pistol and prodded my ribs. "Commun. Up with ye."

"Maybe the others don't agree with you. Don't the rest of you want to double your money?"

Seth and Abel looked sullenly interested, but not enough to challenge Ash's authority. Tully continued to snore. Drummond had heard, but rejected the offer with a contemptuous snort of disbelief. There would be no sundering of loyalties in this group.

Ash grinned "Commun, ye cowardly bastard. Move yerself or you'll get it right 'ere."

It was hardly a statement to inspire encouragement. Inside or out, I was to die. Where might not matter, but when . . . I wanted more time. They weren't giving me any. Not one more minute.

"You must help me. I can't stand. Dizzy." There was no point trying to plead for my life. They'd only find it amusing, especially Ash. I desperately wanted . . . needed time to think.

"Commun."

"I can't." It wasn't all an act; my legs were like water.

Think . . . but no miraculous idea popped into my head.

Expressing considerable disgust, Ash backed off so Drummond could assist me. With his now familiar lack of gentleness, he bent, hauled one of my arms around his neck, and stood, taking me with him. The sudden move to my feet was bad, but not as dreadful as I'd anticipated. I sagged, though, making him support me. He stank of ancient sweat and I could smell the remains of his last meal in the grease smearing his face.

I could also smell something else, something that woke me up more thoroughly than his rough handling or Ash's threats or even my own paralyzing fear.

Blood.

His blood, not mine. And the scent of it was good.

So very, very good.

Unaware, he pulled me along, my weight of no concern to him, paying no attention while I was stumbling in surprise at this inner realization. He had no mind for anything but to get the job at hand finished. I had no mind for anything but the fact that he was awash with what I needed to live. He carried satiation for my roused hunger, healing for my injury, strength for escape.

Red life, rushing, pulsing, *roaring* beneath his coarse skin.

Blood.

Dear God. I was *hungry*. Terribly so.

I stared without seeing anything as he took me through the door into the needle-sharp cold outside.

It was almost as though I were back in the wagon again, drifting in and out of consciousness, only now I was drifting between need and the shock of learning the true immensity of that need. Drummond marched me along over an empty field, the ground sloping slightly upward. I barely kept pace with him, distracted by trying to break free of the spell of my hunger, and succeeding to some degree.

Blood was blood to me, whether it was in a horse or a human. Even the miniscule amount I took from Molly Audy was food, when it came down to absolutes.

I looked sideways at Drummond. He continued to steadily and stolidly walk me on toward an ignominious death.

Dare I try it?

And more importantly, dare I *not*?

I could get on without. Perhaps.

Survival and escape were all that were important. It might be utterly revolting to have to drink from this man's filthy throat, but my instincts, those newly formed by my changed condition and those already innate to my being, told me that this was my best chance to get out alive, if not my only chance.

In the overall scheme of the world, I judged myself to be of considerably more value than Ash, Drummond, or any of the others in their miserable, brutal troop of killers.

So be it.

Now I had to find a way of arranging things to my advantage.

We crested the top of the slope, and the wind clawed at my inadequately protected body like a vengeful animal. I was shivering again and held on to Drummond for warmth as well as support. Snow clung to our boots, slowing us. Ash cursed as he struggled along in our footsteps.

The other side of the slope led down to the Sound. Had I known we were this close to it, I'd have made some mention in my note to Father. This part of the coast was vaguely known to me, and my heart rose a little. It was absurdly comforting to find I wasn't totally lost in an unknown land.

The water was gray and dangerous in the tormenting wind; I should not have cared to venture onto its restless surface in such weather, and I worried that that was what Drummond and Ash were planning.

Making myself more of an impediment than usual, I managed to get Drummond to halt by having my legs give out completely.

"A moment, for pity's sake," I cried in a thin, strained voice.

Ash caught us up. "Keep movin', let's get it over with."

"What . . . what will you do with me?"

"What do ye think?" He grinned down, mistaking my need to have details for more cowardice.

"Tell me! I've a right to know!"

My forceful insistence set him back a little, but he was too grudging to provide an answer.

I looked up at Drummond. "Please, sir. Tell me. If these are my last moments, let me not disgrace myself further."

Reluctantly, he said, "Yer to be shot."

Interesting way to put it, I thought, as though someone else were to do the dirty work.

"With honor, as for a soldier?" I asked, my manner pleading for him to say yes.

"Aye, with honor." There was amusement deep in his eyes. I pretended not to see it.

Ash spat, clearly having no use for what he must have perceived as a useless and trivial concept except when it suited him. He was dancing from one foot to the other from the cold. "Let's git to it."

We reached a level spot on the slope and turned into the wind, taking a path that eventually wound itself down to the shoreline. The wind seemed to grab the air from my lungs, so it was just as well I had no need to breathe.

"Will you bury me?" I gasped out.

Drummond gruffly said, "At sea."

I looked past him at the heartbreakingly bleak water. Truly it was to be a cold, deep grave for me in every sense of the word.

He correctly interpreted my expression. "Have to. Orders."

"Orders from whom?"

He made no answer. Ash, probably. Or Knox. It hardly mattered.

We came to the point on the path where it went down to the shore, but Drummond ignored it and continued to go straight ahead, breaking a way through virgin snow. It was much deeper here and the footing more treacherous, but his size helped. He had tremendous strength and bulled through the increasingly higher drifts as though they weren't there. The extra exertion was of no benefit to my head whatsoever. All I could do was hang onto him for balance and try not to fall.

We were rather far from the house.

Good.

Drummond paused, waiting for Ash, who was having a harder time of it. The wind was dying, I noticed, and the sky . . . growing lighter. Even with the thick clouds of winter between me and the sun, I'd be unable to hold myself conscious once it cleared the horizon.

"Right," said Ash. "Put 'im over there."

I was guided to what I first thought to be a taller than usual drift. It proved to be a slight rise that cut off sharply on the other side. It dropped straight down into water. All they had to do was shoot me and roll the body off and let the sea carry it away or drag it to the bottom. It might never, ever be found.

Ash watched as I worked it all out and enjoyed my reaction of horror. Drummond remained impassive and told me I'd have to stand on my own.

"I—I should like a blindfold, please."

Ash's face transformed into a study of indignant amazement. "*What?*"

"May I not have a blindfold? I should find it easier to take what is to come if I don't have to see."

He was practically speechless. "Of all the—"

"A last request, sir."

He worked himself into a spate of name-calling and I winced and clung to Drummond like a child seeking shelter.

"Let 'im," said Drummond, as I'd hoped he would. He was exasperated, but with Ash, not me. Ash was using more time venting his anger than it would have taken to grant my request.

"What?"

" 'Tis not much to ask. 'E can use yer scarf." Without waiting, Drummond let go his hold on me and backed away.

Damnation. I'd wanted one of them to go back to the house in order to fetch something suitable. Separating them would have made things so much easier for me.

"Might I also have some Bible verses?" I asked with rapidly increasing desperation.

"Got none, lad."

Well. I should have expected as much from a house where no one could read.

"The blindfold," I said. "Please . . . I—"

Drummond looked expectantly at Ash. With more cursing and complaint, he reluctantly untied the length of scarf that held his hat in place. He had to give his pistol to Drummond in order to do it properly. When he came forward to wrap it around my eyes, I lifted one hand in a begging gesture.

"Please . . ."

"What now?"

"A moment to pray. Just a moment for a prayer. Just a—"

I got another curse for an answer, but he made no other objection. I sank down to one knee. Drummond was now too far away to reach, but Ash stood right before me, clutching the scarf, impatient to finish the job and get out of the cold. I bowed my head.

"Heavenly Father, forgive me my sins . . ." I began, and I meant it. To undertake such actions while in the middle of prayer must certainly be sinful, but I had no other choice left. Surely God would understand.

I smashed my fist into Ash's groin.

He made no scream; I think the agony was too great to be vocalized, but his face was eloquent as he doubled over and fell writhing into the snow. Then I forgot about him as Drummond came up.

He had the pistol ready and could not possibly miss at so short a distance. He was hardly two yards away, holding it centered upon my chest. The muzzle was as big as the door to hell, but I had to wrench my eyes from it to look at Drummond. Unlike the display I'd put on earlier, I would face my death, if that was what was to come. I'd survived other woundings, but was very weak now and unsure of what might happen next. I braced myself for the shot, glaring at him and trying to see if there was a soul behind his eyes.

He held off firing. Only stared. We stared at one another for what seemed like hours and I couldn't imagine why he was waiting. He paid no attention to Ash, who lay between us, curled around himself and grunting with agony; all he did was look right back into my eyes, unblinking, like a madman.

What was it? Was he hoping I'd beg? Why was he so still? Was it to break my nerve? What—?

Dawn. It was lighter now than . . .

Light. Enough light for him to see clearly. To see me. For me to . . .

With sudden comprehension, I staggered to my feet and told Drummond to throw his gun down. He did. I told him to get on his knees. He did. His impassive face remained the same, hard as stone . . . maybe just a little vacant about the eyes. That had been the delay for me; I didn't know him well enough to read any inner changes when my influence had taken him over.

My hunger, held in abeyance by so many distractions, now clawed its way back. Ravenous. Undeniable.

Unsteadily, I walked around Ash until I was quite close to Drummond. I told him to shut his eyes. He did. Then, with trembling fingers, I ripped away his rag of a neckcloth.

What came next didn't take long. Fortunate, since it was singularly unpleasant.

Except for the blood, of course.

I pushed his head away and to one side to draw the skin taut over his exposed throat. The scent coming through it— the bloodsmell—overmatched the stink of his unwashed skin and clothing. My teeth were out and my belly gave an inward twist, anticipating. Bending low, I cut hard into him, breaking through the tough skin and drinking in that first glorious swallow of life as it flooded forth.

He made a gagging sound once, and not long after sobbed once, but otherwise held himself as quietly as any of the other beasts I'd fed on in the past.

His blood was different. Tainted in some way I couldn't identify, but I liked the taint. It was comparable to the kind of difference one finds between beef and venison. Both fill you, but one has the tameness of the farm and the other yet holds to the wildness of the wood.

I drank deeply and well and felt the heat of it warming me from the inside out. Strength I thought lost returned and the pain . . . the dreadful pain from the disastrous blow he'd inflicted began to subtly fade. It had been so constant that it seemed strange not to have it anymore.

Pain gone, hunger abated . . . no . . . *fulfilled*. I'd never had better.

When I drew away and licked my lips clean, I found that I'd never taken such total satisfaction from any food in all my life. Perhaps it was because it had been human blood, perhaps it was because it had come from an enemy and was suffused with his fear of me, for Drummond was shuddering with it. Tears from his now wide-open eyes streamed down his cheeks. At some point he'd woken up from my influence and had been hideously aware of all that was happening to him.

I breathed in a great draught of air through my open mouth and released it as laughter. It soared up and was caught by the last of the wind and whipped away into the brightening sky.

It . . . was not a wholesome sound. And when it died away, I felt ashamed.

But why? I'd fed from a man as I'd have fed from any brute beast, and the wild predators of the world feel no shame for what they must do. They kill in order to live; that was their nature as given to them by God. I had been no different prior to my change, having eaten animal flesh, having killed in order to live. I'd felt the triumph of a successful hunt, but this . . . wasn't the same.

Then I understood. My sudden shame came not from my change, but rather from the fact that I'd used my new abilities to play the bully. I'd taken enjoyment from this man's terror. There's a vile streak of that kind of cruelty in all of us, and I'd given into it.

Bad. Very bad of me. I could imagine what Father might have to say about this; he'd been clear enough on the subject when I'd been growing up. Though I was no longer a boy tussling with others in Rapelji's schoolyard, the principle remained the same.

"Please . . . don't kill me," Drummond whispered, his voice broken and dry. He was deathly white, but nowhere near to dying. Yet.

Right. He was begging *me* for his utterly useless, damaging life. Begging for life from the man he'd been ready to kill without the least thought or regret.

"*Please* . . ."

A hundred caustic retorts to that sprang to my lips, but never came forth. What would be the point? He was what he was, a killer and a thief, and whatever I said would not change him.

Or would it?

I knew I'd have to protect myself from him anyway.

With another laugh, short and more bitter this time, I said, "Look at me. Look at me and *listen* . . ."

And he did.

I finished with him fast enough, leaving him with no memory of what he'd been through, only a deep desire to seek an honest path for himself in the world. It both soothed and galled me, for I knew I was at least trying to do the right thing, but my baser side wanted very much to throw him over the cliff as he had meant to do to me. So I might have done in a hot rage, but not now. There was no need. Besides, his death was not worth having on my conscience.

He was asleep, or in a state close to it, and would remain so until Ash woke him up. Ash himself had been too lost in his own trouble to be aware of what had occurred but a few yards from him. His back was to us, so I wasn't worried that he had seen any of it. I walked over and nudged him with a foot.

He burst out with a very creative string of curses, not the wisest thing to do, but then I'd already noticed his singular shortage of brain and could shrug off the abuse. It did stop, however, when he saw I had the pistol in my hand.

He gaped, then started to cry out something, a call to Drummond for help, I thought, but I slapped the other hand over his mouth and informed him that he'd get a second punch between the legs if he made another sound. That shut him up completely and he lay silent as I searched him for those items of mine he'd claimed for himself out of the robbery, namely a gold snuff box and my money purse. I also found another pocketful of coins, and a surprising quantity at that, which I thought might have come from other victims. This I put in with my own money. I had no need of it, but intended to turn it over to Father with the request that he donate it to our church. Doubtless that good place could put the funds to a better use than any Ash had ever planned.

It was growing lighter by the minute. If I was to try my influence with Ash, it would have to be—

" 'Old right there, you!"

I looked up to see Abel and Seth standing just this side of the kneeling Drummond. Abel had a pistol of his own, and it was pointed at me. I hadn't heard their approach. I wondered how long they'd been watching and how much they'd seen. Too much, from the stricken looks they wore. Abel kept trying to steal glances at the oblivious Drummond, which made it hard for him to hold his weapon level.

"*Devil!*" he shrieked when he saw the blood on Drummond's throat. "Ye filthy devil!" His hatchety face went red with outrage and disgust and fear. The gun went off. It may have been an accidental firing or not, but he was so upset that it spoiled his aim. The thing roared and the air was clouded with sudden smoke, but the ball completely missed me. He had one instant to regret it, less than a blink of an eye, and I was upon him.

A clout on the jaw was all that was needed. He was stunned, senseless and unresisting. I turned on Seth, but he'd backed away, jaw sagging and eyes popping, too frightened to move. As he watched, I dragged my cloak from his brother's body.

Ash was on his hands and knees and bellowing at Drummond, who looked to be waking up. Damnation to them. If I had more time I could have stayed, changed their memories to my advantage, but the dawn was against me. I had ten minutes, no more and very probably much less. It was hard to tell for the clouds.

I had to get out.

Slogging away from them over the open snow field was the best I could do. I threw the cloak around my shoulders and pulled it close, grateful for the brothers' greed. The only reason I could think why they'd followed out after us was for Seth to lay claim to my boots before his friends dropped them—along with my body—into the Sound. Abel may have come to try for them himself one more time, that, or to enjoy the execution.

I walked as quickly as possible, wanting distance between myself and the growing row behind me. Ash's voice rose high over the wind, suffused with anger. I looked back once and saw him on his feet, shaking a fist at me. Without a doubt, he was a dangerous man, but also stupid and incredibly foolish; I still had the pistol.

A perverse fancy took me. I stopped and turned, arm out in the best dueling style, my pose and posture unmistakable. He ceased moving, caught between horror and surprise. I pulled the trigger and felt the recoil jolt up my arm. The thing made a grand roar and I had the satisfaction of seeing Ash and the others duck in dismay. They weren't injured, I'd aimed just over their heads, but by the time they found enough courage to look again, they'd not be able to see me. I took that moment as the right time to vanish.

The thought belatedly came that they'd follow my trail. They'd find the discarded pistol and my tracks ending in the middle of the field as though I'd vanished into the air, which, indeed, I had. Well, it was too late now. Let them puzzle it out and be damned.

Glad I was that the wind had died. There was just enough of it now to give me a direction to push against, which I did with all my strength and will. I sped south and then west toward home, though I had not the faintest possibility of reaching it in time.

Panic?

Very likely.

There was also the hope that once I'd put enough distance between myself and that band of patriotic cutthroats, I could go solid, get my bearings and find some shelter for the day. All I needed was a shack or barn, someplace to hide from the approaching sun.

I hurtled forward for as long as I dared, then re-formed. The light was nearly blinding. The snow-blanketed fields reflected it, increased it. I shaded my eyes and searched all around for cover. Nothing, absolutely nothing, presented itself.

For want of anything better to do besides stand and gibber with fear, I vanished and continued forward. There were some trees in the distance, widely spaced and naked of leaves. Probably useless. Faster and faster I went until such senses as were left to me in this form gave me warning that I'd reached my goal.

This next re-forming was more difficult. The light much worse. My fear all but choked me. The trees were useless. Even in the high summer with their leaves, their shade would not have been sufficient. They were too far apart. There was no other choice, though. Perhaps my cloak would help . . .

Then I noticed that the trees farther on were strangely shortened. My sight was getting worse, but I was just able to discern that they were not really short, but were actually the top branches of other trees growing upon much lower ground.

The island was pocked here and there with depressions we called kettles because of their general shape. Rapelji said that they'd been carved out of the earth by ancient glaciers. Some were small, others much larger, with names to them. I had no name for this one, but immediately dubbed it "haven."

I charged forward, faded somewhat, and launched my partially visible body over the edge. It was quite different from the tumble I'd taken into one as a child. The landing was much less abrupt.

The high wall of earth on my left blocked the immediate threat of light; the other wall was not all that far away. The bottom would be exposed to sun for only a short time during the day. I could improve that if I—yes, there, where the wall bulged out, creating a little alcove, but to lie as one dead with only a cloak for covering . . . I was afraid Ash and his crew would come hunting and chance upon me while I lay helpless.

The snow. It had drifted in here all throughout the winter, deep and undisturbed.

It might not work.

Oh, but it *had* to.

I faded completely and sank beneath its unbroken surface, sank until I touched upon the more solid barrier of the frozen ground beneath and there stopped. Then gradually, ever so cautiously, I assumed form once more. Not at all easy, but the hard snow gave way to my frantic pushing and I made myself a kind of burrow. I twisted this way and that, but saw not the least hint of light. It would do. It would have to, for all my choices had been stolen away by the dawn.

It was a grave. No other word could describe this kind of darkness or silence. I was acutely conscious of the great weight of the snow above. Had I needed air, I'd have smothered in a very short time. As it was, my mind was in danger of smothering from the memory of my first wretched awakening into this changed life.

And then . . . all my worries ceased for the day.

CHAPTER
—10—

I awoke to utter blackness, immobile from cold, and just disoriented enough to leap into a kind of groggy alarm. As my last thought had been about my hated churchyard coffin, I mentally kicked out in a—literally—blind panic, instinctively tried to vanish, and did.

By increments.

Bit by bit, I faded, feeling myself going at the extremities first as hands and feet, already numb, lost all further bonding with touch. It seeped past my skin and muscle, to the vitals, to the bones, until I was finally incorporeal and bumping gently against the sides of my tiny prison.

Nasty sensation, that.

During this agonizingly slow transformation I'd recovered some of my wits, recalling that I'd buried myself in a snowbank to escape the daylight. I also knew I no longer wanted to be here anymore. So thinking, I sieved slowly upward from the icy sanctuary until I seemed to be free of it, then tried to resume a solid body again.

It was a reverse of the vanishing, only slower, with me struggling to push it faster and not making very much difference at all. For a time, while but halfway formed, I was madly blinking to clear my fogged vision. My eyes were not themselves subject to any injury, but the lengthy return made it seem so. Once they were clear, I knew I was whole. I felt much better—until my legs gave out and I landed facedown in the snow like a felled tree.

After that, I became more cautious.

I was thoroughly chilled through and through, so much so that I had quite forgotten what it was like to ever be warm. My fingers were an unhealthy white and, though they moved, were far too stiff to be of much use. All my joints were stiff, for that matter. I felt as though I'd been hollowed out and filled from the toes up with slushy, half-frozen mud.

While trying to push the ground away, I reflected that if I didn't find some warmth soon, the mud inside would freeze the rest of the way. With that ominously in mind, success followed my next effort to stand; then I endeavored to walk . . . well, shamble. At least I was moving.

The kettle had high walls, but was mercifully open at the southern end, making for an uncomplicated escape. I didn't want to try vanishing again until my condition had improved. My pace was slow, but constant, and became more fluid the longer I stayed at it. When I started shivering, I knew I'd done the right thing, quite probably just in time.

I had to trudge uphill for a bit, then the kettle opened out into empty field. No fences were in sight, no signs of anything civilized, only snow and the stark black silhouette of a tree here and there. The road that Ash and his crew had used lay somewhere ahead. I was reluctant to find it, though. Since I'd determined I was in Suffolk County, the chances of encountering more of his rebel friends was great. It would not be terribly advantageous to my interests to escape one band of cutthroats only to be captured by another, but I supposed I could cope if it was unavoidable. For now I was too miserable to plan for anything more harrowing than the next few steps forward.

Lots of those. I didn't bother to count.

The going was very slow due to the uneven ground beneath the covering of snow. Thank God that Seth hadn't taken my boots away. Thank God I'd gotten my cloak back from Abel. It was heavy with damp, but more preferable to going without. All I needed now was something to cover my head. My ears were like chips of ice. And, as long as I was making wishes, some gloves would be—

Gloves . . . on impulse I checked the inside pocket of the cloak. They were still there. I'd have to give Jericho a special thanks for his foresight and another to Providence that Abel had overlooked these prizes. Though I was barely able to open and close my hands yet, I managed to pull the things on. Maybe they wouldn't give warmth, but they'd hold in what little I might produce and keep the cruelly cold air from stealing it away.

Each step became marginally easier than the last, and the line of footprints behind me grew longer and longer. A mile of it must have stretched back to the kettle when I saw the road. There was little to mark it from the rest of the countryside but the indentations of ruts and marks left by wheels and livestock. I chose the westward direction and walked and walked and walked.

After an hour of it, I decided my fears of meeting with more rebels were not to be realized. That comforting thought kept me in good spirits until the country silence was broken by the sound of hoofs.

Coming up behind. Rebels for sure. Hunting me down.

No place to hide, not a tree or a drainage ditch, no wall or even a bush.

Vanish? No. My insides were too unsettled yet.

Very well, hide in the open. Pretend to be what I must surely look like, a forlorn traveler on his way to shelter. I'd plod on and ignore them and hope they'd return the favor and pass by.

The sky was clear of clouds and there was a bright, nearly full moon out. The light was excellent. They'd probably have a sharp look at me before they went by. That's what I'd do.

How many? A glimpse over my shoulder showed only two riders. That was good. I could probably handle them if it came to it. I fervently prayed it would not.

They clip-clopped up, in no hurry, and came even with me. They stayed even with me. Damnation.

"You, sir! Who are you and where are you bound?"

An educated voice. A gentleman's voice. Familiar . . .

I looked up . . . right into the astonished face of Lord James Norwood.

My own expression must have matched his well enough, for we were both struck speechless. Then the second rider swung his leg over his mount's neck and slipped off.

"My God, Mr. Barrett, is it you?" Dr. Beldon, brimful of relief.

I was very glad to see him and deeply touched by this evidence of his concern for me, and raised a wan smile. It was meant to reassure, but had quite the opposite effect on the poor man.

"Sweet heavens, are you all right? What has happened to you?"

Norwood, prompted by the doctor's actions, also dismounted and echoed those questions and more. Both of them were obviously shocked by my doubtless wild appearance. They each took an arm to support me, though I'd been doing an adequate enough job before.

"You're freezing cold, man," said Beldon. "Here, I've a blanket in one of my bags . . ." He broke away to get it.

"Where have you been, sir?" asked Norwood.

"Some house near the shore," I answered. My voice was thick and strange in my throat. "Not sure. My family? Are they—?"

"They're very worried for you. Your father is out with another search party farther south."

"Search party?"

"Half the Island is out looking for you. As soon as that rascal turned up early this morning with your note, Mr. Barrett sent me off straight as a shot to fetch Lieutenant Nash and his men."

"Here," said Beldon, shaking out the promised blanket. "Get this up over your head. Your ears are quite blue."

I let him fuss, for it was incredibly good to be among friends again.

"Some brandy now . . ."

There was no way of refusing it gracefully, so I lifted the opaque bottle to my lips and pretended to swallow. A drop or two burned upon my tongue, but only for a moment.

"Are you fit enough to ride?" he asked.

"Yes."

"There's a farm not far ahead—"

"No. My own home. Take me right home."

"You're certain you can make it?"

"A dead run would be too slow for me."

Norwood laughed lightly at this. "And dangerous for the horses, but we'll see what we can do. Can you give him a leg up, Doctor?"

Having the larger and stronger of the two mounts, I was to ride behind him, hanging on as well as I could with my numb hands. He sprang into the saddle, held out a steadying arm, and Beldon gave me the boost I needed. I landed with a thud astride the horse's rump and might have fallen right off again if Norwood hadn't caught me. The exertion called back a ghost of dizzying pain from Drummond's initial assault. My balance was off, but I tried not to let it show, lest they hold to a slow pace.

The pace was slow anyway, at least to my mind, but Norwood kept the time filled by answering my questions on what had happened after Knox's arrival.

"The big brute was strutting around as though he owned the place, demanding to see Mr. Barrett. Ill-favored fellow, from what I saw of him. I only caught a glimpse at the time. Your father read the note he had, and you should have seen the look on the man's face when the servants were ordered to grab hold of him. Took a number of 'em, I must say, all the stable lads and those two black housemen as well were needed before they got him on the floor and tied him tight as a trussed bird. And the language. Your father had him gagged as well, to spare the ears of the ladies. Unpleasant business."

"No doubt."

"But that was a brilliant bit of business with the note, and the same for Mr. Barrett for catching onto it so fast. You took a risk over that, though."

"But it worked. That's what matters."

"Now, who were these fellows who captured you? How did you let it happen?"

"I didn't, they did."

"What? Oh, I see. Yes, certainly you didn't plan to let yourself be kidnapped. Well, then, did you get a good look at 'em?"

"Much too good a look. I'll know them the next time I see them."

"Which will be soon, I hope. That is, if Nash and his men can find 'em before they get away."

"And Father's with them?"

"Looking in the wrong place, it seems."

"Sorry. I couldn't be more specific in the note as I didn't really know where I was until later."

"Tell me what happened."

I did so, briefly, leaving out certain details, and could see him swelling with anger.

"Bastards," he grumbled.

And that about summed it all up for me.

• • •

About three miles from home, Beldon said he wanted to run ahead to prepare things for me, kicked his hack to a canter, and disappeared. I approved, for it would mean any anxiety over me would be relieved that much sooner, and so it proved when Norwood and I finally arrived.

Jericho was there to help me from the horse, to help me inside, and to help me strip from my worse-for-wear clothes. Part of Beldon's preparations had included instructing Mrs. Nooth to boil large quantities of water. The bathtub was set up in the now steamy kitchen and my cold and highly abused body was soon ecstatically soaking in wonderful, reviving heat. A hot wet cloth was wrapped around my head to warm up my ears. I must have looked like some sort of down-at-the-heels sultan, but didn't care.

Mrs. Nooth had bathed me as a child and treated me little different now as an adult. Her one concession to the passage of years was to drape a blanket over the whole of the tub, but I thought that it was more for retaining the heat than to preserve my modesty. She added more hot water as it was ready until I felt like a hard-cooked egg, but got no complaints from me. Her instincts were to feed me something, anything. I managed to put her off on that. My past influence upon her helped there, for she didn't press.

The whole house, it seemed, was in the kitchen, eyes on me, full of questions. Even Mother was present, her mouth turned down in fearsome disapproval for the uproar and, possibly, my naked state, but with the blanket in place she had no cause for worry. Propriety, though somewhat strained, was intact.

Elizabeth had been in tears when Norwood and I had come in, and had thrown her arms about me in relief. I'd held her and told her I was fine and then came the first of the questions: What had happened? Where had I been? How did I get away? And so on. I repeated what I'd said to Norwood, with a few more details and a lot more interruptions. As before, I left out some things. No one noticed, or if they did, it was accepted without comment.

"You should have killed the fellow while you had the chance," said Norwood in regard to my bravado gesture of shooting over Ash's head.

I remained silent on that one and wallowed in the incred-

ible glory of hot water. Beldon removed the soaking wet
turban to check my ears and pronounced them to be normal
again. He then made a careful examination of the spot where
Drummond's near-deadly blow had connected.

"I see no sign of injury, sir," he said. His manner was
reminiscent of the time he'd marveled over my miraculously
healed arm.

I couldn't distract him out of it in front of all this crowd.
"Perhaps it wasn't as bad as I thought."

"But your hair is—was quite matted with blood. It had to
come from a cut in the scalp, and I can't find one."

"That suits me well enough, Doctor. Mrs. Nooth, might I
trouble you for a bit of soap and a flesh brush?"

It was no trouble at all, and her bustling and cheerful chatter
got between me and Beldon, as I'd wanted.

The two oldest stable lads had been dispatched on fresh
mounts to find Father. Norwood thought of going, but didn't
know the countryside as well as the lads. They weren't gone
long; Father had been on his way home when they met him
on the road. He'd galloped the rest of the way back and
still smelled of winter night when he pushed his way into
the kitchen to greet me. He knelt next to the tub, took my
face in his hands and pulled me close, resting his chin on
my head for a moment. Neither of us spoke. It didn't seem
necessary.

He drew back and looked me over and combed a damp
lock of hair from my face. "Oh, laddie, what have you done
to yourself?"

"I'm really all right," I said. I'd said that a lot recently.

"Thank God." Then, with a wry curl of his lip, he added,
"Are you tired of all the repetition?"

"Is it so obvious?"

"It's fine. You look all in, though. I'll ask my questions
when you're up to them."

"Not long," I promised.

He told me I was a good lad, then turned to Beldon and
Norwood for the story of how they'd found me. At the same
time he unobtrusively herded the whole lot from the kitchen.
Jericho remained behind. He'd already been upstairs to fetch
me fresh clothes and was examining the old ones with a critical eye.

"There's blood on your coat," he said quietly, so Mrs. Nooth, busy on the other side of the kitchen, could not hear.

"Yes. That motherless—well, he gave me a bad knock. Near as I can make out he grabbed me by the queue and swung me right into the wagon seat like you'd break a chicken's neck. I'm lucky he didn't kill me."

"And one day later there is no injury to be seen."

I shrugged. "It's the way I've become."

His eyes briefly lighted. "Magic?"

I couldn't help but smile. "Why not?"

Bathed, shaved, and decently dressed: such are the things that mark us as civilized creatures. I was looking very civilized before Jericho gave me permission to leave.

They were all waiting in the parlor. Cousin Anne was serving tea. It might have been the same as any other evening at home except for the way they looked at me with the unease in their faces. It wasn't nice to see, and I was trying to think of a graceful way to excuse myself without seeming rude.

Father saved me the trouble by stepping forward. "Come, Jonathan, I've some things to tell you. No need to bore everyone. The rest of you carry on as you are."

A ripple went through them. Their faces all seemed strangely alike, blurred and blank, even Elizabeth's. Father took my arm and led me away to the library. He closed the door.

It was warm there. A fine big fire was blazing, merry as New Year. I was no longer cold, but the memory of it drove me to the hearth to hold my hands out to the flames. The heat baked my skin, soaked into the bones. Father moved up behind and came around, standing next to me. Watching.

"This feels very good," I said, uncomfortably conscious of his gaze.

He made no comment.

"You had some things to tell me, sir?" I prompted.

"When you can look me in the eye, laddie."

It was painful for some reason I didn't understand. Like looking into the sun. His face was as blurred as the others. I tried blinking to clear my sight and was shocked when tears spilled out.

"I'm sorry," I blurted.

"For what?"

"I . . . don't know."

"T'wasn't your fault, laddie."

I nodded and glumly swiped at my leaking eyes with both hands. It was stupid, so very *stupid* of me to be like this. I wheeled from the fire and threw myself on the settee. Snuffling. Father sat next to me. After a minute he put his arms around my stiff body and got me to relax enough to lean against his chest. Like a child. Thus had he comforted me as a child.

"You're all right, laddie," he told me, his voice husky with his own tears.

That's what broke it. That's when I gave out with a breathy hiccup and truly wept. He held me and rocked me and stroked my hair and never once told me to hush, just kept doing that until I was able to stop. I finally sat up, blindly fishing for the handkerchief Jericho always left in one of my pockets. Father had one ready and put it into my hands. I blew my nose, wiped my eyes, and suddenly yawned.

"Sorry."

"Don't be," he said genially.

"How did you know?"

"When you came into the parlor looking like a drawn rope about to snap, the possibility occurred to me. I've seen it before and it's no good trying to bury it. How do you feel?"

"Not so drawn."

He saw that for himself well enough, but was reassured to hear it confirmed. He went across to unlock his cabinet and poured out a bit of brandy, then locked up again. The habit had ingrained itself in him in such a very short time. He sat facing me in his favorite chair, the firelight playing warmly over his features.

"Well. Can you tell me all about it now?"

I could. And did.

It was easier than the previous tellings. I didn't have to pretend to be brave. I didn't have to lie. So very, very much easier it is to be able to tell the truth. I left out one thing only: the part about drinking Drummond's blood. At the time it had been my survival, but here in the light and peace of my favorite room, it seemed unreal, even monstrous. I was not comfortable about it—especially the fact I'd enjoyed the taste so very much—and was not prepared to offer such a burden of knowledge to my dearly loved father. He had more than enough troubles on his mind.

When I was done, he looked me over from top to toe and again I seemed to see myself through his eyes. There was worry there, of course, for my well-being, but I appeared to be strong enough to handle things now. There was also relief: that I was safely home and if not totally undamaged, then at least able to recover from it. "We've got the other fellow, Knox," he said. "Nash put him into that blockhouse he had built last fall."

"Will there be a hanging?"

"I don't know. The man keeps saying he's a soldier and thus a prisoner of war. Said he was doing his duty right and proper before his capture."

"Oh? And just how does he explain the ransom note he thought he was delivering?"

"Denies it ever was a demand for ransom. Claims he was given to understand it was a request from you to ask for help getting home. The other men had captured you by mistake and he'd come to fetch a horse to bring you back. He volunteered to risk capture himself in order to do you a good turn. Very aggrieved, he is."

"Has he convinced Lieutenant Nash of this tale?"

"What do you think?"

My answer lay in my return expression and we both had a short, grim laugh.

Father sipped his brandy, then sighed. "Tomorrow Nash will take him 'round to Mrs. Montagu's home for her and the servants to have a look at him. There are a few other places in the county to go to as well if she can't identify him. He had no commission papers—"

"A hanging, then."

"Quite likely."

Silence fell upon us, lengthened, and was so complete that I was able to hear to the distant kitchen where Mrs. Nooth was supervising the dumping out of my bathwater. Things were quiet in the parlor by comparison, just Norwood talking low, though I couldn't make out the words.

"Is Nash still out looking for me?"

I'd interrupted whatever gray thoughts had been floating between us. "What? Yes, I suppose he is. And in the wrong place. We were miles from where Beldon and Lord James said they'd found you. Oh, well, it'll do him good. He wants the exercise and if he shakes up a few rebels, all the better."

"What made you break off from him and come home?"

"You. I trusted what you said in your note about trying to escape. Worked out that you'd have to find shelter for the day, but you'd come home as quick as you could after dark. Thought I should be here to check, to see if I was right, and I was. Didn't expect that you'd hole yourself up like a badger in a burrow, though. Very ingenious, laddie."

"More like very desperate. Wish it'd been warmer, but if it had, then I'd have been without cover altogether."

"That had me worried, that you'd be out in some open area for anyone to stumble over. Knowing what you're like during the day, I'd feared you'd be taken for dead. There'd be misunderstandings, rumors—"

"Me having to influence everyone all over again." I shuddered. "No, thank you."

Father chuckled.

And I thought of something. "Do you think Nash would let me talk to Knox?"

"To what purpose?"

"I should like to get the truth from him."

He frowned for a time, knowing exactly what I meant. "A confession from him will mean his death for certain, Jonathan."

"At this point I think that's a foregone conclusion."

Another frown. More silence. Then, "Very well. A gift you have and a gift you should use. Let its use be for finding the truth. Besides . . ."

He trailed off; I urged him to continue.

" 'Tis only because I hate to admit it to myself, but I've a streak of vengeance in me. If he's one of the bastards who caused Mrs. Montagu so much distress, then I'll want to be there at dawn to put the rope 'round his neck myself."

Father finished his brandy and asked if I was up to facing the rest of the household.

"Only if there's no fuss. I've had enough to last me for months."

He could make no guarantee against that, but said I could leave whenever it became too much.

This second attempt to rejoin their company was more successful. The pale blurs were gone. Their faces were faces once more.

Thank God.

Elizabeth broke away from Norwood and came over to slip her arm around mine. "You had us so worried," she told me.

Apparently worried enough herself that in her relief she forgot all about Mother. I shot a glance in that lady's direction, but she wasn't reacting to us at all. She wore her usual joyless expression, nothing more. Well, I suppose it was preferable to one of her insane tirades. She hadn't had one of those for a while, certainly not since the night I'd "talked" to her. Perhaps she was building up to one. I hoped otherwise.

"Yes," said Cousin Anne. "Very worried. It must have been horrid for you."

This was about the fourth time tonight she'd expressed that sentiment. I'd heard the other three when I'd been soaking in the tub. I laughed now, more freely than I thought myself capable of, and assured her I was fine.

Her eyes lingered on me. There was a touch more depth to them than before. I wondered if that was from her own growth from this unpleasantness or because we'd shared a few kisses. Perhaps both. I smiled, took her hand and gave it a gentle squeeze to say *everything's all right*. She tossed her head slightly, smiling back.

Elizabeth made me sit in a comfortable chair and Anne asked if I wanted some tea. I accepted a cup with lots of sugar and pretended to sip, but it was easy to avoid drinking when all the questions started flowing freely once more.

Mrs. Hardinbrook had a strong interest in what the men had been like and what they had said.

"No words fit for a lady's ears, ma'am. Indeed, some of them made me blush." This raised a laugh.

Lady Caroline wanted to know why I hadn't come home right away if I'd made my escape so very early that morning.

"Truth be told, I wasn't in the best of condition. A tap on the head and all that rattling around in the back of a wagon for the worst part of fifteen miles—I was fair exhausted. I found a deserted shack and simply fell asleep for the day."

Norwood was curious as to whether the men had given away any clues about where they'd come from.

"Connecticut, for certain. Knox told them to take to a boat if they saw any trouble coming. I expect they're there now, probably sitting in some rebel hostel and telling a very different version of this story."

More laughter.

"But we'll find out the truth tomorrow," I added.

"How so, sir?"

"I'm going to have a little talk with Knox."

"To what purpose? The man's lied his head off from the moment he was taken."

I shrugged to show that that wasn't my fault. "I think he'll be truthful enough once he sees my face. Remember, he thinks I've been killed by his friends and no one the wiser. When I walk in on him the shock will turn him around, I'm sure."

"That should be interesting," said Beldon. "May I come along and observe this miracle?"

"I should welcome your company, Doctor, but would prefer a private interview with the fellow first."

He graciously accepted the sense in that.

"May I come as well?" asked Norwood.

This must have been how Nash felt when, like it or not, the lot of us had decided to go along with him to Mrs. Montagu's. There was no good reason to refuse, though. But Father was coming, and I trusted he would help if any difficulty arose.

"But tomorrow," put in Lady Caroline. "Mightn't it be rather soon for you? You really ought to rest a few days."

"I'd go tonight if I thought Lieutenant Nash would be there."

"You're in such a hurry?"

"There might be a chance to catch the other men once this one starts talking."

"But you just told us they'd be in Connecticut by now."

"True, but it doesn't mean they'll stay there. If they return, it would be very useful to know where and when and be ready for them."

"Good heavens, yes," said Mrs. Hardinbrook. "Why, they might even come here next, looking for revenge." She seemed to find that idea to be both alarming and fascinating.

I found it to be simply alarming.

Norwood bristled a bit. "They could certainly try, but they'd have the surprise of their lives if they did. Right, gentlemen?"

He got general assent for an answer. I went along with the others to be sociable. Norwood's interest in encountering excitement had bemused me before; now it had become something to bite my tongue over. I'd had my share and then some, and knew it for a fool's wish. A nice quiet life was all I desired. I wondered why, if he was so keen to find adventure, he did not join up with Howe's army. Certainly there must be a place for titled volunteers wishing to serve their king. I could only think that he was reluctant to leave his sister on her own. Then there was Elizabeth. If he loved her as I loved Nora, then running off to play soldier would be the last thing on his mind.

But I was fairly sure that he was a bit envious of me. He questioned me over and over about what had happened, eyes shining as he searched out every scrap of information from my memory. He was welcome to it, though I found no real charm in any of my talk. Perversely, the more I touched on the negative aspects of it, the more solid his admiration became.

It was flattering, in its way, but wearing. He had no idea of the true cost to me. To have strangers come in and attempt to destroy your life for their own gain is at best frightening, at worst, shattering. Father understood the hurt my soul had suffered, Norwood did not.

No, I thought, Lord James Norwood was better suited for something "safely" dangerous, more along the lines of riding to the hounds. There was always the chance of falling and breaking one's neck, but if skillful and fairly lucky, one could return invigorated, content that death had been bravely overcome. However, he could choose to ride or not. I hadn't asked to be kidnapped. That loss of control and choice was the single most important difference between the dangers.

I could *not* see him going through what I had gone through and still emerge filled with the same sense of naive enthusiasm. Though he was nearing thirty, I wondered which of us was the older and decided it was me. Experience can be very aging.

Elizabeth came over, put a hand on his arm and said, "Really, Lord James, you're positively exhausting my poor brother."

His attention went from me to her with (to my eyes) visible difficulty, but his face smoothly adjusted into a smile for her.

Elizabeth picked up on it, though. "I'm interrupting?"

"Not at all," he said. "And you're right. I'm being an imposition."

We made mock protests and other such talk, then they drifted away to their favorite corner for more private converse. I watched them and then with suddenly kindled heat remembered Molly Audy.

With all the other events filling my brain, my discovery of his visits to her had been altogether pushed aside. The incident and my questioning of Molly rolled to the front once more, leaving me flummoxed and fuming over what to do next.

No happy solution presented itself beyond a base desire to break every bone in his body. But, as satisfying as this might prove to be for me, I had to reluctantly admit that what went on between them was not really my business. If she found out, Elizabeth was more than capable of taking care of herself.

If she found out.

I could not be the the one to tell her. Any interference on my part would be a most unwise and importune course to take.

Still, if he upset Elizabeth with his actions, I'd be there for her. Fists at ready.

The next night, Father, Beldon, Norwood, and I sedately rode into Glenbriar. Father and Norwood had already been there early in the morning to sort things out with Nash. That worthy officer chose not to complain about their tardy report of my return home, for he was still in awe of Norwood's title and wished to present himself in a good light. He managed to do just that by swiftly dispatching himself with a troop of men to the road where I'd been found. They eventually located the hovel where I'd been taken, but the place was bare of rebels. There was a wagon in the barn, but no horses and no sign of a boat. Nash, with his ever acquisitive turn of mind, had confiscated the wagon, then ordered the burning of the house and barn.

"Why on earth did you do that, sir?" asked Norwood with some justifiable mystification. The four of us were with Nash at The Oak, listening to the account of his day.

"Because it's one less sanctuary for them to use," he replied.

"But the owner of the property—"

"Was not on the premises. A diligent search was made, I assure you."

"Seems to me," said Father, "that you could have quartered some of your men there."

"Possibly, but I considered it to be too far distant." From the long pause preceding Nash's statement, we could tell he hadn't before now considered the idea at all.

"Pity about that. If the rebels had decided to try returning, you'd have had them cold."

Nash reddened. "If they return, I'm sure the Suffolk Militia will be able to deal with them."

This was met with the kind of silence in which much is said. It was well known that the loyalty of Suffolk County was at the best, debatable, and that's what we were all thinking, including, belatedly, Nash.

"I'd like to see this Knox fellow," I said, before things got too embarrassing.

He'd already agreed that I could have my private talk, though he would have guards standing ready outside. The memory of the two escapees last fall was with him, and even if he'd been made to forget who had helped them, he was not inclined to take further chances. Now he fairly leaped at my offered distraction and issued orders for the man to be removed and brought in from the blockhouse.

"Where will you interview him?" asked Norwood.

I deferred to Nash, who said, "This room will suit, I think. The door is stout and the window too small for a fellow his size to squeeze through. Just remember that we'll be just out here if you want help with him."

I thanked him and then retired to a dark corner so Knox wouldn't see me until it was time. Not that it was necessary; I could make him talk no matter what. This was for the benefit of the others.

Soon four large soldiers marched Knox inside, their heavy steps thundering throughout the inn along with the clank and clink of chains. They shoved their charge in with me and came out again, slamming the door.

He was not in the best of condition. His tough face bore some truly colorful bruises, and one eye had swollen shut. He moved stiffly, evidence of more bruising along the rest of his body. His clothes were more ragged than before and much dirtier. He dragged over to the table in the center and dropped wearily into a chair. I had no pity for him. He and his cronies had been all too ready to kill me, and they'd certainly killed others. If I could prevent them from continuing, well and good; I was glad of the privilege.

I stepped from the shadows and slipped into a chair opposite him with the table in between. Folding my hands before me, I looked at him and waited.

Though there were plenty of candles lighting the place, recognition came slowly to him. The last time he'd seen me, I'd been in roughly the same plight he was in now, injured, and with other people deciding his fate. A change of clothing and posture had made a significant difference in my appearance.

" 'O're you?" he asked with a ghost of belligerence. There wasn't sufficient force in his voice for it to be a demand.

I studied him long, then said, "Jonathan Barrett."

The color draining out of his face made the bruises seem that much worse. His one good eye grew wide and his mouth sagged and the breath went right out of him as though I'd hit him hard in the belly.

"I—I didn't ever want t' 'urt you, mister—" he began.

"Never mind that, I'm not interested in your excuses. All I want is for you to listen to me."

"Listen?"

I leaned closer. "Yes . . . listen . . ." I went on, speaking steadily, calming him, putting him in a state that would make him very eager to answer any question at all.

His expression went slack, as they all did. It was a disturbing kind of vacuity, as though I'd stolen his soul, leaving behind a breathing but utterly empty vessel of a body.

Ignore it, I thought. "Now you're going to tell me all about your friends Ash, Tully, Abel, and Seth." I left out Drummond, confident that the fellow was applying himself to more constructive pursuits by now.

"Tell you . . ."

Now that I had him in such a helpless state, it was hard to keep my emotions in check. I sensed that if I allowed myself to let loose of any shard of my anger at this point, the results for Knox would be very distressing, indeed.

"Everything," I said, putting all my concentration into it until my head began to hurt and I had to ease off.

"Wha . . . ?"

He'd need guidance. I couldn't expect to get useful information from him unless I came up with specific questions. Well, I had no end of those; which one first?

Before I could draw breath for it I was interrupted by the abrupt sound of glass breaking, very close. My eyes shot to the small window. One of the panes was gone; bits of it lay on the floor below. The row had made me jump and after that I froze, staring. Nothing happened for what seemed like a long time, but could only have been a second or two. I started to move, though I had no idea exactly what I was going to do. Go to the window and look out, perhaps. I was too startled to call to the soldiers outside. There was no time, anyway. The brief two seconds passed and then came the hard, harsh *bang* of a pistol being fired.

Knox instantly slumped forward.

I must have yelled. The door flew open and men crowded in, but it was all over. They found me with my back pressed hard against the wall, as if trying to melt right through it. They wouldn't have been far wrong, either.

Knox was sprawled over the table with a terrible hole on one side of his skull and his brains and blood spilling out a much larger one on the other. Questions were shouted at me. All I could do was point at the window and one bright lad finally got the idea and bellowed something to Nash. A lot of confusion followed as some went to peer through the opening and others left to run outside.

The bloodsmell was everywhere, all but choking me the way it filled the room. One image impressed itself upon my overtaxed brain: the stream of blood flowing across the table and falling over its edge to the floor. I clearly heard the soft drip-drip-drip of it as it formed a ghastly puddle almost at my feet.

Then Father was suddenly there, looking as sick and horrified as I felt, but *there*, and dragged me out, thank God.

I was shaking, chilled through by sudden cold. Father got me to the common room and made me sit close before the big fireplace, somehow managing to wrest a sanctuary for us from the general tumult. I shut my eyes against it, held onto him, and shuddered once.

"It's all right, laddie," he murmured just loud enough so that only I could hear him. That pulled me away from the worst of it, and soon after, either warmed by the fire or by his soothing voice, my shivering stopped.

Beldon emerged from the death room, shaking his head to confirm what we all knew, that Knox was well beyond any earthly help.

He knelt before me to peer into my eyes and asked if I needed anything. I gulped and began to laugh in his face.

Father gripped my shoulder tightly. "Jonathan, behave yourself," he said in a severe voice.

That worked, helping to steady me. "I'm all right," I said after a minute, and was reasonably sure I meant it. Another gulp and I was able to haltingly tell them what little I knew.

"My God," said Beldon. Both men were clearly shocked.

"Where's Lord James?" I asked.

Father pointed toward the outside door of the inn where many of the soldiers had gone. "As soon as he understood the situation, he was off to the hunt."

Glory-seeker, I thought. "He's welcome to it, if he doesn't get his head blown . . ." My eyes were drawn back toward the room, but I couldn't see anything of Knox's body because of the many other people trying to get in for a look. Just as well.

"I'm going, too," Beldon announced and hurried away. Father and I followed him.

There wasn't much wind, but it slapped enough to sting. I shivered with a cold that was more imagined than actually felt and walked around the building until I reached the little window. It was small owing to the expense of glass at the time this part of the inn had been built. It had shutters, but they'd been pushed back to let in the meager winter light and no one had bothered to close them again; otherwise the assassin might have been stymied.

I thought I caught a whiff of acrid powder on the air, but discounted it as more imagination. The breeze would have swept that away by now. Several soldiers were gathered at this spot and I recognized a few, including my sometime tutor for German, Eichelburger. He and the others were making much ado over two prizes, one a pistol, the other a length of wood.

"What is it?" I asked in German.

He hefted the pistol, holding it so the light coming from the broken window fell upon it. I moved closer and realized I'd not been mistaken. The smell of powder lingered around the thing. "This he dropped, the killer. This"—he waved the piece of wood—"was used to break the glass."

I translated for Father and Beldon. "Where is Lieutenant Nash?"

He gestured at the empty yard around the inn and what lay beyond.

"Did anyone see who fired?"

Eichelburger shook his head. "We'll get him."

I did not suffer from his confidence and broke away to walk toward the limits of the yard. The wind carried vague sounds to me of men crashing about in the dark.

"It's hopeless," I said to Father when he caught up with me. "They can't see a thing in this. They need help."

"Good God, you're not thinking of—" But he saw that I was. "Jonathan, you've had enough for one night, you've had more than enough for a lifetime."

"Perhaps so, but I have to get out and do something."

His patience was thinning, but he was willing to stretch it a bit more. "Do you now?"

I took stock of myself. I'd been badly shaken, but was far from being a complete wreck over the unpleasantness and told him as much. "Those bastards plucked me up, carrying me off like I was just more stolen livestock, and just when I thought I might be able to do something about it, they took that away as well. Perhaps I'm being a fool wanting to find the killer of a killer, but if I have to stand idle, waiting for Nash to come back empty-handed, as doubtless he will, I shall go mad from it."

He frowned for a long time, then finally half-lifted his arms as if to give in. "You're no fool, laddie. I know how you feel. I'd like to come along, but 'twill be better if I stay. This lot around the inn are running around like headless chickens. They're wanting some one to argue 'em calm again. Just don't let yourself be seen. The soldiers out there are liable to be skittish. And for God's sake, be careful."

I gave him my most solemn word on that point.

There had not been any fresh snow in the last day or so; the ground had been well-churned by dozens of passing feet and I wasn't enough of a skilled woodsman to tell old tracks from new under these circumstances. But I wasn't planning to trail anyone if I could help it. I walked as quickly as I could, taking the general direction of the soldiers. They were out of sight and nearly beyond hearing; I deemed it safe to let myself fade away and rise on the wind like smoke.

Practice told me about how high I was: a little above the treetops. There I took on just enough solidity to see and hoped that none of the hunters below chanced to look up.

I spotted a few of them, gray shapes on gray ground, in a hurry, yet trying to be cautious. Willing myself ahead, I saw more and more and by their movements discerned they were all part of Nash's troop. None of them was purposefully rushing forward in that way a fugitive might.

An hour passed, they searching below, me circling high above and ranging far ahead of them. Neither of us saw anything. They headed north, toward the coast, and once there covered the shoreline, but I could have told them it was useless. No boats had been launched that I had seen. Though the killer had had a good head start and just might have escaped that way, I was not inclined to think so. He'd probably gone to ground in one of any number of places. Nassau County was loyal, but there were pockets of sedition here and there that a rebel might know about. Whoever had done for Knox was probably sheltering in any of a hundred innocuous buildings between the inn and the Sound.

Pale and tired from all my skyward exertions, I returned to Glenbriar and found Father and Beldon waiting for me at The Oak. Lieutenant Nash had come back a little earlier, just as weary and tremendously disgruntled.

"I'll hear your story of what happened, if you please, sir," he said to me.

I told him, unable to add any more details, though he very much wanted them.

"You saw nothing through the window?" he asked, just on the polite side of exasperation.

"Only a vague shape. The candles in the room made reflections on the remaining glass. I glimpsed the smoke, but that was all. At first, I couldn't believe what I'd seen or what had been done."

We were in the common room, surrounded by a few more soldiers and many more townspeople. Cold as it was, the front windows were open, and others outside had draped themselves over the sills to catch the news.

"And you found no sign of where he'd gone?" I asked in turn.

Nash frowned mightily. "My men are still looking. Lord James thought he saw something and took himself away after it."

"Not alone, I hope."

"No, certainly not."

Mr. Farr, supremely unhappy that such an awful murder had occurred in his house, pushed forward. "What I want to know is why anyone would do such a wretched thing. I run a very respectable place and this—" He clenched his hands, shaking them for want of words to express his outrage and fear.

"Revenge, possibly," said Dr. Beldon. "There are people aplenty hereabouts who would be happy to see someone like Knox in hell."

"He'd have been sent there soon as we were done with him," Nash grumbled. "First those two escapes and now this one shot before we could hang him. Mark me, I think his own rebel friends murdered him so he wouldn't betray them to us."

This inspired a rumbling murmur of agreement from the crowded room. Not one of us—least of all I—had any doubts over the viciousness of the so-called patriots who had troubled the whole county. That they should turn upon one of their own to save themselves was a dreadful and cowardly act, but not terribly surprising.

Nash was not only partial to his idea, but more than willing to act upon it. "Mr. Barrett, I'll want a complete description of the men who kidnapped you, as much as you can remember right down to the least scrap of clothing on their backs. Write it out. I want something I can pass along to my men. I'll be finding these traitors if I have to turn over every stone in the county."

CHAPTER
—11—

May 1777

"You're more quiet than usual," observed Elizabeth.

"I didn't know it was usual for me to be quiet."

"It has been lately. What's been bothering you?"

"Long days and short nights." For me, such a complaint had quite a bit different meaning than it did for other people.

"And nothing else?"

"Waiting for Nora to reply, or at least for Oliver to send a letter. It's been ages." Plenty of time for a letter to find its way to the Warburton family in Italy and for them to pass it on to Nora. I worried that it had gone astray somehow, undelivered while I sat half a world away impatiently fuming for an answer that would never come.

"I thought it might be because of those men," she said.

That was how the household had come to refer to Ash and the other cutthroats. "Why should you think that?"

"Because that's when you started being so quiet."

And also when I discovered Norwood's liaison with Molly Audy. I didn't like having the knowledge, and keeping it a secret was affecting my behavior with Elizabeth. I was tempted to unburden myself about it, if not to her then to Father, or perhaps even Beldon, but since that time Norwood had not gone whoring. Of that I was sure since I'd made a habit of "questioning" Molly whenever I paid my respects. At least, a whispering voice in my head said, he hadn't been whoring with *her*. With all the soldiers around, there were any number of camp followers about, and if not as pretty or as skilled as Molly, they were cheap. I remembered her mention of his parsimony over the price.

A little "talk" between us would clear the air and either cancel my doubts or confirm them. If the latter, then Norwood and I would have a very serious talk, indeed. But I'd been putting it off, as one does any potentially unpleasant task.

"You haven't said much about it." Elizabeth brought me back to the present with her misplaced assumption about my reticence.

"Haven't really wanted to. Or needed to," I added, looking up at her with as much reassurance as I could muster.

She met my eyes over the mound of sewing piled before her on the dining table and hopefully saw that her gentle concern was appreciated, but not necessary.

"What about yourself?" I asked. "Getting nervous?"

"Only about whether I'll have this finished in time." She indicated the satin and silk she was sewing together.

"You will."

"So everyone tells me."

"The others would help if you'd let them."

She smiled and shook her head. "No, thank you. Sewing my own wedding dress has long been a fancy of mine, and I'll not ask others to share it with me."

The initial formalities had come and gone months ago. Lord James Norwood asked Elizabeth if he might petition Father for her hand in marriage and had been answered in a most positive manner. Father had granted permission in his turn, with the reluctance and pride all fathers experience when they must give up their daughters, and since then the house had been busy with preparations for the wedding. Much of it had to do with the making of many new clothes for the bride, and while Elizabeth had gratefully accepted help for her other dresses and things, she'd reserved the most important project for herself.

It was taking longer than expected. Amid the housecleaning, the hiring of new servants, the parties of congratulation and celebration and the thousand other details that seemed to arise when two people decide to join forces, Elizabeth hadn't had much time for her project. She rose early before the sun to work and was still at it long after dark. I kept her company, for the time was fast approaching when we would no longer be able to have these quiet talks. Soon Norwood would sweep her away and things would never be the same again. Well could I understand Father's mixed feelings in the matter. I was happy for Elizabeth's happiness, but sorry for myself at losing her.

I'd picked up a slight edge in her tone, or thought I had. "Has Mother been troublesome?"

"What do you mean?"

"I just wondered if anything had happened today."

"No. *She's* been quiet enough."

True, very true. Since that one talk I'd had with her, Mother had been behaving with remarkable restraint. She still ignored us as much as possible, but was otherwise almost civil. There was a marked lessening of her biting sarcasm, no shows of temper, no tantrums, no berserk fits, and far more important to me, no laudanum turning up in Father's tea. He commented now and then about the change in her, but thought it to be a result of Elizabeth's physical confrontation with her last December. I knew better, but still did not care to enlighten him about it, and if he'd guessed, he kept it to himself. As he cautiously (and more discreetly) resumed visiting with Mrs. Montagu, I found a great easing for any strain my conscience might have felt over the matter.

"What about her toady, then?" Things had been rather uneasy between Elizabeth and Mrs. Hardinbrook lately. The lady's disappointment at Elizabeth's marrying Norwood instead of Beldon had festered into bitterness.

"She's a fool and a wretch," Elizabeth said in a low voice. She flushed deep red and promptly pricked her finger on her next stitch.

I picked up the bloodsmell right away, but easily dismissed it. "What's she done?"

"It's what she says, and she says it in the nicest way possible. I'd managed to forget about it until now."

But not very well, since I'd noticed something wasn't quite right with her. "Tell me."

She stopped sewing and heaved a great sigh. "It was this afternoon when we were receiving some of Mother's cronies. Even if she doesn't look at me if she can help it, I had to be there. It's usually bearable, but Mrs. Hardinbrook had her head together with that awful cat, Mrs. Osburn. She was talking just loud enough for me to hear, but not enough so that I could really make a comment about it. You know how they—"

"Yes, I've seen it in practice. Go on."

"She was all pleasantries about me, but what she was saying was still full of spite."

"What did she say?"

"Well, it was about how *lucky* I was that Lord James had picked me. So very *lucky* that I hadn't ended up an old maid, after all. You'd think that James and I hadn't come to our determination together or that he'd taken pity on me or something."

"The bitch," I said evenly.

"Then she started going on about all the money he'd come into once we were married and as much as implied that *that* was why he'd proposed. They laughed about it, because she'd make a joke of it, but it wasn't nice laughter. I looked at her to let her know I'd heard and all she did was smile back, pretending otherwise. How I hate her."

"She's a fool, definitely, and not worth your notice."

"I try to think that, but it's hard. I don't know how a person can go to church every Sunday, appear to listen so closely, and then act as she does toward me. It's wicked."

"The more so because she knows what's she's doing to you."

Her lips came together a moment and there was an excess of water in her eyes. "You don't know about this, but when you came home hurt from Mrs. Montagu's . . ."

"What?"

"Well, I overheard that beastly woman asking our mother who would get your share of Grandfather's estate should something happen to you."

That left me stunned at her bad manners, but not too terribly surprised.

"I—damnation—I'm finding myself cringing inside like a child whenever I see her, waiting for the next bit of poison to come spewing out. Sometimes I know what she's going to say next and then she says it, as though she's hearing my very thoughts. I don't know how Dr. Beldon puts up with her. Sometimes all I want to do is . . ." One of her hands formed into a fist, then she let it relax. "But if I did that then I'd feel awful afterward."

"Not nearly so bad as Mrs. Hardinbrook. She'd feel *much* worse."

She glanced up, her eyes slowly kindling with the beginnings of a smile. "You think so?"

"Oh, yes. She'd feel terrible. Can you imagine her consternation trying to cover the bruises with rice flour? There wouldn't be enough of that stuff on the Island to do a proper job of it."

Elizabeth fell into my humor, speculating, "I could black her eye . . ."

"Knock out a tooth or two in the front . . ."

"Cut her hair and throw her wigs down the well . . ."

"I wouldn't go that far, it'd foul the water."

By then she was laughing freely and when it had worn itself out, I saw that her usual good spirits had reasserted themselves.

"There," I said. "The next time you see her, try thinking of her as looking like that. She'll go mad trying to figure out what's amusing you so much."

"I don't know how I shall manage without you, little brother."

"You won't be living that far away. I shall visit so often, you and James will be sick of seeing my face."

"Never." She went back to her sewing again. "But I know that things will change. They always do when someone gets married. I've seen it happen to my friends, how they break away and move on like leaves dropping from a tree. The wind catches them up and off they go. I shouldn't like that."

"Then make sure James knows and perhaps you can avoid it."

"I can tell him, but there are some things that can't be avoided. You know he's talked about taking me to England. We'll probably even stay there. I might never see you or Father ever again." She looked in danger of tears.

"You can always call off the wedding."

The danger instantly passed. "I can't do that!"

"Well, then." I spread my hands.

She made a kind of growling sigh. "All right. Perhaps I *am* getting nervous."

"You've every right to be considering what you're taking on. It's not only getting married, but setting up your own household, getting the servants to work together . . ."

She nearly shuddered. "I can handle the ones I engage well enough, but that Harridge fellow makes me feel like I should curtsy every time he walks into the room."

In the front hall or the servants' hall, Norwood's valet was not a popular man.

"He's going to be a perfect ogre to the others, I know it," she said.

"Keep him busy enough with duties and maybe he won't have the time for it. That should be easy with all the work to be done in the new house."

She muttered a guarded agreement, but I could see the reminder of what was to come had been a cheering one. She was very much looking forward to setting up her own home.

By some miracle Norwood had found a suitable dwelling halfway between Glenbriar and Glenbriar Landing and had rented it, calling it their "nuptial cottage." The miracle had been finding anything at all. By now Long Island was not only flooded with soldiers, but with prisoners of war, and all of them in need of lodging. I suspected that Norwood had used his own kind of influence to secure it, trading on his title as much and as often as possible.

It was no vast hall, but certainly much more than a cottage, having belonged to a gentleman who had had the misfortune of being home when the zealous Colonel Heard and his troop of traitors had come calling over a year ago. Heard had already been to Hempstead hell-bent on extracting oaths of loyalty for his American "congress." Father had been caught up in that farce himself and had managed to shrug it off, but this other gentleman had not. Keenly feeling the humiliation of being forced to take an oath to support an illegal government he'd neither voted for or wanted, he'd put his place up for sale and packed his family off to Canada that summer—just before Lord Howe's arrival.

The house stood empty for only as long as it took for some officers to claim it and move in, and, being gentlemen, they hadn't the faintest idea how to organize anything of a domestic nature. It became very run-down, very quickly, enough so that any prospective buyer would turn away before passing the gate. The officers had long moved out, following Lord Howe to New York. With no owner present and the agent for the sale desperate for any kind of money, he'd been most eager to agree to the pittance Norwood had offered in the way of rent. His lordship had pointed out, quite correctly, that the house needed repairs and the only other likely occupants would be prisoners with little or no money at all. An agreement was made, and Norwood and his bride would soon be taking up residence.

Far too soon for me. I would miss my sister very much. Far more than when I'd been packed off to Cambridge. It didn't matter that she'd be living only a couple of miles away, things would change between us.

I supposed that it would be easier if I liked Norwood better, but that business about Molly had infused me with a difficult to overcome prejudice. For Elizabeth's sake I'd tried not to let it bother me and had been fairly successful. Time would inform me on whether I could maintain the attitude with any degree of sincerity.

"You're quiet again."

Time to make an effort, I thought, and assumed a sadly serious face. "Well, I . . . had a question for you."

She caught my tone and put aside the sewing once more, giving me all her attention, and bracing herself for whatever was to come.

"Tell me, when you write letters will you sign yourself as 'Elizabeth' or as 'Lady James Norwood'?"

She threw her thimble at me.

The spring lambing had been good, despite the best efforts by the army commissary, and it looked like we'd be having if not a profitable year, then at least a comfortable one. Nash kept himself very busy, ranging farther afield searching out the Island's bounty, but under my "tutelage" he'd turned into quite an honest fellow, paying the farmers for their goods. Mind you, it was a terrific wrench against his basic nature, so he was never too comfortable whenever he saw me coming. The lukewarm smile he wore when I walked into The Oak's common room tonight was the best that could be expected given the circumstances.

I hailed him like a long-lost friend and asked if I could have the pleasure of buying him a drink. Several of the regular customers, hoping to take a share of my generosity, soon crowded in to give me their greetings. Eternally parched Noddy Milverton moved in right next to me without my having to trouble myself to arrange it.

Nash accepted the offer and somehow all the others were included, and they drank to my health.

"Anything in the post, Mr. Farr?" I asked.

"A few things did chance to come in today," he said, fetching them. Chance indeed, for the post had not been a model of efficiency lately. He lay a string-tied packet before me and I made use of my penknife to cut it open. Had my heart been beating, it would have been audible from my surge of hope. But the hope was short-lived and the dashing of it was not unnoticed.

"Nothing from England?" sympathized Farr. He knew from my almost nightly visits to his place that I was expecting an important letter from there.

"No." Some stuff for Father from Hempstead, some things for Elizabeth, a note for Beldon. My disappointment was very acute. Noddy Milverton took the opportunity to swiftly drain my ale and continue his simpleminded innocence.

"Sorry."

"Another time, then." I asked for and got the latest gossip. There had been a raid at Sands Cove, with stock carried off in whaleboats. A valuable bull had been part of the haul, and the unhappy owner was both enraged and sickened that his breeding animal was probably already hanging from a hook in some distant butchery.

"What's to be done about it?" I asked Nash, rather unfairly putting him on the spot in front of everyone.

But he'd heard that question often enough and was ready for it. "All that can be done. The men up there watch the coast like hawks, but they can't be everywhere at once."

"There oughter be a way o' stoppin' 'um," someone put in.

"There is. The army is doing its best to track down the traitors across the Sound. Once order is restored you'll be free of trouble soon enough."

No one was encouraged by this pronouncement, but they'd not get anything different from him and knew better than to try. Most retired to other parts of the room, grumbling a little, but not to the point of rudeness. Nash was content to ignore them.

"This raid at Sands Cove," I said in a lower voice. "Any familiar faces there?"

He knew I meant Ash and his lot. "The descriptions were too vague to be sure. The fellows were definitely from Connecticut by their talk, according to the farmer. The rest of his family had been badly frightened, but he—well, I've rarely seen a man so spitting mad before. Thought he'd burst a blood vessel from it."

He must have been angry indeed for Nash to notice, having so blithely annoyed quite a lot of people with his collections. I made no comment on it. "Then there's been no fresh word on any of them?"

"None."

As there seemed little point in continuing the conversation, I bade him a polite good evening and retired to one of the chairs to listen to the other men's gossip. Nash, I thought, glimpsing at him from the corner of my eye, looked relieved. It must have been hard on him, always being vaguely uncomfortable about me and never knowing why.

The talk was more of the same, but leavened with a curse or two directed at the troublemakers. Occasionally the British army or the Hessians were the targets of their ire, but only in the lowest of tones. I fell under the eye of Mr. Curtis, who gestured for me to come closer, which I did. Room was made and I sat next to him.

"Well, Mr. Barrett, is that reward you're offering still good?"

Months ago I'd put up a sum of money for the arrest of my kidnappers. So far no one had been able to claim it. "It is."

"Real money?"

"In gold. What do you know?"

He didn't quite answer the question. "Just wanted to be sure of it in case we ran into 'em."

My brows went up. "You think there's a chance of that?"

He and the others were amused. "I reckon we might see a new face an' it wouldn't hurt to be wise about it."

"No, not at all."

More amusement and I joined them, albeit grimly now that I understood what they were about. Connecticut had its raiders, and so now did Long Island, and I was sitting with a few of them. It was a clear night, with a bright full moon, though, else they'd already be out trying to repay the many insults our neighbor across the Sound had made to us. I could imagine both sides passing each other in their whaleboats, all unknowing, the next time conditions for a stealthy crossing occurred.

"Mr. Curtis, I was wondering if you'd heard anything about raiders coming in from Suffolk County."

"I'm not as near there as you are. You'd know more'n me, wouldn't you?"

"Yes, but you have been blessed with a sharper ear than most. I thought some word might have come your way."

He shook his head. "What's your idea?"

"It's something Mr. Nash just said about the thieves he missed catching." I won a smile from them at Nash's expense.

"What 'uz that?"

"He said they must have been from Connecticut from their talk, and it seemed to me to have two meanings, that they either spoke of the place or the place itself was in their speech. An accent."

"What of it?"

"Well, I was recalling how those men spoke to me, and I don't think one of them had a Connecticut accent."

"It don't mean that they weren't from there, though. Lots of folk have had to move around with this war on."

"Perhaps so. But it was a very windy night back then and even after the wind had died, the sea would be no friend to anyone in a boat trying to make the crossing. I was thinking it might be easier for them to row along the shore for a few miles until they were deeper into Suffolk County."

"I'm no whaling man, but it makes sense to me. What'll you do about it?"

"There's not much I can do, except pass the word on to Mr. Nash and hope some good comes of it."

"Then good luck to you both, I'm sure."

Now the laugh was at my expense, I took it good-naturedly, knowing full well the seed had been planted. If any of them heard a whisper, I'd know about it. I wished them good luck in turn and took my leave.

Even after spending some time with (and money on) Molly Audy, I was home again just before midnight, and slightly startled to see lights still burning in the music room. I peered in the window. Mother, Mrs. Hardinbrook, Beldon, and Lady Caroline were at cards. Beldon and Lady Caroline were yawning their heads off. This was the latest I'd ever seen any of them stay up to play, but Mother was quite addicted to the games after all. If she insisted on another hand or two, she could count on Mrs. Hardinbrook to enthusiastically join in, dragging her brother along. Lady Caroline played, I thought, to be polite.

The rest of the house was dark and quiet, with everyone else presumably in bed. Father wasn't home, having left for an overnight trip to Hempstead, though I knew him to really be at Mrs. Montagu's. I wished him well. No doubt he'd left a stack of work for me in the library, but it wouldn't hurt to delay my start on it for a while. Molly had, as usual, put me into a mellow frame of mood and mind; I was content to stand outside and watch.

And wait.

The game went on, with Beldon and Lady Caroline growing more sleepy by the minute. Even Mrs. Hardinbrook was starting to droop. Mother was quite alert, though, her movements crisp. There was a certain nervousness in her manner, but that was familiar to us all. She had been staying up later and later over the months, asking for just one more hand, or continuing a conversation beyond its natural close. I don't think she slept very well, for I'd heard her pacing in her room at odd hours. Beldon gave her sleeping draughts when she asked for them, and though she drank them straight down, they must not have been doing her much good.

Now she looked to be trying the patience of her staunchest supporter, for when the hand was finished, Mrs. Hardinbrook made a great show of weariness and rose. Beldon lurched to his feet as well, then Lady Caroline. Mother remained seated and I felt an unexpected stab of pity for her as she looked up at them. She looked . . . lost. I hadn't forgotten how she never let herself be alone if she could help it.

It was probably awful for her, but there was little I could do about it. I had other things to concern me.

Beldon escorted Lady Caroline out of the room. They'd likely go straight up to their respective beds. Excellent. Mrs. Hardinbrook lingered, putting the cards away and offering one-word replies to anything Mother said. She put out all but two of the candles, taking one for herself and giving the other to Mother.

I pushed away from the window and, fading slightly, willed myself to silently drift around the house toward the back. It was still a clear night, but this side was in deep shadow, so I thought I could risk such behavior. The late hour was very much in my favor as well; all the servants would be asleep, even the lordly Mr. Harridge. I let myself rise up to a second-floor window, faded away completely, and sieved through the shutters. There was a moment of brittle discomfort as I crossed the glass barrier of the window, then I was floating free in the hallway.

Waiting still, but not for long.

A door closed down the hall and around a corner. Mother's. Now Mrs. Hardinbrook would be coming along to her room. I went solid and saw that I was right. The glow of her candle announced her approach. She didn't half give a jump when she saw me standing by the window.

"Oh! Mr. Barrett, whatever are you doing there?"

"Just making sure the window is bolted. Can't be too careful these days."

"One certainly can't. Well, good night."

"A moment, please, I had a question for you."

That also surprised her, for I never spoke to her if I could avoid it.

"Yes, what is it?"

I stepped closer into the light so she could see me.

It didn't take long. And I'd had plenty of practice with people like Nash . . . and Drummond. I got her attention, saw her brightly empty face grow a little emptier, and that was that.

"I want you to cease being so cruel toward Elizabeth. Do you understand me?"

She whispered that she did. The candle began to tremble. I took it away before she dropped it.

"There's no room in this house for any of your spite. You can be civil or you needn't say anything at all. Understand?"

"Yes . . ."

Unpleasant woman, but perhaps less so now. "That's very kind of you, then." I released her from my influence. "I shall bid you a good night, Mrs. Hardinbrook."

She blinked several times and became suddenly puzzled at how her candle had jumped into my hand without her noticing. I didn't bother to explain, but gave it back to her with a little bow. Disturbed, she scuttled into her room and shut the door between us. I turned away, only just managing to keep my laughter silent. Though I'd not mention it to her, this was one of my wedding presents to Elizabeth. With all the other things claiming her attention, she could do without Mrs. Hardinbrook's little observations and innuendos. After the wedding it wouldn't matter, but at least until then there would be a bit more peace in the household.

I stopped dead cold. *Damnation.*

Beldon was standing at the corner, holding a candle high in one hand, with a book in the other. He'd probably been on his way to the library and had obviously seen and heard everything. I knew that what I'd said to Mrs. Hardinbrook had been innocent enough, if a trifle rude, but it might still be taken as a very odd exchange. From the look on his face, he'd correctly interpreted it in that manner. He stared and stared and stared, not moving, hardly even breathing.

I stared back, not knowing what to do or say until the long silence began to pile up between us, thick and dreadful, and I came to the reluctant conclusion I'd have to influence him as well. To make him forget what he'd seen.

But he never gave me that chance. He whipped around, heading for his room. Heart in my belly, I went after him.

"Dr. Beldon," I whispered, putting some urgency, not unmixed with exasperation, into it.

He surprised me again by stopping cold in the hallway. He did not turn to face me, but did wait, back all stiff, for me to catch him up. When I was even with him, he gave every evidence of acute discomfort.

"Doctor—"

"Mr. Barrett—"

Knowing ahead of time that I would certainly have the last word, I indicated for him to go ahead.

"I'm sorry," he said. "I did not intend to intrude upon your conversation with Deborah."

"You what?"

"I should have said something when I passed by, but I thought it best to . . . well . . ."

That's when I abruptly realized that his reaction was not that of fear, but rather tremendous embarrassment. *Well-a-day.*

"Deborah," he continued, "often forgets that we are your guests. She's not a very clever woman, that is to say . . . I've tried to talk to her, but she's never been one to listen to me."

I started to speak, but he raised one hand.

"No, please, I just wanted to apologize for her behavior. I'm very sorry if she's caused any distress to your family, especially to your dear sister. I also wanted to say that I'm very glad that you did talk to her just now. It's . . . long overdue. My chief regret is that I have not been more firm with her in the past."

"I . . . don't know what to say, sir," I muttered. "If I have been overly brusk with—"

"No, you spoke your mind to her and that was what was needed."

"You're uncommonly kind, sir."

"As you have been to me, sir, many, many times over." I knew that he harbored a genuine affection for my family, but often as not his natural reticence prevented him from expressing it. I also knew that he harbored a particularly deep affection for me, but had never acted upon it. Now he did look square upon me, and I saw what it was costing him to be so direct. He was skimming rather close to issues that we had long since tabled and was perhaps afraid I might misinterpret his gratitude for something else.

I smiled back at him, offering reassurance. "'Tis my honor to do so, sir," I said, and gave a little bow.

His relief was hardly subtle, his shoulders visibly relaxed, and a tentative smile crept over his own worried features. "Thank you, Mr. Barrett."

"At your service, Dr. Beldon."

"Good night, then."

"And to you." Having apparently forgotten the errand that had taken him out to start with, he returned to his room. With a light step.

Well-a-day, I thought again.

Despite his sometime toad-eating manner, I'd come to regard Beldon as a friend, never more so than now. I'd influenced him before, but only to protect the secret of my changed nature. Such intrusions upon so inoffensive a man often plagued my conscience; I was more than happy to forgo another experience. Thank heavens for his parochial mind, that he'd seen no more than what had seemed natural to him and had not attributed anything outre to it.

With an equally light step, I made my way downstairs, so vastly relieved that I forgot the late hour and began to whistle.

Nights came and went swiftly, blurring together so that I sometimes had the illusion of living through one very lengthy night punctuated only by changes of clothes. The conversations all seemed to be the same, since they concerned but one topic: the wedding. The people were certainly the same. It might have been tedious, but my past experiences had taught me a hard lesson on the priceless value of boredom. Better to be inactive and at peace in the world than to be subjected to the frantic racing about brought on by catastrophe.

Father saw to his practice, Elizabeth sewed on her dress, and I kept them company or went down to The Oak to hear the news. As expected, Mrs. Hardinbrook ceased to be quite so hatefully annoying and looked after Mother, who had come to be remarkably restrained in her manner. She worried me, for I thought she might still be suffering from fright. I tried to catch her eye now and then, but hers would slide past as though I were not there. She played cards, or sewed, or gossiped when such friends as she had came calling, but if she were afraid of me, it did not show. Several times I overheard her requesting sleeping draughts from Beldon, but they must have had an indifferent effect on her, for I'd still hear her moving about in her room late at night and on into the early morning hours. She looked a bit haggard from the lack of sleep and was more withdrawn than before, but that was preferable to her fits.

No one else marked it, though, being so busy with their own projects, and I had no plans to draw it to anyone's attention. After a time I came to consider it to be just another in a series of unpleasant incidents no one ever talked about and was content to let life run on as usual.

There were plenty of genteel distractions in the early hours of the shortening summer evenings. Cousin Anne had persuaded me to join her in reading some Shakespeare to the others by way of entertainment. Her first choice was the first play I'd recommended, *Twelfth Night*, and she turned out to be something of a natural actress—once she understood what she was saying. Of course, most of the base jokes in the text escaped her and the whole room had a moment of bald embarrassment when she stopped the reading once to ask the meaning of the word "eunuch."

Elizabeth, gallantly stifling a laugh, came to my rescue, saying that it was a boy who would never grow to become a man. Anne's comprehension was questionable, for we continued with no further pauses. Afterward, she sought out Elizabeth for a highly intense conversation.

I found myself too curious to resist. When Anne had finished and glided off, I moved in. "What did she ask you this time?"

Elizabeth kept her laughter quiet and kindly. "Goodness, she should be more observant about what's going on around her here in the country. Then she'd know about these things."

"What things?"

"She wanted to know how a boy could not help but grow into a man, what could possibly prevent it. So I tried a comparison employing the gelding of horses—"

"Good God, Elizabeth!"

"It's close enough," she defended, still trying not to laugh. "I said that since a stallion has private parts to be gelded, then so does a man, and if he is deprived of them at a certain age . . ."

I was all but choking. "Then what?"

"Well, she did want to know . . ." Now she stopped and blushed a very violent red.

I leaned forward, looking expectant.

She gave me a mock-severe look in return. "You're being coarse and prurient, Jonathan."

"Absolutely. What did she want to know?"

She gave up in disgust. "Appearance."

I did choke on that one and fought in vain to hold onto a sober face. "And what did you tell her?"

"*Jonathan!*"

Time to retreat, which I did, laughing, but vowing to avoid any solitary interviews with Anne for the time being. She'd been curious about kissing, which I'd been happy to help on, but I wasn't at all ready to provide answers should she decide to question me on this particular topic. Some days later, Elizabeth informed me that a solution had presented itself during a visit to a friend with an infant boy. When the child's natural requirements dictated a change of diaper, Elizabeth volunteered to do the task for the mother and took Anne along to help. The experience proved to be sufficiently educational to satisfy our sweetly innocent cousin, so I was safe once more.

Also after that incident, having learned the value of discretion, Anne made a point to reserve further inquiries about unfamiliar words until the end of an evening.

And then one day the wedding dress was finished and the event itself was upon us. I was unaware of most of it, being confined to my usually quiet bed in the cellar, but the first thing I heard the instant the sun was gone was one of Mrs. Nooth's many helpers clattering around in search of some supply for the kitchen. I was glad not to have to breathe, for the place reeked of cooking and baking. As soon as the helper was gone, I vanished and let myself float up through the very floors of the house, reappearing in my upstairs room.

Jericho was waiting there for me and only jumped a little when I arrived.

We shared chagrined smiles, then I asked, "How have things been today?"

"Fairly easy. We have not yet run out of food and the young son of one of the guests provided some unexpected entertainment by tumbling from the hayloft and breaking his fall in the muck heap outside the stable."

"Oh, lord."

"Precisely what his mother said, plus quite a bit more. Their own servants saw to his cleaning up, I'm glad to say. It could not have been an especially pleasant job."

"Is everyone else all right?"

"Oh, yes. Mr. Barrett is making sure all the gentlemen have sufficient food with their drink, so there have been no incidents even when politics are being discussed. Miss Elizabeth is well enough, considering."

For the last week Elizabeth had been harried by all the last-minute tasks and planning. She had a true talent for organization, though, otherwise she might not have made it this far.

"Everyone has been asking for you throughout the day," he said, letting me know that I should hurry.

My best clothes had been carefully laid out on the bed and he had the shaving things ready, the water still gently steaming. He must have walked in seconds before me. The man had impeccable timing. Without another word, we fell into our long-practiced routine. He had me shaved, powdered, and dressed fit for a royal audience, or even my sister's wedding, without hurry, yet in a very short time. I'd discovered that it went much faster when I did not argue with him on his choice of clothes for me and offered none now.

He had me very well trained.

Once downstairs and giving belated greetings to the vast number of guests, I felt as though I were back in London again, attending one of the Bolyn family's many lavish parties. War notwithstanding, everyone else was also in their best, either made new for the occasion or refurbished to look like new.

Molly Audy had had a surfeit of custom for her legitimate business and scarcely time for anything else, even if it did pay better. After one of our necessarily briefer liaisons, I asked why she even bothered with the sewing and was informed that she derived a great deal of satisfaction from it. This inspired a further query from me, asking if the two businesses—or pleasures as was the case—were remotely comparable in terms of enjoyment, and I promptly got a pillow in my face.

Though discreet herself, her workmanship was strongly in evidence tonight. I recognized many of her completed commissions on the backs (and backsides) of a number of gentlemen, having seen the fabrics and garments in various stages of development in her workroom. They had me wondering which of them availed themselves of both of Molly's services, and doubtless they were thinking the same thing as they eyed each other. I was made exempt from this, in that my clothes had been made in London.

Norwood, too, I noticed with approval, wore a familiar-looking coat, though the waistcoat was new. A gift from Elizabeth. His innate thriftiness had probably encouraged him to use what he had rather than invest in any expansion of his wardrobe. Like me, he might also have a preference for London tailors. I didn't care so long as it meant he was keeping clear of Molly.

I greeted my prospective brother-in-law with a light thump on the back and was relieved to see that he wasn't even remotely drunk, though he seemed rather relaxed for a groom.

"What, have you done this before?" I asked with a gesture at the wedding party.

He laughed. "I don't know why everyone expects me to be nervous. I'm not, really. Really I'm not. Really."

Ah, now *there* was a bit of strain to him, after all. Very cheering, to be sure.

Elizabeth, when I found her, was in the center of a virtual garden of gowns. So thickly were her friends gathered 'round her that their wide-reaching dresses scarcely left any space in the room. I was bumped and crowded and made over and teased as I made my way to her, being very careful where I put my feet, especially around the seated ladies, who had spread their skirts out to show them off. None, I thought, were more beautiful than Elizabeth's, and certainly none of the women wearing them were as beautiful, either.

I bowed deeply and kissed her hand and wished her the best of all possible days. My throat was clogging and my eyes stung a bit.

"Thank you, little brother." She smiled back at me, looking utterly radiant, and I was ready to burst with pride in her. "It's been a truly marvelous day, but now . . ."

"Night is here with my arrival, or is it the other way around?"

"You ass!" But she softened her humor. "You wonderful ass."

"Coming soon, is it?"

She gulped. "Yes, very soon."

"I'm glad you arranged things so I could be here to see."

"That's all Father's doing."

"How is he?"

"Being fatherly. When I came downstairs he had to use his handkerchief a lot. Tried to pretend he had dust in his eyes, but I knew better."

"I know how he feels. All I can say is be happy, Elizabeth."

"I will. I know I will."

And within the hour she married Lord James Norwood amid tears and laughter and glorious celebration. Thus did we observe and acknowledge the change that came to all our lives.

CHAPTER
—12—

June 1777

Though larger campaigns of destruction were being undertaken by the armies in the greater world outside, we were naturally most concerned for our own area, having endured a number of raids, both bold and vicious. Some of the thieves were caught, and those without commission papers were hanged. Hardworking farmers made desperate by the loss of their produce to the British and the rebels turned to thieving themselves as a means of survival and revenge. Some of them joined with the local militia, others preferred to work on their own. One such group included Mr. Curtis, Mr. Davis, and even Noddy Milverton on occasion. Whenever they were absent from The Oak, it was generally accepted they'd "gone fishing" along the Connecticut coast. No one objected to it, least of all Lieutenant Nash.

Some of the Hessian troops had been transferred out, both to the relief and annoyance of the locals. Our barn was empty once more, as was Mrs. Montagu's. They were hated company, but their presence had been a curtailment to the raids. Father worried for her and visited as often as he could. He'd gifted her with several pistols and a good hunting rifle and had gone to no little trouble to teach her and her servants how to shoot well. The lady had also taken to increasing the numbers of geese around her home, being of the same opinion as the old Romans that they were better than dogs for giving the alarm.

But though the times were hard, we knew they were much worse elsewhere, so we thanked God for our lot and prayed for a swift victory over our enemies and the restoration of peace.

The sun rose later each night and arrived sooner each day, but I'd gotten over the feeling of being deprived of my waking hours. When I lay my head down, the dawn brought such complete oblivion that I had no knowledge of the day's passage, hence the continuation of my illusion of living one endless night. I seemed to find plenty of time to do all that I wanted; I had no more complaints.

I did become a frequent visitor to Elizabeth's new house. She'd made it into a very pretty place despite Norwood's objections to the expense.

"I think it's because of his plans to go back to England," she confided to me. "He thinks it's a waste of money to put it into a house we won't be staying in for very long."

"What's he mean by that? Are you to leave so soon?" The idea had been there for some time, but only in the abstract. Now Elizabeth was speaking as though they were already starting to pack for the journey.

"Oh, not for a while, perhaps. Maybe a year or so."

"That's something, then," I said grudgingly. Though my perception of time had been skewed by my change, a year still seemed a very great interval. "I mean, if you really want to leave . . ."

"Actually, I don't, but I should go and meet his family. I'm rather curious about how a duke lives."

"Doesn't he tell you?"

"Not always. I hear more about his dead ancestors than the living relatives. Do you know his people were at Agincourt? It seems that I've married into a very famous family."

I looked on as she sewed away on some humble task, her head bowed over her work. She'd changed, a bit, and would change more as most of her interests came to center upon her new life. "Are you happy about it?"

"It's not very real to me yet. All I know is James. He's what's real."

"Are you happy with him?"

"Yes, certainly I'm happy. How can you ask such a thing?"

"Just playing the protective brother, is all."

"That can't be all. Don't you like him?"

"Well, yes, but you can't expect me to be in favor of his taking you away to England someday. Father and I would miss you terribly."

"And I would miss you both terribly, but I have to go with my husband. That's the way things are."

"Then it's not right. You should have a say in where you want to live."

"I know, but I'm sure things will work out for the best no matter where we are."

She was in love and would follow her husband. I was only her brother and it wasn't my place to object.

Lady Caroline had come over earlier that day for a visit and had stayed longer than expected. My arrival soon after dusk was greeted with surprise. She had been going to spend the night rather than risk traveling after dark, but at the conclusion of my visit she asked me to escort her home.

"But the roads might be dangerous," said Norwood.

"It will be perfectly safe," I replied. I had confidence in my ability to see and hear a potential hazard long before it saw me. "I'll be going by way of Glenbriar to check the post."

"For that letter from England? I hope it comes soon, or you shall wear out your welcome at the inn."

"I shouldn't want to be any trouble," said Lady Caroline.

"No trouble," I told her. "Besides, Anne will miss your company. She had her heart set on reading that scene with you of Portia and Nerissa discussing the suitors in *The Merchant of Venice*."

"So she did. I recall she wanted you to play the Prince of Morocco."

"And the Prince of Arragon—and Bassanio, too, if there's time."

"She's turned into quite the scholar."

"Actress, more like. If she continues like this, Mr. Garrick will have to come out of retirement."

"Who?"

"David Garrick, the actor."

"Oh, goodness, of course. For some reason I thought you meant one of the farmers hereabouts."

"You'll not catch many of them with time for reading Shakespeare."

"Or aught else, I'm sure."

"I'll go see to the horses, then." I went off toward the miserable-looking structure that served as a stable. Elizabeth had once mentioned her desire to repair and improve it before the winter, lightly complaining when Norwood asked to put it off a while longer. I wondered if his tight-fisted nature would soon be a source of discontent for her.

They had no stablemen, not even a lad to see to their own beasts. Norwood claimed that he enjoyed looking after them himself, which was understandable to me, but I thought it odd for a man in his position not to have at least one servant for the task. There wasn't that much work to do, though, with but two horses. He had a hunter and Elizabeth had brought along her favorite from home, Beauty. So far they had not yet acquired a carriage, not that there were many to be had these days. When Sunday came along, Father would send a man along in ours to pick them up for church.

I'd taken up riding again to give Rolly some much needed exercise and make a change for me. This included my wish to avoid being seen floating about. I'd been spotted twice, but fortunately both times the men had been rather drunk and no one believed their story about a "flying ghost." After that I became more careful.

Taking Rolly's reins and those of Lady Caroline's horse, I walked back to the house in no particular hurry, but unwilling to waste time. Elizabeth had already said good night and gone upstairs, leaving Norwood and his sister in the front entry. They were speaking in low tones and looked to be having some kind of a disagreement. Before I'd quite gotten close enough to hear anything above the noise of the horses, they broke off and acted as though nothing were amiss. Well, if they wished it to be so, then I would act in kind. I helped Lady Caroline up to her sidesaddle, swung onto Rolly, and bade farewell to Norwood. He stood in the doorway and watched us until we were out of sight down the lane.

"Was there anything wrong between you two?" I asked.

"Not really. He's just worried about my being out, but I told him that we'd be fine."

It had looked more interesting than simple concern, but if so, then she was determined to keep it to herself.

"You are armed, I hope?" she asked.

"I'd feel undressed without these." I touched the specially made case hanging from my saddle that held a set of duelers

I'd bought on a whim in London. Since my abduction, I took them everywhere, loaded, and ready at hand. "And you?"

Instead of the "muff gun" favored by some ladies, she pulled out a formidable brass-barreled specimen made by Powell of Dublin that was capable of firing six shots, one after another. It was an amazing piece of work, and I had hopes of someday acquiring one myself. Its appeal lay in the fact that after an initial priming, all one had to do was to pull back the trigger guard after each shot, turn the cylinder, and push the guard forward to lock it, then fire again. Six in a row without reloading. An absolutely marvelous invention.

Our safety assured by our arms collection, we kicked the horses up with confidence and cantered toward Glenbriar. It wasn't far, and I found the ride shortened by her pleasing company. Almost before I knew it, we were reining up before The Oak. As this night I was only interested in the post and not buying a round of drinks and time with Molly Audy, I would only be a moment. There was a room on the side reserved for the ladies if Lady Caroline desired to come in, and I asked her as much, but she professed that she was content to wait without.

I was hailed by a somewhat thinner crowd than usual. It being a calm night, it was easy to conclude that Nassau County's own irregulars were out prowling the Sound for booty. I didn't approve or disapprove of their work, but did hope that they harmed no one and could avoid capture if at all possible. Their treatment as prisoners would doubtless be short and brutal, for the hangings had made many of the Connecticut "militia" very bitter.

"Anything at all, Mr. Farr?" I asked after giving him greeting.

With a flourish as though he'd brought it across the Atlantic himself, he placed a battered packet before me, smiling broadly. I let out a crow and fell upon it like a starving man to a loaf of bread. This gave much amusement to the other patrons, so I made something of an ass of myself, but I didn't care. I cut the thing open then and there with my penknife and unfolded the sheets within.

The date, as nearly as I could make out from Oliver's atrocious handwriting, was late in February, indicating that he'd replied immediately after the arrival of my last missive to him. So it had taken a solid four months to get to me. Old news by now, but much better than nothing. My eyes flew over the crabbed words, searching for Nora's name.

And when I found it . . . well, I'd hoped for more . . . expected more.

He told me that he'd forwarded my letter to Nora to the Warburtons as per my request and hoped that I should get a speedy reply. He'd had no word from them other than a note from Mrs. Warburton saying that her son, Tony, had improved a little in the temperate Italian climate, though he was still far from recovered.

Damned murdering bastard, I thought, my mood turned foul from this lack of news. I didn't care about him, I wanted news of *Nora*.

"Not bad tidings, I hope?" said Mr. Farr.

"More like no tidings at all," I grumbled.

The rest of the letter reflected the one I'd sent him, chatty and full of comments about things long past and near forgotten. I was to the point of folding it to read later when I caught the name "Norbury," and went a bit farther. I'd asked him for an opinion of the family and he had provided one.

I was reading it for the fourth time when Lady Caroline, apparently impatient with waiting, came in. Mr. Farr went to her and asked permission to show her to the ladies' portion of his house, but she put him off and came smiling over to me.

"Mr. Barrett? I've no wish to rush you, but I thought you might have forgotten that your cousin is waiting for us."

Couldn't speak. Could barely hear her. Could only stare at her face, familiar for so many months, pretty, friendly, intelligent, charming, an entirely lovely woman. I stared and felt a terrible illness creeping up from my belly.

Farr noticed something was wrong. "Mr. Barrett? What is it? Mr. Barrett?"

My eyes jerked from her face to his and I struggled to form an answer. Impossible. The whole world was impossible.

She said my name again. Questioning.

Still couldn't answer. Shock, I suppose. Made it hard to think.

". . . some brandy, sir?" Farr was saying.

I shook my head. Put a hand to my eyes, rubbed them. When I blinked them clear, the horror was still before me. Undeniable. It would not go away on its own. It would have to be dealt with, and the damnable job had fallen to me.

Once I understood that, a kind of acceptance and resolve took hold. Without another word, I seized her by the arm and guided her toward one of the more private receiving rooms. I grabbed up a candle from one of the tables in passing, much to the startlement of the men there. Ignoring their comments, I pushed her ahead of me into the room and shut the door.

"What is the matter, Mr. Barrett?" she demanded, non-plussed if not angered by my abrupt behavior.

"That is something for you to explain, madam." I put the candle on a heavy oak table and placed Oliver's letter next to it. "Read," I ordered, pointing.

"This is ridiculous," she protested. "What on earth—?"

"Read, damn you!"

She went pale with true anger, but there was a sudden wavering in her eyes.

Doubt, I thought. Most definitely doubt.

She kept anger to the front, though, and showing it in her every move and gesture, sat in one of the chairs and plucked up the pages. It was slow going, she was not used to the handwriting, but I knew how things stood as I watched her grow paler and paler until she was deathly white. Then there was a strange reversal and her color returned until she was flushed and hot, with two crimson spots high on her cheeks.

Oliver had been fairly succinct on the subject:

"I'd not heard of any Duke of Norbury, but thought if Cousin Elizabeth were considering on adding a peer to the family it wouldn't hurt to improve my knowledge, so I started asking around. The news isn't good, I fear, as it turns out there is no such duke and never has been. The only Norbury I can turn up is some nothing of a little hamlet south of London that doesn't even have a church, much less a duke. There *is* a village called Norwood and I understand it has a rather fine inn, but again, no duke lurking about the place. I'd question this fellow and his sister very closely as they're bound to be bounders, don't you know."

She shook her head, putting on a wonderful puzzlement. "Really, Mr. Barrett, there has been a awful mistake, that, or your cousin is playing a miserable joke upon us all. My family is an old and noble line, why, we even had ancestors with Henry at Agincourt."

"I don't give a damn if they were with Richard at Bosworth Field, you will explain yourself."

"But I tell you there's nothing to be explained, 'tis your cousin who needs to . . ." She saw my look and tried another tack. "This is ridiculous. We've lived with your family for months. You *know* us well. How can we be anything except what we are?"

And for a moment I did experience a twinge of doubt. Oliver was often a rather silly fellow, after all. He *might* have gotten things muddled . . .

"This is a mistake," she said firmly. "You must realize that."

No. He could be an ass at times, but he was no fool.

Unlike me. Unlike all of us.

I fixed my eyes hard upon her. "You will *listen* to me . . ."

She hissed as though burned and flinched. After that initial reaction she was as still as stone, expression wide open and blank. Soulless.

Certainly heartless.

Sweet God, *how* . . .

I broke away to pace up and down a few times, trying to calm myself. I was sick and angry and ashamed, with a thousand other similar damnable feelings crowding mind and cowing spirit, filling me with their turbulent hum, making it impossible to think clearly or do anything. No good trying to question her while I was so upset, it could kill her . . . or worse.

Sweet God, it *hurt*.

And it was like this for me for many long and silent moments until it finally settled into something I could control. Only then did I dare look at her and form my first question.

"Who are you?"

"Caroline Norwood."

"Where are you from?"

"London."

"Is your oldest brother the Duke of Norbury?"

"I have no brother."

God. "Then who is James Norwood?"

"My husband."

Turned away. Quickly. Had to, to save her, to save myself. The sickness returned tenfold. For a time I just couldn't do anything, the horror of it was too much. I kept my back to her, breathing in huge gulps of air, trying to clear my mind, and, after a time, succeeding. When I was calm again, I resigned myself to the fact that everything to come was probably going to hurt like blazes, but there was no way it could be avoided. All I could do was to get on with it and over with as quickly as possible.

Pulled a chair out opposite her. Sat. Clasped my hands before me on the table.

"All right, Caroline. I want you to tell me everything about yourself."

It was a wretched story, made more so by their utter lack of conscience.

They'd come across from England over a year ago with some fine clothes and finer manners and posed as Lord James and Lady Caroline, complete with a duke as their elder brother along with a distinguished family history. The pair had had much contact with nobility in England, after all; she had been a music teacher, he a dancing master to scions of the peerage. Both were natural actors. Both were highly discontent with their lot and prepared to do anything to improve it. The titles had been predictably irresistible to certain members of Philadelphia society, and it wasn't hard to dupe the lot.

They made shameless use of their new status to acquire goods, services, favors, and stayed as guests of some of the best families in the city. Though they took out many loans they'd no intention of paying back, they were always short of cash and on the lookout for a means of getting more.

But the trouble in that city from the approaching war made it impossible for them to fulfill such plans as they'd made; escape was necessary. Enter my innocent cousin, Anne, not terribly smart, but possessing relatives with a luxuriant sanctuary far from the conflict.

Possessing money . . . at least on one side of the family.

Once they arrived and got their bearings, it was determined that one of them should try to marry into that money. James would come to pay court to my sister, as there was less difficulty for a husband to control his wife's property than the other way 'round. All he had to do was be what he essentially was, handsome, genial, naturally charming, but without a speck of real feeling or guilt for what he was doing.

Caroline was the same way. They were perfectly matched.

Then they'd found out that Elizabeth was my heir. Her money alone would be a fortune, but how much better would it be to double it. That's when they made their first attempt on my life. During the happy confusion of a tea party, it had been easy enough to keep Anne distracted. Caroline had slipped a good dose of laudanum into my tea and watched with approval as my blameless cousin stirred in plenty of sugar, which would mask the taste for me.

The plan was that I should simply fall asleep, never to wake. If anybody at the party noticed me dozing off in a chair, one or the other of them would prevent any attempt to rouse me. The greater likelihood was that once I felt sleepy enough, I'd go upstairs to bed, never to return.

They couldn't know that I would not be drinking it; I'd long planted that provision into their minds as I'd done with everyone else: that they should entirely ignore the fact I never ate or drank anything.

What a shock it had been to them when Rapelji had come in and raised the alarm about Father.

Father . . . my poor father . . . he might have died in my place, all unknowing.

And Mother . . . all these months ignorantly bearing the stigma of a poisoner.

I roughly pushed the stabbing rage aside and made Caroline go on.

Made cautious by this blunder, they held off for a time, until things could fall back into their usual routine. They did not for a moment believe Beldon's story about the flying gout and noticed right away the new lock on his door. After much speculation and observation, later confirmed when Elizabeth decided to confide in Norwood, they knew it was Mother we all suspected, not them. With relief they watched and waited for another opportunity, and James proceeded with his courtship of Elizabeth.

Caroline apparently had little objection to her husband's conquest of another woman and none at all to his going to a prostitute for the easement of such urges as come to a man forced by circumstances to be celibate. After he'd finished with Molly one night, he'd gone to The Oak for a fortifying drink and had overheard the regulars joking amongst themselves about my recent departure to pay my respects to the lady.

He wasn't aware at that time of Molly's reputation for discretion. He knew that one careless word from her to his prospective brother-in-law could endanger his chances with Elizabeth. Besides, there was the additional gain of inheritance to consider. I had to be silenced.

And the men to do it were right there. Ash, Drummond, all the others.

For they were Norwood's men.

He'd met them and secured their services on one of his frequent trips away to see to "business." Faster and more certain than marriage, he'd made lucrative arrangements with them, finding likely places for a raid and taking a portion of the profit. They'd been in Glenbriar that night to plan the next one and he ordered them to kill me, saying that I'd found them out and would talk.

There were two problems with that, though: Ash had decided on his own to try for a ransom on the side . . . and I was no longer the ordinary man I appeared to be. No wonder Norwood had been so completely astonished to see me alive on the road the next night. I was supposed to be dead and drifting somewhere at the bottom of the Sound.

Also to his misfortune, Knox had been captured. He'd been closemouthed, but then I'd promised to make the man talk. Norwood's wife had to see that he did not.

"You? How were you involved with that?" I demanded. My influence upon her had lowered her guard so much that she was readily answering questions as though they were part of a normal conversation, requiring only a word or two from me to keep her going. It was just as well. The initial effort of concentration had been painless, but to sustain it for any length of time made my head ache terribly.

"I left the house carrying some of James's clothes," she said. "I changed into them, then cut across the fields to get to town, before any of you arrived."

Sweet heavens. She must have taken the idea from the play I'd given Anne to read. Certainly she she would have greater mobility and be less noticeable in men's clothing.

"What did you do?"

"Watched and waited. When I saw Knox in the room with you, I broke the window and shot him, then ran. James led them in the wrong direction, away from me. I got back, changed again, and went on to the house with no one the wiser."

"Then what?"

"That was all. The whole thing had been so much of a risk and all for nothing because you obviously didn't know anything harmful against us. I then told James to work on the girl. Marriage to her was safer and more profitable. Besides . . . there would be others soon enough."

Others? I didn't take her meaning right away. It was too awful to see, I suppose, and when I did, I wished that I hadn't.

Elizabeth was only to be the first in a series of marriages. Now that they'd worked out their ploy, they would eventually venture forth to take full advantage of any number of other women with money. Over the years they would be able to make thousands of pounds with very little effort or expenditure of their own funds.

Of course to do so, they would have to find a way of divesting themselves of Elizabeth's company fairly soon, but in these unsettled times it would be simple enough to arrange something with Ash. They'd already made mention of it to him. It had been what Norwood and Caroline had been discussing while I'd seen to the horses. Their disagreement had been about whether to keep me there or let me leave. Caroline had wanted me well away from things. Her plans had been laid; she did not want me around to risk the least disruption of them. But to get me out, she'd have to go as well, and Norwood hadn't liked it. His dear and loving wife was the more clever of the two, after all; he'd wanted her with him, just in case anything unexpected did arise.

The idea was to make it look like another rebel incursion. Norwood would emerge to tell the sad tale of how he'd been knocked unconscious trying to defend his house, awakening after all was over to discover the body of his bride, foully murdered by the pitiless raiders in their quest for booty. How easy for him afterward to collect his inheritance from her estate and leave, playing the part of a grief-stricken widower.

I had been able to control myself up to this point. Their attacks upon others, their murder of Knox, their murders using Ash as their weapon, their attack upon me, even upon Father, none of it had been pleasant to hear, but I'd just been able to stand it.

But not this. Not hearing her coldly explaining the fine points of how they would be killing my dearly loved sister. It was impossible for me, impossible for any man with a heart to endure. Until the words were out of her mouth, I thought I'd already reached the limit of my rage. Now a raw and roaring blast of it tore through me like a wild nor'easter.

I was lost to it . . . and then so was Caroline.

Blind and deaf to all reason, all restraint, it clawed its way out of my brain—

And right into hers.

When I came to myself, I was on the other side of the room, face to the wall, hands covering my eyes. I was aware that something had happened, but felt as disoriented as a newly wakened sleeper. It was taking me a moment to sort dream from reality.

The dream was a fading memory of a shapeless dark *thing* that had bounded up from some deep place in my soul. Ugly and huge, if my anger could have taken on a such an amorphous form and size, it might have looked like that. It had been full of force and fury, erupting forth, filling the room, filling the world, overflowing it, overwhelming it. It bellowed and raved, smashed and hurled this way and that before finally driving itself into another vessel other than myself. It seemed too large for the other to hold without breaking.

And so it proved.

I became aware of the reality where it sat slumped at the table.

Caroline's eyes told me the tale of what had happened. I'd seen such eyes on Tony Warburton after Nora's temper had exceeded all control and broken free. She'd snapped his mind like a twig, and now I'd done exactly the same thing to Caroline.

She stared at nothing, shivering a little. Each time she blinked, her whole head twitched slightly. Her hands rested easily upon the table, inches from the incriminating letter.

I plucked it from her reach, folded, and tucked it away, hardly aware of the action. I also eased one hand into the pocket of her riding coat and drew out her pistol, placing it into my own coat pocket. It struck me that it would not be a good idea to leave her armed.

But it would not have mattered. She paid no mind to me. With hard certainty, I knew that she had no mind left. It was just the same as before with Nora and Warburton.

Nora had regretted her loss of control, though; I could not. I regarded Caroline with a cold satisfaction. I could not raise the least shame in me for what I'd done to her, nor was there any desire to try. If that made me wicked, then so be it; it could hardly compare with what she and her husband had planned for Elizabeth.

There was a sudden and strange peace within me, as though Caroline had somehow drained away all my doubts about myself, about what I would have to do in the very near future. For I had determined that Elizabeth would not spend one more hour in that bastard's defiling company.

I walked steadily out into the common room and was somewhat surprised to find that all was as right and normal as could be. I'd had some idea that they might have heard a row coming from our private room and be alert to trouble, but though I got some curious looks, no one said anything. All the noise had been in my head, it seemed, part of the dream . . . or rather, the nightmare.

Only Mr. Farr, who had witnessed my initial reaction to the letter, took it upon himself to come over and have his curiosity answered. "Are you all right, Mr. Barrett?"

Some dissembling was required, then. Very well. I knew I could manage. It did not take much to look stunned and put a small tremor into my voice. "A little brandy for Lady Caroline, if you please. I fear she has suffered some sort of a fit."

"A fit?" he questioned, even as he turned away to find the right bottle.

"One moment we were talking and the next she put her hand to her head and seemed to fall asleep. I got her to wake up, but she seems very dazed. I'd like to send one of your lads to fetch Dr. Beldon as quickly as possible."

"Certainly, sir." He came back with the brandy, full of bustling concern, which blossomed into a fearful shock once he saw the woman's blank face. He immediately sent for his wife to look after her, then dispatched two of his stablemen off to my house to get Beldon.

It went very smoothly, better than I'd hoped. I simply mirrored his feelings, then announced that I'd go to fetch her brother, Lord James. This was met with grim approval. Yes, it was far and away the best thing that could be done, by all means her closest relative should be with her during this strange illness.

He and Mrs. Farr were already speaking in hushed tones about apoplexy as I hurried out the door and jumped onto Rolly's back.

No lights were showing when I arrived. Everyone had gone to bed. Theirs was a small household, just Elizabeth and James and the valet, Harridge. There was a cook, maid, and a scullery boy, all part of the same family, but they lived in their own house a quarter mile farther along. So convenient for the Norwoods, so convenient for Ash.

I dismounted and quietly walked to the front door, vanished, and slipped through the narrow space of the threshold, reappearing on the inside. I had no plan, no idea of what I was going to do, only blind faith that the right path would present itself now that I was here.

Going to the front parlor, I busied myself with the tinder box by the fireplace and soon had a number of candles burning throughout the room. I wanted a lot of light. When I was done, I went out to the staircase landing and bellowed out my sister's name. I couldn't bring myself to go up to their bedroom.

After a moment, Norwood called down. "Jonathan? My God, man! What are you doing here? Has something happened to Caroline?"

"Jonathan?" Elizabeth hesitantly called.

"Come down, please," I said, in a softer tone. I was not talking to him. For a tiny instant, I nearly fled. I was about to deliver a hideous hurt to someone I loved dearly. Perhaps I should wait, go get Father to help.

"What the devil are you about, man?" Norwood demanded, sounding highly aggrieved.

No. I crushed my doubts. *Not one more hour with him*.

Soon they came, Elizabeth wrapped in some sort of loose gown over her nightclothes, Norwood still dressed except for his coat and waistcoat. They hurried into the parlor and stopped, faces full of worry and curiosity and with a touch of anger at this unorthodox intrusion.

"What is it, Jonathan?" asked Elizabeth, coming over to me.

"Yes," said Norwood. "Is it the war? What's wrong?" He stopped short, staring at the pistol in my hand. It was Caroline's.

I had it pointed at the floor, but he was plainly wondering why I was in possession of it.

Elizabeth noticed as well. "What is it? What's wrong? Was there trouble on the road? Is it Father? Is he ill or hurt?"

"No, nothing like that. I've learned something that you need to know."

"Learned what?"

I drew out the letter. "This arrived from Oliver. It's on the top page." A cowardly way to tell her, but if I'd tried to speak the words would have choked me on the spot.

"Really, Jonathan," said Norwood. "What is so important that you had to come by at this hour? Where's Caroline?"

Elizabeth took the letter and held it so the candlelight fell upon the damning page and read. Then she let out with a moaning gasp and sat heavily on one of the chairs. "My God . . ."

"Elizabeth?" Norwood was made uneasy with her failure to reply and turned back to me. "See here, Jonathan, I won't be having you barging in and just standing there without a word of explanation."

"Be quiet."

He flushed. "And I won't be spoken to like that in my own house even if you are my brother-in-law!"

"You're no relation to me and you know it. Be quiet or I will kill you."

His mouth dropped open, but nothing came forth. He saw how I looked and finally, finally the true meaning behind my actions began to dawn upon him.

"Elizabeth?" I went back to her. She had become smaller and was trembling as though chilled to the bone. The letter shook so much in her hand that she had to press the rattling pages against the chair arm to read it again. She'd have to read it several times, even as I had.

She looked to me. "This is true, isn't it?"

"I'm sorry."

"It's not some silly joke of Oliver's . . ."

"No. I showed this to Caroline. I made her talk. She was . . . unable to lie. She and Norwood are married."

She let the letter drop and looked past me, not to her husband, but to the man who had betrayed her. Her eyes blurred and grew blind from the welling tears.

"How could you?" she asked him in a broken voice that pierced me right through the heart.

"How could I what? Elizabeth—" He reached toward her, putting on a most convincing show of hurt and tender concern.

But she ignored him and looked to me once more, pleading for me to make things right again.

"If I could change it, I would. You know that."

And this confirmation made her smaller still. Elizabeth hunched in on herself, unable to hold back the grief any longer. She gave up fighting it and the tears and sobs came on, leaving her helpless for a time as her emotions overwhelmed her. If she had the least doubt about the truth of things, she had only to look at Norwood. He remained quiet and made not the slightest protest of innocence, nor any gesture of compassion toward the people he'd so callously hurt or displayed a jot of shame for any of it. If anything, he appeared to be disgusted at this turning of events.

Soulless and heartless, the *bastard*.

I put my arms around Elizabeth, offering what small comfort I could, but sickening as it was just to look at him, not once did I take my eyes from Norwood.

"What shall we do?" Elizabeth asked.

The first shattering shock had been the worst, but Elizabeth was a strong woman. She'd recovered for the present, blew her nose, dried her eyes, and braced herself to listen to the full story behind the letter. I told her everything, including what Caroline had imparted to me. The fact that I'd gotten so much information from her both puzzled and frightened Norwood. When it was over, Elizabeth voiced the question that had begun to hammer at me as I talked.

"I don't know," I answered. "We'll have to tell Father. He'll help us work out something."

"I don't see how."

Neither did I, but she didn't need to hear that. "He will."

She nodded dully, accepting it, not really thinking about it. Just as well. "What about Caroline?"

Norwood's eyes flickered and sharpened.

"She'll be no trouble to us, I promise," I said. "Go upstairs. Put on some riding clothes. I'm going to take you home. We'll talk to Father."

"What about him?" She glared at Norwood.

"He'll be here when we come back. I'll make sure of it."

"You'll—"

"I'll do that which is necessary. Now go."

Elizabeth stood, stiff as an old woman one moment, then swaying as though about to swoon the next, but she got hold of herself and paced over to where Norwood was standing. He had no real expression on his face, just a trace of watchfulness, nothing more. She looked him up and down, a tall and handsome man, husband for a month, betrayer for a lifetime.

She slapped him, then spit in his face.

He flinched, but didn't otherwise react. I was right behind Elizabeth and Norwood must have seen his own murder in my eye if he dared to make the smallest move against her. He was not even tempted to wipe away the spittle.

Elizabeth turned her back to him and left the room by the parlor's other door, which led to the kitchen. I wondered why she'd gone that way until I heard the soft splash of water. Yes, she'd want to wash her face first, part and parcel of making a new start on things. I listened to her quiet movements until she was done and slowly climbing the servants' stairs to her room. When her steps faded and a door closed, I told him to sit, but Norwood remained standing, the better to offer arguments in his favor.

"Look, now," he said. "I know it's been a blow to you, but there's no need for this to go any further. You've caught me out and we all know it, but do you want all the rest of the county to know it as well? Do you really want Elizabeth to have to face the scandal, the pointing fingers, the whispers?"

"You don't give a damn for her, so don't try using that excuse to save your skin."

"But it will happen if you turn me in, make this public. Let me go and Caroline and I will leave quietly, we won't ever come back, we'll say nothing."

"Leaving Elizabeth to explain why her 'husband' deserted her?"

"You can say I'd been called back to England, say anything you like. We'll be out of your lives, we'll stay away, I promise."

"You've tried to kill me twice, nearly killed my father, and God knows, you were planning to kill Elizabeth as well and you think that I could cheerfully let you go free just to avoid a little gossip?"

"But—"

"You're a murderer already with blood on your hands from the people killed and robbed by your men, you even slaughtered one of your own to keep him quiet, and by God, I'm going to see that Nash knows all about it. I could strangle you where you stand, but I won't. It'll give me far greater pleasure to wait and watch you dancing under the gallows. There'll be no one pulling on your heels to speed you to hell, I'll see to that."

He went whiter than his shirt and backed away, not far, only into a chair into which he sat rather heavily. He embarrassed himself no more with protests. He finally saw their futility. Some new thought came to him, though. "You'd let them hang Caroline, too? If you turn me in, then she'll have to be part of it. You'd let them hang a woman?"

My hard silence was not the answer he wanted. Caroline was beyond the rope, but I saw no reason to inform or explain to him her condition.

"You *must* let me go." Tears were in his eyes, his voice, but I'd seen them first in my sister. I was not about to be persuaded to pity for this creature.

"Aye, let 'im go an' we'll take care o' things," someone advised me.

Ash's voice.

He blocked the doorway that led to the kitchen, holding a pistol in each hand, both aimed at me. I knew they were primed to fire, having done it myself since they were the duelers I'd left on my saddle. Behind him were other men I recognized: Tully, Seth, Abel. Drummond wasn't with them.

"Stand clear of 'im," Ash ordered.

I did just that, smoothly, without haste, and holding my own pistol along the line of my leg, keeping it out of his sight for a moment longer. I presented only my side to him, like a fencer.

"That's far enough."

Norwood was on his feet again, pointing at me. "Look out for him, he's armed."

But Ash had me well covered. " 'E won't make no trouble. 'E's too smart by 'alf to even try. Am I right, ye young bastard? Am I right? Thought as much. Now put that on the table. Reach for it 'n' you'll make me a happy man, 'n' that's God's honest truth."

As instructed, I placed my gun on the table, but did not move from my spot.

Relief flowed out from Norwood so strongly I could almost feel it as a physical presence in the room. "Excellent work, Mr. Ash. I'd nearly despaired of your coming tonight."

"That bloody idiot you sent to fetch us put up more of a fight than we'd reckoned on."

"What? Harridge?"

" 'E squealed a bit, but Tully got 'im quiet. 'E won't be makin' no more noise ever ag'in." Ash chuckled, the others joining him as they separated out over the room.

"Where is he?"

"We drug 'im into yer scullery. It'll look like it's supposed to, you've naught to worry about on that."

"You sent your servant off to be murdered?" I asked Norwood.

He smiled. "Couldn't be helped. He was beginning to realize a few too many things, anyway. It's a good night for the work, right lads? Quiet and dark, just as we like best."

Yes, it was a quiet, moonless night, a rare night for mayhem be you rebel or Loyalist. That was why Norwood and Caroline had chosen to take advantage of it.

Tully sniggered, as did the rest. "Not what I like best. Where's that Tory bitch ye been keepin', yer lordship? I've 'eard she 'ad a fair face. I've a mind t' see it."

And so while Caroline and I rode home, where we planned to sit with Anne and read Shakespeare aloud to each other, my sister would be suffering God knows what horrors at their hands until they finally . . .

"*Devil*," whispered Abel, staring at me. "See the fire in 'is eyes? 'E's a bloodsucking devil, I tell ye!"

They all looked, and things were silent for a moment, but Ash snorted, waving one of the duelers. "Then 'e won't mind us sendin' 'im back to 'ell, will 'e?"

"Not at all," agreed Norwood. But the man looked uneasy, for my gaze was wholly focused upon him. "Send him along now, if you please, Mr. Ash."

"Oh, but 'e'll need a bit of company to go with 'im."

"The sister? Yes, I'll fetch her down. It'll be less fuss if I—"

"We'll take care of yer Tory doxy soon enough, yer lordship. First I want t' know what this bastard meant when 'e said 'slaughtered one o' yer own.' "

Norwood did not take his meaning right away. "What are you on about?"

"We 'eard 'im talkin' with ye afore we showed ourselves. What did 'e mean?" Ash casually let one of the duelers swing in Norwood's direction.

"He wants to know about Knox," I said, my voice very thick, very low.

The meaning now dawned on him, but his acting skills were so ingrained that he was able to shift his thoughts 'round without showing so much as a flicker of change in his face. The others saw nothing, but in that deathly still room *I* was able to hear the abrupt thump as his heart lurched and pounded in reaction.

"What about Knox?" he asked with just the right touch of annoyed puzzlement.

None of it worked on Ash, who was already predisposed to suspect a lie. "You tell us, yer lordship. What did 'e mean?"

"I haven't the faintest idea. Poor Knox was killed trying to escape—"

"Aye, that's one o' the stories. The other is 'e were 'anged by a mob, 'n' 'nother were 'e were shot through the 'ead while 'e sat 'elpless 'n' chained."

"That's the true one," I put in, slowly, deliberately, watching Norwood with an unholy delight burgeoning within me. "His lady wife shot through a broken window and blew out his brains just as you said."

"Be that true?" Ash demanded of him.

"Of course not! How could it? What a ridiculous idea! He's trying to confuse you—to get you to spare him. He knows you'll be killing him—"

"So I've no reason to lie," I said.

"You do if you want to drag me down as well."

"Norwood was afraid Knox might talk," I went on. "Afraid Knox would betray him. That's why he was murdered."

"But that's—"

"*Norwood . . . look at me!*"

He looked. He couldn't *not* look.

I drove into his mind like an axe. "*Tell them the truth.*"

He gave a little gasp and fell back a step.

"Devil," Abel murmured.

"*The truth, Norwood.*"

He all but strangled on the words, but they did at last come forth. And when he was done, I released him, and he dropped to his knees.

I bowed my head, tired and suddenly aware of the sharp pain crashing around inside my skull. I had not lost control as I'd done earlier; this was the price of it, perhaps. When I came back to myself and glanced up, they were staring at one another, at Norwood, at me. Tully and Ash with fearful wonder, Seth and Abel with fear alone as they shifted nervously from foot to foot as though ready to run. I half-expected Abel to call me a devil again.

Norwood made a breathy sob and grabbed at his chair to keep from falling completely over.

Ash turned full upon me. "I don' know 'ow ye done it, but 'tis done, 'n' I believe it."

"No, Ash." Norwood made a valiant effort to straighten himself. "It's a terrible mistake."

"Don't see 'ow it can be, since we all 'eard the story from yer own lips."

"It wasn't true, I swear it! I was forced to say those things. You saw what he did. He made me lie, he made me—you saw! He's not natural, he's—"

"Bastard! I don't give a bloody damn what 'e is, devil, angel or whatever's in between, you've a debt to pay for the murder of a good man."

"But it wasn't even me! Caroline was the one, you know that! I didn't want her to, but she—"

"Oh, now, listen to 'im squeal. Ye make me sick."

And with no more prelude than that, Ash aimed one of the duelers at Norwood and fired. The ball struck him square in the chest and he collapsed forward, his last cry lost in the deafening blast of the shot. Smoke billowed out from the pistol, obscuring things for a moment, long enough—more than long enough—for me to grab Caroline's gun.

Without thinking, without loss of motion, I raised it and fired at Ash where he stood now half turned from me. The gun cracked sharply and more smoke clouded my vision, but he gave out with a surprised shriek, jerking away, one arm flailing. I was distantly conscious of the others tumbling over themselves to get out of the way.

" 'E's a devil!" screamed Abel, ducking from the line of fire. I wasn't paying much attention, being busy with pulling back the gun's trigger guard.

Turn the cylinder. Push the guard forward . . .

Lock.

Tully's reactions were better than the others. He charged at me, arms out to bring me down. I got the muzzle up just in time, but he made a grab at my wrist and the shot went wide. He hadn't expected it, though, and the flash and burn made him jump. I dropped the gun, seized Tully by the shoulders, and hauled him sharply around. His feet left the floor. I swung him like a sack of grain and let him go. He all but flew across the room to smash into a wall with such force as to break bone. Hardly wasting a glance at him, I stooped and retrieved the pistol.

Pull back the guard, turn the cylinder, push, lock . . .

Fire.

Seth and Abel had seen it coming and had scrambled for the door, both in a panic to get out. I followed them through the kitchen. They stumbled over Harridge's body in their haste to gain the scullery.

Pull back, turn, push, lock . . .

Fire.

By then I wasn't even trying to aim. They were routed, and that was enough. I didn't care if they lived or died as long as they were gone. They broke free of the house and fled away into the summer night. I could have followed them, but simply fired over their heads, inducing them to greater speed.

They ran back the way they'd come: up the road to the cook's home, probably where they stayed when they weren't making raids. I'd allowed for the thieves coming over from Suffolk to prey on us, but it had never occurred to me that they could just as easily work their scheme from Nassau County. If they had any brain at all between them, they'd take to a boat and be long gone before Nash could catch them.

I didn't care. To hell with them.

Returning to the others, I found Ash, Tully, and Norwood as I'd left them. The scents of bloodsmell and powder and fear and death filled the room.

I rolled Norwood over. His eyes were just beginning to film and fade. His last expression was of hurt disbelief. Ash had gotten him right where his heart would have been had he possessed one. He was now past any worldly cares.

A pity. I would have *treasured* the chance to watch him swing, to see the this dancing master's legs twitching in his final jig. Too late now.

Tully would trouble us no more, either. His neck had been broken. His spine, too, from the look of things. I took in this indirect evidence of my strength with barely a shrug, as though it had nothing to do with me, as though some other person had gone mad and—

I was numb inside and just a little cold. It was impossible to tell whether it had to do with my body or my soul. A iron hard heaviness dragged at me, slowing my movements, my thoughts. I roused myself just enough to go check on Ash.

He lay on his back, a fearful wound just below his heart and the look of death settling a gray shadow upon his face.

"Curse ye fer a bastard," he grunted as I knelt next to him.

"No doubt."

"That were a righteous execution. 'E were a traitor."

"Yes."

"Curse ye . . . oh, God 'a' mercy." His hands clutched at the wound, unable to stem the outflow of blood or push away the pain.

"Let it go," I told him, knowing exactly, *exactly* what he was going through.

"Wha . . ."

My eyes hard on his, I said, "Let it go. The pain will stop."

"Stop?"

"Yes . . ."

We stared at one another for a long minute, me silent with concentration, he gasping out his last breaths. Then his breathing eased, the moans lessened. His eyes were growing distant, starting to focus on something else. I recognized the look. Knew what he saw. Had felt that comforting drowsiness stealing up. I'd been there. Briefly. He would stay forever.

"Go to sleep, Mr. Ash," I whispered.

And he did.

I shut his eyes for him.

I shut my own.

But could not shut out the sights and sounds of what had happened. Of what I'd done.

God have mercy on us all.

"Jonathan?"

Only Elizabeth's voice could have possibly roused me from the blackness that had stolen its way so swiftly and completely over my soul. But I hardly recognized her. Could that thin and fear-filled whisper possibly belong to her?

She called to me again, and I somehow found my feet and went out to the hall. She was at the top of the stairs peering fearfully down at me. She clutched a pistol in one hand.

"It's over," I said.

"I heard them . . . I heard everything—"

Hurried up to her. Held her. "It's over. They're gone."

"I wanted to help, but I—"

"No, you did the right thing by staying out of it. God bless you for your good sense. If anything had happened to you . . ."

She pushed away from me. "What's happened to James?"

He'd been the lowest kind of scoundrel and though betrayed in every sense of the word, she had, after all, loved him.

Still loved him, if I read her rightly. Such feelings don't die in an instant, no matter how great the killing anger may be. They linger on, full of pain and giving pain.

She saw my answer in my face, then tried to break away from me to go to him. But I held her tight and kept her from rushing down into the hell-pit below.

EPILOGUE

Day by day, Elizabeth fought to regain herself. She spent a lot of time in Father's library, just sitting and reading, or sewing, or doing nothing much at all. He talked to her when she felt like it, or listened, or held her when she cried. On nights when she could not sleep, I took his place and kept her company.

I was unable to attend the funeral, which was thought of as strange by those outside the immediate family. But if Mother worried about what people might think, she kept it to herself for once. I heard all this afterward from Father, as well as an account of how Elizabeth had startled not a few by insisting that they call her by her maiden name again.

"The man I married is dead," she told them. "I am content to bury him with his name and get on with things."

Brave words, though it took a while before she was up to fulfilling them.

But even the worst wounds can heal, given enough time and care. Father and I did our best for her. Her grief was genuine, her healing slow, but she had no want for support and sympathy from all who knew her.

How terrible it was, they thought, wedded but a month and then to have her husband killed by rebels . . . and her poor sister-in-law gone simpleminded, too. It was wicked, outrageous. Something ought to be done. At least her brother had been there to roust the bastards. He'd gotten two of them, by God, that was something. Well done, Jonathan.

That was the story that was put about, anyway.

Nash had gone after the remaining men and the cook and her family. He missed catching them, which was just as well. We certainly had no need for any truth muddling up the facts at hand.

"How could I have been so wrong?" Elizabeth asked us many, many times.

"You weren't wrong, he was," Father and I would tell her.

She wore mourning clothes and went through the motions and rituals expected of widows, and people assumed that her reason for not wanting to talk about Norwood was a measure of the depth of her grief.

Given the times, other events soon crowded the tragedy from peoples' minds as the realization asserted itself that the war was not going to be over within the year as they'd hoped. More raids took place, more raids were staged, crops matured for the commissary to take away. Summer waxed and waned, and little by little my nights began to lengthen.

I wrote to Oliver about the marriage and enjoined him to say aught to the rest of the family about the business of the false title. As far as they were concerned, she'd married "Lord Norwood" and he'd been killed by the war. His sympathetic answer assured me that they knew nothing of their Cousin Elizabeth's true plight and never would from him.

He had no new word on Nora, except to say that the Warburtons had not seen her for some months. They did not know where she had gone. I grew restless with worry, snappish with unexpressed anger, and by the close of September had made a decision.

I would go back to England.

It had been a long year full of too much waiting. The time had come for me to look for Nora myself, to let her know what had happened to me, to ask her such questions as still remained. After much talk with Father about the practicalities of the journey, I won not only his consent, but full support. He and I began making arrangements for the passage.

Elizabeth was anything but overjoyed. "But how will you feed yourself?"

"I'll be taking along some livestock, of course, though Father thinks a sea voyage might be rough on them. But I shan't be doing any flying about, so each meal should last me a few nights."

"I don't see how you can do it. You're utterly helpless during the day. You'll need a guardian."

"That's why Jericho will be with me, but I should really like some more company, just to be safe . . . will you come?"

That surprised her. In fact, it took all the speech away from her for some minutes. "*Me* go to England?"

"You'd love it there. I did, when it wasn't raining. Damnation, I loved it when it was. Please say yes."

"But what should I do?"

"Anything you like. You're independent now."

That won me a sharp look, but I knew what I was saying. Her marriage had been illegal, but the law did not know that, and to save face we were not prepared to say otherwise. She'd come into her inheritance money. I saw no reason why she shouldn't get some enjoyment out of it.

"There'd be parties . . ."

She shuddered. "I'm not sure I'm ready for those."

"Sight-seeing, then. Cousin Oliver can take you 'round. You can skip Bedlam, if you like."

"Oh, thank you very much."

"You know what I mean. Please come."

"Is this as company for you or to get me out of this house?"

"Both and neither."

"I don't *know* . . ." And she didn't. Not really. Not at all.

My heart sank. She'd been like this for far too long, withdrawn, visibly hurting, and in doubt of herself. No matter how much help and love she had, it would never truly be enough. At some point she would have to learn how to help herself. Elizabeth had not yet reached it and I sadly wondered if she ever would.

Then out of nowhere the idea came to me, or perhaps it had been thrown up from some past memory of a time when my sister had been a happy and confident woman.

"Tell me this, then: if you had never met him, would you go?"

She answered without really thinking. "Why, yes." Then she thought about it . . .

And the thought surprised her.